8/13

D0090692

OTHERWORLD CHRONICLES: BOOK TWO

The SEVEN SWORDS

NILS JOHNSON-SHELTON

HARPER
An Imprint of HarperCollinsPublishers

Otherworld Chronicles: The Seven Swords
Copyright © 2013 by Full Fathom Five, LLC
All rights reserved. Printed in the United States of America.
No part of this book may be used or reproduced in any manner whatsoever
without written permission except in the case of brief quotations embodied
in critical articles and reviews. For information address HarperCollins
Children's Books, a division of HarperCollins Publishers, 10 East 53rd
Street, New York, NY 10022.
www.harpercollinschildrens.com

Library of Congress Cataloging-in-Publication Data
Johnson-Shelton, Nils.
  The seven swords / Nils Johnson-Shelton. — 1st ed.
    p. cm. — (Otherworld chronicles ; bk. 2)
  Summary: "Twelve-year-old Artie Kingfisher has only ten days to
gather a team of knights to wield the mythical seven swords, or his
mission to save the Otherworld and claim his throne as King Arthur
will be lost"— Provided by publisher.
  ISBN 978-0-06-207094-4
  1. Arthur, King—Juvenile fiction. [1. Arthur, King—Fiction.
2. Adventure and adventurers—Fiction.] I. Title.
PZ7.J6398Sev 2013   2012019088
[Fic]—dc23   CIP
                                                       AC

Typography by Torborg Davern

12 13 14 15 16   LP/RRDH   10 9 8 7 6 5 4 3 2 1

❖

First Edition

TABLE OF CONTENTS

From The Fairy Book of Pretelling
How Comes Thy Newest King

The incomparable sword, from the depths of the Lake.
See Merlin Ambrosius, with tongue like a snake.
He slithers and lies, and waits long in vain
For the orphan king of Lady Igraine.

At last he arrives and dons his mail
And, with his fair knights, parts open the veil.
Gate one is refound and quickly thrown wide;
Now Arthur the Next no longer can hide.

Lo! See the many changes in store:
The wizard is free, imprisoned no more.
As the king surveys and crisscrosses the field,
The Worlds are rejoined and the earth, it is healed.

Have faith, young king, be noble and ready;
Make haste for the Seven, surefire and steady.
Fail not—
Else the Worlds will rot.

𝕼𝔴𝔬𝔫 𝕺𝔫𝔞𝔨𝔢𝔞'𝔰 𝔠𝔩𝔬𝔲𝔡𝔢𝔡 𝔪𝔦𝔫𝔡 𝔣𝔩𝔲𝔱𝔱𝔢𝔯𝔢𝔡 in and out as she was carried over a large kid's shoulder.

Her senses returned slowly. First came the pain of hunger in the pit of her stomach. Then the sounds of the boy's footfalls and his labored breathing. After this was the heady smell of new rain and dirt. Then there was taste, which was totally unpleasant; Qwon was ridiculously thirsty, and her mouth was coated with a dry, bitter film.

Last came sight. Some things she recognized—the green and wet ground, a small campfire at night, the boy's leather boots—but a lot of what she saw looked like it came from another world.

For instance, the boy carried a long sword and wore a strange mash-up of armor—part leather, part chain mail, part denim—which in her more lucid moments Qwon thought was pretty strange. Who carried a sword and wore armor these days? No one. No one who wasn't loony, anyway.

Loonier than this was the boy's traveling companion. In shape and size it resembled a rat, but it was covered with iridescent blue scales like an exotic snake; its tail was fat and furry like a squirrel's; and its face was comically scrunched like a pug dog's. Qwon couldn't explain how, but she could swear that sometimes when the boy talked to this animal it answered back.

With words.

The boy called the animal Smash, and Smash called the boy Dred.

Where was she? Not Pennsylvania, that was for sure. Racked by hunger and half-deluded, Qwon wondered if there was a Red Lobster nearby. Qwon kind of loved Red Lobster. Those endless salad bars rocked. Maybe they were in Canada or something. Did Canada have Red Lobsters? She didn't know. Probably. But then, she'd never been to Canada.

Qwon was unconscious a lot and couldn't be sure how long their trip lasted. Twice daily the boy lowered a canteen to her mouth and made her drink a cool liquid that was both sweet and bitter, like children's medicine. Qwon knew this concoction was doing just enough to sustain her, but she also believed it was keeping her in a state of paralysis, for she couldn't twitch a finger or even utter a word.

Dred never spoke to her and she never saw his face because he wore a weird medieval-looking helmet all the time. He walked and walked and walked some more. It was always cloudy and it rained constantly. Qwon's clothing clung uncomfortably to her body as the relentless patter of raindrops seemed to go on forever.

But then, on what turned out to be the last day of their journey, the land around them changed. The clouds parted and the sun broke through, crashing over her back. It felt glorious.

Dred stopped at the edge of a swamp. Qwon watched Smash scurry up his leg, pausing midthigh to take a long look at her. The creature was strange but very cute. Its eyes were deep black, and like most animals, it looked like it knew things that people never would.

Dred resumed walking, and Qwon found herself thinking about her house back in Shadyside, and her parents, who'd separated just over a year ago. Then she thought about Artie and Kay Kingfisher and that weird sword they'd had in their backyard. That seemed significant for some reason, but she couldn't place it, and for the life of her she couldn't remember exactly how she'd been kidnapped.

Dred's feet crunched on a road that wound up a steep hill. They passed others, who Dred greeted with a cheery "Hallo!" or "Whassup?" Some commented on the turn in the weather, and they agreed that it was long overdue.

Not one of these people mentioned the girl draped over Dred's shoulder. Qwon figured maybe this kind of thing was normal around here. Qwon figured she was dealing with some very eccentric but very professional kidnappers. Qwon also figured she probably wasn't in Canada.

The road finally leveled and they stopped. Dred lowered Qwon to the ground, propped her against a pile of stones, and grabbed her chin. Smash jumped onto her thighs and dug his claws into her filthy blue jeans. Dred held her head up so she could see what was in front of them.

It was a castle. A real, honest-to-goodness castle with normal castle things like a drawbridge, a moat, and a curtain-like wall surrounding a cluster of towers and buildings. But it wasn't normal, not at all. One of the towers was made entirely of dark-green glass, like a huge empty bottle. Wisteria covered with thick cones of purple flowers crawled around its walls, and many of the stones in these walls were rose-colored or bright green. The closed drawbridge was painted a garish pink and appeared to have the world's largest lace doily pasted on it. Over the drawbridge, in a bubbly script, were the words *Castel Deorc Wæters*. The *o* in *Deorc* was shaped like a heart.

Qwon thought it looked more like a dollhouse in a fairy garden than a fortress. She rolled her eyes, which was all she could manage in her paralyzed state.

Dred sighed and said, "I know." It was the first time he seemed at all sympathetic to Qwon's feelings, though she had an inkling that Dred thought *she* was the one being sympathetic to *him*. "She's nuts," he said, though Qwon had no idea who he was talking about. "You better hope she's happy today and doesn't do away with you on the spot."

Qwon shut her eyes and wished that she were back home, in her room, wearing clean clothes. She wished that she were able to run.

But she wasn't.

Dred heaved Qwon back over his shoulder. As he walked toward the castle, she heard the sounds of great chains clanking, then a thud that reverberated in her chest. The drawbridge. They walked across, and the water in the moat looked like ink. This must have been the "Deorc Wæters" that the "Castel" was named after.

Dred entered the fortress and walked for a long time down cavernous halls, turning corners and going up and down at least six flights of stairs. The place was well lit and smelled like a flower shop—two more things Qwon thought of as being distinctly un-castle-like.

Finally they reached a large room with thick white carpeting. Qwon's head lolled back as Dred plopped her into an upholstered chair, and she saw sunlight pouring in from high stained-glass windows. Then her head fell forward and she saw that Dred was strapping her ankles and wrists to the chair with leather belts. He pulled them tight, and the pain reassured her that her body was sound.

A sugary voice from across the room said, "Hello, my pets!"

"Mum," Dred said as Smash ran enthusiastically toward the woman.

"So this is the girl, hmm?" the woman asked. She sounded like a well-meaning aunt, the kind who always brought candy when she came to visit.

"Yep," Dred answered.

"And was she difficult to secure?"

"Kind of. He was there. He had Excalibur."

Excalibur!

The word rang in Qwon's ears.

All at once Qwon remembered her kidnapping: she was sitting in her room listening to her iPod when a person covered in—*moss?* yes, in moss—flew through her open window and grabbed her. Then Artie was knocking on her door, and then he was cutting it to pieces—*with a sword!*

Excalibur!

Dred—who evidently had been this moss-covered person—gagged Qwon as Artie demanded that she be released. Then Artie said, "Darkness!" and the room became as black as tar. The next thing Qwon knew, she was on the floor with Dred's knee in her back. She recalled hearing something hit Dred. Then she passed out and all was quiet and dark, and her journey through the strange wilderness was under way.

The woman approached. She was chubby, very pretty, and looked about fifty. She was dressed in a bright-green pantsuit, wore red-rimmed glasses, and had cute silver shoes on her feet. She was absolutely covered in tacky, shiny bangles and wore tons of thin chains around her neck. She had reddish-brown hair, freckles, and a cheerful smile. Like Kay Kingfisher, she had different-colored eyes—but hers were brown and purple instead of blue and green. One of her eyebrows was a shock of white.

She stopped and leaned on a long broadsword in front of Qwon. "I see," the woman said. "He wasn't able to use it on you, was he?"

"He used it to black out the room," Dred recounted, "and somehow he shot at me with an arrow, but other than that, no."

"Well, thank goodness. I don't know what I'd do without you, snookums."

Dred didn't say anything.

The woman said, "Why don't you bring our dear guest back to life, hmm?"

"As you wish, Mum." Dred held a vial to Qwon's lips and poured a liquid into her mouth. She drank. It tasted like water.

At first nothing happened, but then Qwon's arms and

legs tingled like they'd been asleep, and she realized that she could move again. She tried desperately to get up, but the straps stopped her. She also tried to cry out, but no sound came.

"Tell me, dearie, do you know who I am?"

Qwon shook her head.

"My name is Lordess Morgaine. This boy is Mordred, though I'm the only one who calls him that. As you must know by now, he goes simply by Dred, which is a perfectly apt name for him."

Dred nodded slightly.

Qwon stopped trying to escape from the straps and gazed at the sword the woman leaned on. Qwon's grandfather, Tetsuo, who was a kendo master, had taught her a lot about swords. One of the things he taught her was that somewhere in the world there was an ancient blade named Kusanagi that belonged only to her. Qwon never really believed him, and didn't even know if Kusanagi was real. But what Qwon did know, and hoped that this Morgaine person didn't, was that she was actually pretty gifted with a blade. If she could just get her hands on that sword, then maybe she'd have a shot at getting away from these people.

Morgaine pulled back and said, "Tell me, Mistress Qwon, do you recognize this sword?"

Even if Qwon could have spoken, she wouldn't have given this woman the satisfaction of an answer.

"I think you do, dearie," Morgaine said sweetly. "This is Excalibur! None other than the sword of King Arthur himself—or Artie Kingfisher, as he's called these days. And though it's missing its pommel, it's still quite a prize."

Qwon felt the room tilt. Wait. Artie was *King Arthur*? That was downright nuts.

Morgaine continued, "I was lucky enough to steal it from him while you and Mordred were traipsing through the swamp. I know that you are special to young Kingfisher, Mistress Qwon, which means that for the moment you are special to me—until the next new moon rises, anyway."

Qwon surged forward, straining even harder at her restraints than before.

Morgaine beamed. "Feisty. I like that. Listen here, Qwon of Shadyside. You're going to help me, whether you like it or not. With you, I will draw this 'Artie' out, and once I do, I will retrieve the pommel and mend Excalibur. Then it will be truly priceless. What I do after that doesn't concern you, because your usefulness will have expired." She cupped Qwon's chin in her hand and said, "I wonder what I'll do with you. . . . No matter. Whatever it is, trust that it will not be pleasant."

Morgaine turned to Dred and said, "Be a dear and show Mistress Qwon to her quarters. Put her with that feral fairy. Observe the manner of their, er, *acquaintance*, and report back to me."

"Yes, Mum," Dred said unenthusiastically.

Morgaine waved her hand and, as if by magic, Qwon's body went lifeless again. Dred unbuckled her and threw her back over his shoulder. He sighed quietly and they left the room.

"Hail!" Bedevere saluted with his remaining arm as he waltzed into the Kingfishers' game room.

Artie, clutching the golden controller he'd gotten at the Invisible Tower, blurted over his shoulder, "One sec, Beddy."

Bedevere looked at the new forty-six-inch flat-screen mounted to the wall, where Artie's *Otherworld* character, Nitwit the Gray, was up to his old tricks. He was dealing with a violent and unruly giant with a red Mohawk, who was swinging at him with a massive hammer. Artie had the game switched to first person, so only Nitwit's hands could be seen. The right hand held a long and terrifying mace, complete with spikes, and the left was charged with the green glow of magic. Nitwit was a warrior-mage—good not only with weapons but also with spells.

Nitwit jumped, then ducked a swipe and threw some of the green magic at the giant, poisoning the monster. Its health bar began to plummet. But the poison didn't stop the giant from scoring a hit that knocked Nitwit to the ground. Dazed, Nitwit couldn't move as his enemy jumped into the air and came down on top of him. Now it was Nitwit's health bar that jumped alarmingly toward death.

Artie fumbled manically with the controller, switching spells. The ball in his left hand turned golden yellow, and the margins of the screen sparked with the same energy.

Bedevere smiled and said, "Damage Conversion, eh, sire?"

"You bet," Artie said, not taking his eyes from the screen.

Bedevere sucked at video games, *Otherworld* especially, but that didn't mean he didn't understand them. In fact, Bedevere had insisted that Nitwit learn Damage Conversion even though Artie didn't want to waste Spell Points on it. A totally unglamorous conjuration, it converted all damage into healing for ten seconds. When the spell was on, the harder Nitwit got hit, the better he felt.

"Nice," Bedevere said as Nitwit's power was restored. "You should drop that mace and use your spear. It'll keep some distance between you and that . . . *thing.*"

"Duh," Artie said quietly, switching weapons. "Why didn't I think of that?"

Artie's fingers danced on the controller as Nitwit jabbed the giant in the chest. For nearly a minute he scored cheap hits as he waited for his spell-casting mana to restore. Finally, he threw caution to the wind, chucked the spear at the giant's midsection, downed a booster potion, and hurled a huge two-handed fireball at his adversary.

That did the trick. The giant fell, throwing up a cloud of sand, and died unceremoniously.

"Take that!" Kay said, catching the final blow as she entered the game room.

Artie turned to his sister and smiled. "Yeah, take that," he said with a lot less enthusiasm.

Kay plopped next to her brother. Artie paused the game and looked into his sister's crazy, mismatched eyes. "The game's not doing it for you, is it?" she asked.

Artie shook his head.

He wanted so badly to go back to the real Otherworld and finish what he had started. Morgaine had stolen Excalibur and, worse, his dear friend Qwon. Every day Artie spent away from the Otherworld was like torture. He *had* to go back as soon as possible.

But of course he couldn't go back. Not yet. He'd promised to wait to hear from Merlin. But Merlin had been totally AWOL since they'd freed him from the invisible tower back in Cincinnati a few weeks earlier, and Artie was beginning to lose his patience.

"I can't stop thinking about her, Kay. Q must be so miserable and scared. And I can't stop thinking about what I need to do in the Otherworld," Artie lamented.

"Well, what's going on in the video-game version of the Otherworld?" Kay asked, trying to change the subject slightly.

"Some quest for a magic sword, which sucks because all it makes me think about is Excalibur. I can't believe that stupid witch snagged it from me."

Bedevere said, "Give yourself a break, sire. She is extremely powerful." He pointed at a pair of long scars on Artie's leg. "Don't forget what she did to you that day."

"I know," said Artie. "At least if I mess up in the video game, I won't get fried by a bolt of lightning."

Kay lifted her shirt a little to reveal a long crescent-shaped scar on her stomach. "Or get gored by a giant boar."

Bedevere twirled the stump of his right arm through the air. "Or get your arm shot off by a half-crazed wood elf."

Artie said, "I'm sorry about the arm, Bedevere."

Bedevere shook his head. "You've said that a million times, sire. I'm fine. I'm a knight. Knights lose things like arms from time to time."

"I guess," Artie said, still not convinced that Bedevere really didn't care. "But, seriously, if Merlin hasn't turned up by next weekend, we're going back."

Bedevere started, "I don't—"

"King's orders, Sir Bedevere," Artie said.

"Hey, guys!" Kynder yelled excitedly from the kitchen before Bedevere could respond. "Come check this out!"

Artie bolted upstairs, Kay and Bedevere right on his heels.

As Artie stepped into the kitchen, he found Kynder wearing a very authentic-looking medieval robe. It appeared to be made of hay, burlap, and wool, and Artie thought that it must be the itchiest thing ever worn by anyone in the last five hundred years.

"Well?" Kynder asked, the overhead light reflecting harshly off his square, owlish glasses. He did a little twirl and asked, "What do you think? Don't I look *exactly* like a fifth-century druid?"

Since they had returned to Shadyside, Kynder had become obsessed with general Arthuriana. He spent most of his time on the computer reading about the old days, when Romans were a scourge, and magic roamed freely over the cliffs and through the dells, and knights battled regularly and with much honor.

In short, he'd become a Dark Ages Dr Pepper head.

Kay rolled her eyes and pushed by him. "No, Kynder,"

she said loudly, "not *exactly*. I don't think druids wore Nikes. And if they had glasses, they sure didn't look anything like yours." Kay opened the fridge and stared into it.

"Oh, well, besides that," Kynder said. "I'm sure they didn't wear underwear, either."

"*Gross*," Kay said, closing the fridge without taking anything out.

They heard the front door open and close. Lance clambered into the kitchen carrying a couple of big empty buckets and a short two-by-four. "Hey, dudes! Who wants to help me put some new sparring dummies together?"

"I do!" Kay said, quickly moving toward the patio door. She loved making things that she could later destroy with Cleomede.

Lance followed her and paused next to a silent Artie. He knew how hard it had been for Artie to wait to return to the Otherworld to save his friend. "C'mon, dude," Lance said. "Don't mope. It'll be good to work. Go get the circular saw and meet us in the yard."

"All right," Artie said softly.

"Good," Lance said. He went out back and Artie ambled after him.

Artie did actually feel a little better as he and his knights worked on the dummies. Lance measured, Artie cut some two-by-fours, and Kay and Bedevere assembled. They'd made dozens of dummies over the past couple of weeks and had it down pat. Artie liked the growl of the saw and the smell of the sawdust. Lance had been right: working was good.

Artie finished cutting the last batch of lumber and turned off the saw. His ears rang a little from the noise, but this unpleasant sound was quickly replaced by a vigorous burst of birdsong.

A lot of birdsong.

Too much birdsong.

The high-pitched vibrato got so loud that everyone had to cover their ears. Looking around, Artie realized that the surrounding oaks and maples were dripping with songbirds. It was as if they had simply materialized in the trees. Some were extremely colorful, but most were jet-black with little red tufts on the tops of their heads.

Artie got a sick feeling in the pit of his stomach, and the back of Kay's neck went cold. The siblings could feel each other's unease—a special gift they shared. A slight breeze sifted through the yard. Kynder walked onto the patio to see what was going on, and as he did the birds stopped singing, as if following a command.

Total silence reigned for a few moments, and then *BOOM*! A blast of blue light sparked the middle of the yard, and the birds took wing away from the explosion, expanding outward in a ring.

The blue light chased the birds and then fell back, gathering above the grass like a little supernova. It became very bright, forcing Artie to shut his eyes as a strong wind swept through, blowing leaves and sawdust everywhere.

When the air around them settled, Artie cautiously opened his eyes.

Collapsed amid a mess of building supplies was Merlin, a great spike of wood driven through his left thigh.

"Merlin!" shouted Kay.

Everyone rushed to the fallen wizard, and Lance gently rolled him onto his back. Kynder inspected the wound in his leg, and Kay asked, "Should we call nine-one-one?"

"No," Merlin wheezed. His eyelids fluttered and his skin was ashen. His tattoos were blurred and faded, like they'd aged a thousand years.

Artie stepped forward. Bedevere, fearing some unseen treachery, went to the shed and grabbed his claymore.

"What do you need us to do?" Lance asked with a soldier's urgency.

"There," Merlin said, using his eyes to indicate a white canvas bag gripped tightly in his hand. "In there."

Kynder grabbed it and peered inside. "But it's empty!"

"Reach in. A bottle. A wooden cane."

Kynder stuck his hand into the bag. What a wonder! It was full of furry things and slick things; hard things and gummy things; rocks, dirt, and leaves. Kynder felt small bones and claws, and sifted his hands through a mass of marbles. He thrust his whole arm into the thing, even though from the outside the bag was only about a foot long.

"I can't find them." Kynder panted.

"Deeper," Merlin ordered. Kynder pushed farther into the bag. "There," the wizard whispered.

Kynder felt a cone-shaped bottle and a length of wood. He wrapped his fingers around both and yanked his arm out.

The bottle was full of a brown, unappealing liquid. The piece of wood was a gray walking cane, the handle carved like a roosting owl, one eye shut, one open.

Merlin stared at the liquid. Kynder pulled at the wax stopper, but it didn't budge.

"Mr. Kingfisher, hold it out," said Bedevere. Kynder did, and with a clean stroke Bedevere used his ginormous sword to slice the wax-covered top off the bottle.

An unholy stench of rotten eggs, wet dog hair, and gym socks shot from the opening. Kynder held it at arm's length, and everyone took a step back.

"Put it to my lips, please," Merlin said.

Kynder did, and Merlin gulped down the elixir like it was chocolate milk. Merlin's color returned, and he held his hand out for his cane. Kynder passed it to him and, with Lance's help, Merlin sat up.

"Now, Mr. Lance, please push that blasted thing through my leg," Merlin said, indicating the piece of wood in his thigh.

Lance nodded. One end of the shaft stuck out of the top of Merlin's thigh by less than an inch, while the other end protruded from the hamstring at a handsbreadth. "This looks like a crossbow bolt," Lance said.

"'Tis. Get rid of it," Merlin said.

"It's gonna hurt."

"Nonsense. Do it!"

"Right," Lance said, propping Merlin's leg against his own. "On three. One. Two. Three."

Lance pushed the tip of the crossbow bolt through the wound as Kay let out a long "Ewwwww!" The old man grimaced but didn't make a noise. Then Lance grabbed the other end of the bloody bolt and yanked it out.

Merlin grunted and said, "Thank you. Please throw that as high as you can."

Lance flung the bolt into the air with a great under-hand motion. When it reached its apex, Merlin pointed the carved end of his cane at it. The owl's closed eye opened briefly, and the bolt exploded into a million little pieces.

"There," Merlin said, satisfied. He looked totally spent.

"Dude, you need a tourniquet," Lance said as he applied pressure to the wizard's thigh.

Merlin nodded weakly as his color faded again.

Bedevere dropped his claymore and ripped off his T-shirt. He handed it to Lance, who quickly and expertly stanched the flow of blood from the wizard's leg.

"Water," Merlin said. "I'm so thirsty."

Bedevere ran into the house.

Breathless, Artie knelt next to his friend and asked, "Merlin—what happened?"

Merlin's head rolled toward Artie. It took all his effort to say, "I tried to find Qwon. I tried to go to Fenland. But Morgaine . . ."

And before he could say any more, he passed out.

𝕸erlin was moved to the guest bedroom, and Lance dressed his wound properly. For the rest of the day and through the night, Merlin slept.

He woke at noon the next day and asked for water, toast, and four Advils. "Magic is good, but magic plus medicine is great," he said faintly. He ate, swallowed the pills, and went back to sleep.

He woke again at dinnertime. Artie was in the room reading a comic book. Merlin looked at the thin boy who had freed him from his prison, the invisible tower. Merlin couldn't believe it: after all these centuries, after all his suffering, after all his scheming, his plan was working.

Merlin whispered, "My boy, how are you?"

Artie looked up from his comic book and said, "Good,

I guess. But how are *you*?"

"I'll be fine," Merlin said, a smile creasing his face. "I'm sorry I didn't come sooner."

Artie shrugged. "Don't sweat it."

Merlin propped himself up. "It must have been hard to wait. I know how badly you want to get your friend back." He paused for a moment before adding, "In fact, Artie Kingfisher, we *need* to get her back."

"Of course we do—she belongs in Shadyside, not in the Otherworld!" Artie insisted, but clearly Merlin meant something more. Artie stood and asked, "What's going on?"

Merlin started to get out of bed. "It's better if I tell everyone. Are they here?"

"Yeah, they are. But I want you to tell me first. I am the king, after all."

Merlin gave Artie a hard look. "As you wish, my liege," he said with a little less sincerity than Artie would have hoped for. "Qwon's in trouble. She doesn't have much time." Merlin raised his head and looked Artie in the eye. "We need to get her so she won't be killed."

"What?" Artie asked, taking a step backward.

"I'm sorry, my boy. We have ten days."

"*Ten days?* What are you talking about?" The fact that Artie wasn't already there, actively helping Qwon, was killing him.

Merlin stood. "When you and Mr. Thumb opened the

crossover at Serpent Mound, things were set in motion. Things that can't be stopped," he said. "The worlds became aware of one another. If they are to continue to reunite— and then remain united—you must open the King's Gate on Avalon before the next new moon rises."

"I don't understand—" Artie began.

"It really would be easier to explain this to everyone at the same time, my boy."

"Okay," Artie blurted, his heart beating through his chest. "But tell me one thing."

"What is it, sire?"

Again, Merlin's tone sounded slightly condescending, which Artie didn't dig at all. "Is she all right?" Artie asked.

"As far as I can tell, yes."

"Good," Artie said, his heart rate easing. "Let's go see the others then."

Artie helped Merlin downstairs and into the living room, where everyone was engrossed in some TV show. "Ahem," Merlin said.

Kay spun and exclaimed, "Merlin!" Bedevere switched off the tube, and they took turns giving Merlin a heartfelt welcome.

As they settled down, the wizard asked what they'd been up to while he was away. "Not much," Kay answered. "School, chores, sword practice, video games, school."

"Target practice," added Lance.

"Trying to understand algebra," Bedevere lamented.

"Preparing the store to reopen," Thumb said from a small chair on the coffee table. He'd been in Cincinnati until the night before, taking care of the IT, which had been closed since the actual invisible tower had come crashing down around it.

They chatted idly for a few more minutes, awkwardly avoiding all the things they wanted to talk about. Finally Artie, his knee bouncing furiously, leaned forward and urged, "Forget us, Merlin. Tell them what you told me!"

All eyes whipped to the wizard.

Merlin tried on a well-meaning smile. "Qwon is in trouble," he said.

"What kind of trouble?" Kynder asked.

"I'm afraid her life is in danger."

"And we've got *ten days* to rescue her!" Artie said desperately.

Kay stood and said, "Ten days? What are we waiting for?"

Merlin held out his hand and patted the air. "We can't be hasty, dear Kay," he said. "You saw what happened to my leg. I was lucky to get out of there alive. Morgaine is quite powerful."

Kay plopped back down and asked, "But why only ten days?"

"Something about the new moon. Something about Avalon," Artie said.

Bedevere huffed as Merlin said, "Yes. If the next new moon rises and Artie hasn't yet gone to Avalon to open the King's Gate, then all crossovers—whether open or closed—will be sealed for a thousand years. Excalibur's pommel will no longer work, and everything we've fought for will be for nothing. You will not become king—"

"And Qwon will be trapped in the Otherworld," Kynder said.

"Precisely," Merlin said gravely.

"Then let's go to Avalon!" Artie blurted.

"Yeah, like, tonight!" Kay said.

"Ha!" Bedevere laughed. "No one has been to Avalon in ages. Isn't that right, Merlin?"

Thumb answered for the wizard. "That is right, Sir Bedevere. But *we* will go there. And once we do, the game is changed."

Artie leaned forward and said, "It'll be my whatchama-callit . . . my coronation, won't it?"

Merlin and Thumb nodded together. "Yes, sire," Merlin said. "Once you are returned to Avalon, you will be the king of Otherworld, and all there must bow to you, including Morgaine, who will be forced to return your friend. If not, she will pay the price." The wizard looked giddy with anticipation on this last point.

"How do they get to Avalon then?" Kynder asked, a little nervous to let his children go off on another quest for the ancient wizard.

"By retrieving the Seven Swords," Merlin said matter-of-factly.

"Ha!" Bedevere repeated, even more defiantly than before.

"Hey, c'mon, Beddy," Kay scolded. "What's so hard about getting a few more swords? We've proven that we're pretty good at that already."

"The Seven Swords aren't your average swords, Kay," Bedevere scoffed. "They're only the seven most magical blades of the Dark Ages. One of them is Excalibur, which, inconveniently, is being held by our enemy. Most of the others have been hidden for a very long time!"

"Not anymore," Thumb said, nodding at Merlin.

Bedevere's eyes widened as Merlin said, "It wasn't easy, my dear Bedevere, I'll give you that. Researching the locations of the Seven Swords was a major project of ours during my detention in the invisible tower, and all the work has paid off. We have found nearly all of them!"

"And while Excalibur may be under wraps at the moment," Thumb said, "we already have one in our possession."

"Cleomede!" Artie exclaimed.

"Precisely." Merlin beamed. "The others are Gram, a

Norse broadsword; Kusanagi, a Japanese katana; Orgulus, a French rapier; The Anguish, a bizarre fairy blade; and lastly the mysterious Peace Sword. This one has special meaning. In the old days it was used by the traitor Mordred to kill Arthur the First."

"Whoa," Artie said.

"Gram, which like Excalibur can only be retrieved by its rightful owner, is in Sweden," Merlin said. Lance quietly pumped his fist, happy that this time he might be able to help—even if he couldn't go to the Otherworld, he could definitely jet to Sweden.

"Kusanagi is in a strange part of the Otherworld," Thumb said, "that can only be accessed from a crossover in a remote corner of Japan."

Merlin continued, "Orgulus is in a castle that exists simultaneously in both this world and the Otherworld."

"And The Anguish," Thumb added, "is safe in the hands of its rightful owner—a fairy named Shallot le Fey—in the Otherworld land of Leagon."

There was a pause before Artie asked, "And what about the Peace Sword? The one that killed the original Arthur?"

Merlin frowned. "A guard in Fenland wields it. Sadly, we haven't yet discovered who this guard is."

"We'll have to figure that out," Thumb said.

"In the next ten days," Kay added with a note of sarcasm.

"Yes, lass," Thumb confirmed. "We will do it."

They were silent for a few moments as this news sank in. Artie's mind spun, but no matter where it went, it kept returning to Qwon. He had to get her back, alive and well. He thought about the last time he'd hung out with her, when she caught Artie and Kay playing with Cleomede in the backyard. She'd taken a turn with Kay's sword, and Artie remembered how expert she was at wielding it. Then it hit him.

"Qwon's important for another reason, isn't she?" Artie asked Merlin directly.

Merlin squinted as he said, "Yes, she is."

"Kusanagi—the Japanese sword—it's Qwon's, isn't it?" Artie guessed.

"Yes, my boy," Merlin said with a smile.

Kay couldn't believe it. She threw up her arms and said, "And I suppose Gram belongs to Erik Erikssen? I'm pretty sure he's like a thousand percent Norse, or Swedish or whatever."

"Ha! Right! Can you guys imagine?" Artie said with a laugh.

But neither Merlin nor Thumb returned his laughter.

"Actually, yes," Thumb said.

"*What?*" Kay blurted.

"This is all pretty convenient," Kynder said. "Artie, Kay, Qwon, Erik. All in Shadyside?"

"Convenient my foot," Merlin quipped. "Do you have any idea the lengths that I had to go to get these children's families to move closer to you? The Onakeas are from Hawaii. Imagine how hard it is to convince Hawaiians that their lives will be better in Pittsburgh—nothing against Pittsburgh, of course, lovely place. The Erikssens were easier since they were from Ohio, but even so."

"So it's not all a coincidence?" Kay asked. The idea that she and Erik, who happened to like her a lot, were *meant* to spend time together was slightly nauseating.

"No, Kay, it's not," Merlin said.

"It makes sense," Artie said, standing up. "It's why Qwon knew what she was doing with Cleomede that day, Kay. It's why Morgaine could key in on her. She's like us. She's . . . different." Merlin nodded, and Artie continued, "All right. How do we go about this?"

The wizard smiled. "Using the pommel, you will leapfrog around this world and the Otherworld, opening crossovers as you go, seeking out the Seven Swords. Naturally Morgaine will try to stop you when she can. Of course she wants to prevent you from returning to Avalon, but she also does not want the crossovers opened. They devour magical energy through the ether, so more open crossovers equals less power for Morgaine, and the less power she has, the easier she will be to defeat!"

At this Merlin clapped his hands excitedly.

"Fine, but how are we going to get Excalibur?" Artie asked.

Merlin sighed and said, "I'm still working on that."

"Great," Kay said flatly.

Artie wasn't totally satisfied either, but what choice did they have? He said, "Okay. Let's get started. Like, now."

"Tomorrow, lad," Thumb said. "We've got to recruit Erik first, and also ready ourselves."

"Yes—tomorrow," Merlin said. "I've drafted a half dozen magical letters that will enchant whoever reads them, making them unaware that you're not around. They're for Erik's parents and your school, since you'll be absent for the next week or so. Lance—can you run them to the post office in the morning?"

"Course," Lance said. "Then can you send me to Sweden? I really want to help find Gram. I don't enjoy feeling like a fifth wheel so much, you know?"

"Of course, Mr. Lance," Merlin said with a broad smile. "But this time you can help in any way Artie sees fit. You will be joining us in the Otherworld!"

"*What?*" Lance barked.

"That's right! I've brought back some talismans that will enable you to cross as easily as Artie or Kay or Mr. Thumb."

"Hoo-ah!" Lance said, standing up and knocking his

chair over. He bounded into the backyard whooping and hollering.

"That's awesome," said Kay, happy to know they'd have another ally over there.

"Seriously," Artie agreed.

"Well," Kynder said, smacking his thighs and standing up. "Merlin—why don't we let the guys take this all in? I have to go and do some dishes. Do you feel well enough to give me a hand?"

"Yes, of course," the wizard said, easing out of his chair. He joined Kynder and they went into the kitchen, leaving Artie, Kay, Thumb, and Bedevere to talk about going back to the Otherworld.

Kynder rinsed dishes and Merlin loaded them into the dishwasher, and for a while they didn't speak. Kynder broke their silence when he said, "Merlin, there's something I've been meaning to ask you."

"Yes?"

"A few weeks ago you mentioned that Arthur was genetically engineered by someone in the Otherworld." Merlin nodded. "Do you know who it was?"

Merlin put down a plate and removed a smooth, dark pebble from his pocket. "Take this, Kynder, and keep it with you at all times. I need you to do something for me. You must come to the Otherworld this time as well and go to the Great Library of Sylvan. I need you to do some research for us."

"Okay . . . ," Kynder said cautiously, taking the pebble.

Merlin cleared his throat and said ominously, "The children cannot know what I am about to tell you. Promise you won't tell them."

Kynder's grip on the little stone tightened. "Okay, I promise," he said hollowly, almost like the wizard was casting a spell on him.

"Morgaine, Lordess of Fenland, made Artie. I know it sounds crazy. But King Arthur needed to return so he could get Excalibur and free me. And I needed to be freed so that Morgaine could try to kill me. She never could have reached me in the invisible tower. It was my prison, but it was also my refuge. Her plan went awry—she never intended for Artie to be stolen from her—but the end result is the same. I stand here before you a free wizard."

"Whoa," Kynder said, his hairs rising along his neck.

"I know. Now, this is what I need your help with. According to the Lady of the Lake, it's not just Morgaine who wants to kill me. Excalibur does too. I need you to find out *why* the sword wants me dead."

Kynder pursed his lips. "Okay," he said, feeling a little dazed. "But what should we tell Arthur?"

"We'll tell Artie that you're being sent to the Library to try to discover the identity of the person who wields the Peace Sword."

"Got it," Kynder said, clutching the pebble with purpose.

Already he could feel the Otherworld's power pulsing through it.

This time, when his kids went to the Otherworld, Kynder Kingfisher would be going too.

Once again Dred carried Qwon up and down many stairs, and in and around many turns. The effect was disorienting; she had about zero idea of where she was being taken.

Eventually he stepped outside and walked the length of a long portico. Birds chittered and trilled. The air was still.

They stopped at the end of the portico, and Dred dropped Qwon onto the damp flagstone. He knelt and uncorked a small bottle and held it to her lips. She drank eagerly, knowing it would allow her to move. But before she could drink it all, Dred pulled the vial away. She could hold her head up, but couldn't move the rest of her body yet.

"You can talk, if you like," Dred said matter-of-factly.

His voice had a nasal quality it lacked before, like he was really, really stuffed up.

Qwon started to ask, "I can?" but all that came out was a weak "Ike?" Her body, still mostly paralyzed, wasn't quite ready to speak.

Talking was not what she wanted to do, though. What she wanted to do was scream. She wanted to snatch the sword from Dred's belt and show him a thing or two about how to use it. She wanted to see her kidnapper's face, but he was still wearing that stupid helmet. So annoying.

Dred studied this girl. He'd never seen one like her before. Her hair was thick and black and straight and cut like a boy's. Her dark, unwavering eyes were slightly slanted. Her face was flat and broad, and her cheeks were high and round.

He thought she was pretty, but he wasn't about to say so.

"Who're you? Where's'iss place?" Qwon's mouth was starting to feel better, and she was regaining the ability to form clear words.

"You heard. I'm Mordred. And you know where you are. Castel Deorc Wæters."

Qwon shook her head, never allowing her gaze to shift from the narrow slit in Dred's faceplate.

For the first time, the oddness of the helmet registered with her. Its general shape was unremarkable, like an upside-down, handleless pot with a crease rising from the forehead. A section was cut out for Dred's face, but this was covered with the faceplate, which was shaped like a giant leaf. There were perforations over his mouth and nose, and a long slit for the eyes. Rising from the top of the helmet were a pair of crooked deer horns, one red, the other blue.

"I mean, where's th'castle?" Qwon asked.

"Oh, right," Dred said, turning away. "The castle is in Fenland, and Fenland is in a place known simply as the Otherworld. The Otherworld is your side's dark reflection. Fairies live here, and dragons, and shadows—and bad people like me!" He whipped his head toward her, and her heart skipped a beat.

"Forget it," Qwon said, frustrated that this Dred guy wasn't making any sense. "Just take me to my quarters," she said, fully regaining her speech.

"As you wish," he said. Dred stood and unlocked a super-thick yellow door that was covered with bands of dark metal and rivets and spikes. In there were her quarters. In there was this feral fairy Morgaine had mentioned.

Dred pushed open the door, but instead of tossing her

in, he gave her the rest of the liquid. She drank it quickly as he said, "Well, I'll be seeing you, Qwon of Shadyside." Then he stepped through the doorway, pulled the door shut, and threw the lock.

Wait. She was being left outside?

Energy coursed through Qwon's body from her shoulders to her toes as the liquid took effect. She moved her arms and shook out her legs. She cracked her neck. She put her hands on the ground and gingerly stood.

The portico ran around three sides of a square courtyard that was about fifty feet across. A high stone wall at the far end marked the fourth side. Beyond it, Qwon could just see the top of the dark-green glass tower. By the position of the sun, she guessed that this marked the southern end of the yard, and somewhere past that was the drawbridge. She hoped all of this information would prove helpful in eventually escaping.

The roof of the portico slanted down toward the inside of the courtyard, and it was covered with shards of broken glass jutting up at all angles. The pillars supporting it were also covered in jagged glass. No escaping that way.

There were several doors along the walkway under the portico. All were heavy-looking, each painted a different ridiculously bright color, and, Qwon presumed, locked from the inside. In the middle of the yard was a chest-high birdbath made from some kind of turquoise metal. Qwon stepped onto the grass. The ground was soft. The courtyard smelled good.

It smelled *remarkably* good. Like . . . like shavings of Ivory soap and fresh-cut grass and newly plucked honeysuckle all at once.

While she was enthralled by the smell, Qwon was knocked in the back of the head. She fell onto her hands and knees, and something whisked by her in a blur of pink and black, disappearing in the shadows.

"Who's there?" Qwon demanded of the blur.

A high-pitched giggle came from her right, and Qwon realized the source of the smell was there too. Still on the ground, she whipped her head around and saw the end of a wooden stick as it disappeared at the far end of the yard. *Aha!*

Qwon sprang to her feet and followed her nose. Adrenaline fueled her movements. She looked desperately around for anything to fight with, but there was nothing.

She raced to the western side of the portico, but when she got there, the thing—which must have been this fairy—darted to the other side.

"Stop moving!" Qwon yelled.

The fairy answered by giggling again.

Just then a long pole came shooting out of a little window in Dred's yellow door. Qwon knew exactly what it was: a quarterstaff. Qwon ran for it, but the fairy somehow tripped her, and Qwon fell on her face, taking a mouthful of grass. As she was about to get up, the fairy bolted across the length of her body. The fairy's feet felt like little hooves on her back.

Qwon thrust her right arm forward and snagged the ankle of the lightning-quick sprite, causing it to fall face-first in the grass, too. The fairy squealed. And then—and then it *sprayed* Qwon, just like a skunk!

Only the smell was amazing.

Qwon's grip loosened as she was transported to a field of lavender and flowering sweet peas. A smile crawled across her face. Her eyes brightened.

The fairy wriggled free and churned toward the staff. Qwon came around and yelped, "No!" just as the fairy bent to pick it up. But before it could, it was plonked on the forehead with a stone that Dred had thrown from the little window. "Ouch!" the fairy barked.

Qwon got her first good look at the fairy. She was very thin and stood a little less than five feet tall. Her shoulders were only a foot across, and her legs were so long she hardly had a torso. Her arms were also disturbingly long, and she had pink hair drawn into an athletic ponytail that nearly reached the back of her knees. Her hair had three thick black streaks, one down the middle and two on either side above the ears, which added to the skunk effect. She was barefoot, but was otherwise dressed in plain cotton pants and a matching shirt.

The fairy bent to pick up the staff again, and this time a small fusillade of stones sailed from the window. She screeched and bolted away without looking back.

Qwon sprinted forward and slid feet first, scooping up the staff as she passed it. She threw her back against Dred's door and said through the opening, "Thanks."

"Don't thank me yet," her kidnapper replied wryly.

He was clearly enjoying this.

Jerk, thought Qwon.

She slid left along the wall to the corner, turned, and continued moving until she reached the middle of the next wall, where there was another door. She tried it. Locked. Just as she'd suspected.

Qwon let the staff fall into the crook of her arm and quickly tore two small strips of fabric from the bottom of her T-shirt. She balled them up and stuffed one in each nostril. She had to do something to defend herself from the fairy's intoxicating scent. Then she stepped toward the clearing, but before she even reached the grass, the fairy came from nowhere and poked Qwon's back. She tumbled forward, her staff in front of her, and wheeled around.

The sprite was in a semicrouch, her stick held across her body. Her face was twisted into a gnarly grimace. She was small but powerful.

Her eyes were the color of tropical seas, and their pupils were as deep and limitless as the night sky. Something about the balance of her features, the clear hue of her skin, and her tiny, knowing smile made Qwon freeze.

She was almost achingly beautiful. How was Qwon going to strike this creature?

But then the fairy hissed like a cornered cat, and sprayed again.

Qwon's nose plugs didn't block the scent completely, but they helped. She lunged forward and twirled her staff, knocking the fairy in the shoulder. The fairy did not retreat. She hissed again—revealing a mouthful of pointy teeth that belied her beauty—and continued fighting with a flurry of jabs and swings. Qwon parried them all, mixing in attacks of her own.

They were too equally matched.

Finally each jumped back. Qwon could hear Dred's muted laughter, which she did not appreciate. She did not like this game.

Qwon looked the fairy squarely in the eyes and said, "My name is Qwon Onakea, and I've been kidnapped. Who are you and why are you here?"

The fairy cocked her head. She said something that Qwon had a hard time understanding because, like her smell and her beauty, her voice was borderline enchanting.

The fairy repeated herself, taking pains to suppress whatever it was that made her voice so enrapturing. "I am Shallot le Fey," she said. "I was taken too, from my home in Leagon. I have been in this yard for a month, and until today have not seen a single person."

Qwon nodded slowly and said, "Well, Shallot, I'm from Pennsylvania, and I think we're going to be prisoners here together. Wherever this place is."

Qwon dropped her staff to her side. Shallot did the same.

Shallot took a few cautious steps and asked, "Are you also here because of the prophecy?"

Qwon frowned. "Prophecy?"

"From *The Fairy Book of Pretelling*. The one about the sword," Shallot explained. "The one about Excalibur. The one about Arthur and Merlin Ambrosius."

Qwon said weakly, "You mean the one about Artie Kingfisher?" As she said the words, she couldn't help but feel like they were the beginning of a bad joke.

Shallot stepped forward. She held out her hand palm down, in some unknown gesture of greeting, and said in her lovely voice, "Yes. The one about Artie Kingfisher."

𝕿𝖍𝖊 𝖒𝖔𝖗𝖓𝖎𝖓𝖌 𝖆𝖋𝖙𝖊𝖗 𝖙𝖍𝖊 𝕶𝖎𝖓𝖌𝖋𝖎𝖘𝖍𝖊𝖗𝖘 were told about the next phase of their adventures, Erik Erikssen showed up at their house complaining of a headache, saying, "I don't know why, but I just had to come over to your guys' house."

Merlin hadn't given advance warning about the spell he used to call Erik, and to her revulsion, Kay was the one who answered the door—in her nightgown. Thankfully, Erik was so out of it that he didn't seem to notice. He pushed by Kay, made for the living room, and dropped onto the sofa. Before Kay could get a word out, Merlin floated into the room and asked Kay to fetch a glass of warm water. She did. Merlin poured some powder into it and stirred the mixture with a finger. Then he gave the glass to Erik and with a velvety tone said, "I suggest you drink this, my boy."

Erik drank. No sooner had he handed the glass back to Merlin than he fell completely asleep.

"Knock him out to take him to the Otherworld," Kay observed. "I like it."

"Yes," Merlin said. "Erik should see the Otherworld before he's told about it. He'll be more easily convinced that way, I think."

Kay narrowed her eyes, nodded, and then bounded off to her room to get ready.

That morning the Kingfisher house buzzed with anticipation. Lance made sure his bow and arrows were in top shape. Kynder packed a large duffel bag with his Arthurian research and another with clothing. Bedevere sharpened his claymore and checked his armor. Kay packed the infinite backpack and made sure they had some warm clothes.

At eleven in the morning Artie was in his room looking over the stuff he'd laid out on his bed: Excalibur's empty scabbard, a pile of headlamps, and his trusty dagger, Carnwennan. He twirled Excalibur's pommel in his hand. And that was when it came to him!

He ran downstairs and found Merlin in the kitchen eating a peanut-butter-and-jelly sandwich.

"Merlin! I've got it!"

Merlin swallowed hard and wiped his mouth with the back of his hand. "What's that?" he asked.

"I know how we can get Excalibur! And rescue Qwon at the same time!"

Merlin tilted his head and asked, "How's that, my boy?"

"We just go there!" Artie exclaimed, holding out the pommel.

Merlin put down his sandwich and looked at it seriously. "You know, I never had a P-B-and-J before breaking out of the tower. It's so simple, yet so scrumptious!"

"Merlin, did you hear me? It'd be like a special ops raid or whatever—drop in behind enemy lines, get what we need, and get out. It's perfect!"

Merlin gave Artie a forlorn look. "Yes, it sounds perfect. And it *is* true that the pommel can take you anywhere. But you first have to know where you're going, Artie, or at least have a very good mental picture of it. You can transport to the Library now, for instance, or your court-in-exile, or even Tiberius's hidden cave—but only because you know those places. Remember when you ordered Excalibur to take you to the Font a few weeks back?"

"Sure," Artie said as dejection began to settle around him like a fog.

"Did it take you right to it?"

"No . . ."

"Right. Listen, my boy, even if you could get into the Castel, there's no guarantee you would be anywhere near Excalibur. What if you transported into a trap? What if you landed in Morgaine's bedroom? You could materialize inside a wall, or in midair over the moat! I'm sorry, Artie, but we can't risk it. However . . ."

Artie looked up eagerly. "Yes?"

"If we could *find out* where Excalibur is being kept, then your idea may be quite effective. What we need, then, is—"

"A spy!" Artie yelped.

"Precisely. But where to get one?" Merlin thought for a few moments and then snapped his fingers. "I've got it. Thumb and Tiberius were planning on meeting Lord Lot, the leader of the fairy kingdom of Leagon, to request the service of Shallot le Fey and her fairy blade, The Anguish. While they are there, they will also ask him for a spy. Fairies hate Morgaine and her minions, so Lot should be eager to help. Plus, Leagonese spies are the absolute best."

"Great!" Artie said. "Sounds like a plan." And before Merlin could say anything else, Artie bolted back to his room.

They were finally set.

Kynder, Merlin, Lance, Thumb, Bedevere, Artie, and Kay circled up in the game room, where all this craziness had started. Lance carried Erik, who was still fast asleep, over his shoulder like a wounded soldier.

Before going to the court-in-exile, they were stopping at the Library to drop off Kynder and Merlin. The wizard would help Kynder get set up so he could find out more about the identity of the person who wielded the Peace Sword (and also look into why Excalibur wanted Merlin iced—but that was a secret). Then Merlin would leave and go to a secret location he called The Bunker, which was where the wizard had learned much of his magic back in the day. He told them it contained no end of arcana and scrolls and ancient magical instruments—more even than what he had managed to gather in the fantastical basement of the Invisible Tower. It was from this location that Merlin would do his part to disrupt the lordess of Fenland.

Artie readied the pommel but before he could open the moongate, Merlin said, "Wait! I have some things to hand out." Merlin rummaged through his magical bag and pulled out three flat objects, each the size of a thin magazine.

"Are those iPads?" Kay asked.

"They are! Jailbreaked too!" Merlin said proudly, and then he mused, "Fascinating contraptions. I've kept one for myself, of course." He gave the others to Artie, Kynder, and Bedevere. "Since my escape, Mr. Thumb has been working on a port of the *Otherworld* game and several very special apps."

"So, what, you want us to play *Otherworld* while we're in the Otherworld?" Kay asked. "Isn't that, like . . . redundant?"

Erik rattled out a loud snore. Lance shifted him on his shoulder.

"I don't expect you to play it, although I wouldn't stop you if you wanted to during your downtime," Merlin said jovially. "But it's the apps that are important. There are atlases of both sides, and also an app with loads of information about each of the Seven Swords."

"And," Thumb added proudly, "I've modified the tablets to link up with the Otherworld's cellular network. So we'll be able to video-chat!"

Bedevere shook his head in wonderment. Kay said, "Far out."

As they put them away, Thumb clapped and said, "Well, lads, what do you think? Master Artie, shall we?"

"Yeah, Tom, we shall." Artie stepped into the middle of the circle. Kay took Kynder's hand and gave it a squeeze. She was glad he was coming with them this time, even if they did have to leave him at the Library. Kynder squeezed back. He was glad too.

Artie knelt and looked at his knights. Bedevere had donned his black suit of plate armor, minus the right arm. Lance sported his usual mix of commando and Robin Hood gear plus a thick down vest, his compound bow—decorated with American flags and screaming eagles—slung over his shoulder. Kynder was dressed like he was about to do some gardening, but since he was going to stay at the Library, that was just fine. Thumb was dressed casually in his little linen suit. Kay had on blue jeans and sneakers and a leather-and-ring-mail jerkin under a sweatshirt. Like Artie, she also wore one of the titanium-laced undershirts Merlin had given them over the summer. Artie was dressed almost exactly like his sister, plus he had his trusty buckler strapped to his left arm.

Artie closed his eyes. He held out the pommel and said quietly but forcefully, "*Lunae lumen.*" A moongate swung open and engulfed them, leaving the game room in Shadyside, Pennsylvania, completely empty.

After dropping Kynder and Merlin at the Library, the rest of the group moved on to the court-in-exile. Lance had spent so much time with Merlin and Thumb at the Invisible Tower back in Cincinnati that he took the wonders of the Otherworld in stride, dropping right into military grunt mode, ready for anything.

But Erik, who they woke with a packet of smelling salts, was another story.

All the weirdness left the newest knight in a state of shock.

First, there was Bercilak. As the Green Knight ambled up to the party with his arms held out for a hug, Erik's jaw dropped to the floor.

"My good knights! How I've missed you!" Bercilak said.

"Bercy!" Kay said, running to him. She embraced Bercilak and slapped him hard on the back, sending a loud sound reverberating through his bodiless suit of armor.

"My lord! Sir Kay! Bedevere! I've taken fine care of your feline. And Mr. Thumb! How is the old gnome? And we've added an archer, I see!" Lance gave Bercilak a deep nod. "And who's this? Another new knight, sire?"

Artie walked over to Erik, who was sitting down, and whispered, "Don't worry, you'll get used to it."

"To what?" Erik gasped. "The no-head thing?"

"Yeah," Artie confirmed. "And that he's a little, well, weird."

"You can say that again," Erik said.

Bercilak approached Erik and said, "Hallo! I am the Green Knight, the Empty Knight, Bercilak the Hollow! It is my esteemed pleasure to meet you, Sir . . ."

Erik stared up at this walking, talking suit of green armor and said, "Uh, Erik?"

"Uh-Erik! Fabulous! Tell me, are you related to Uh-Enmo? Or maybe Uh-Elring?"

"Uh, no?" Erik said.

"Uh-No? I've not met him."

"No, Bercy," Artie explained. "He's not related to any of those people. This is Erik. He's from our side, and this is his first time here, so go easy on him, all right?"

Bercilak took Erik's hand and shook it. "Of course! Sorry for the confusion, Erik the New."

Erik looked at the empty space where Bercilak's eyes

would have been and said, "No problem, I guess."

"Good!" Bercilak dropped Erik's hand and spun around. "Now—where is Wilt Chamberlain? The dragon is out by the stable and wants to parley with him."

"Dr-dragon?" Erik stammered.

Lance said quietly, "Yeah, pretty cool, right? I can't wait to meet one either."

Cool was not what Erik was thinking, since he had no desire to meet a dragon. None.

Artie answered Bercilak, "Merlin—Wilt Chamberlain— is at the Library. He's with Kynder."

Bercilak tilted in a way that clearly meant, "Who's Kynder?"

"Kynder's our dad," Kay explained.

"I can parley with the dragon," Thumb said. "He and I need to shove off for Leagon soon anyway."

Artie stepped forward. If he was really becoming a king, he'd better start acting like one. "And I can talk to him too, you know."

"Of course, sire," Thumb said, bowing slightly.

"Let's to him then, shall we?" Bercilak boomed.

Artie ushered a dazed Erik toward the door as the group followed the Green Knight to the stables, where sure enough there was a great green dragon sitting in the paddock.

Artie and Kay ran to Tiberius, eager to greet him.

Thumb took his time. He was still peeved about having been frozen in Tiberius's rock breath on their last adventure. Lance was extremely impressed and let out a long whistle.

But Erik Erikssen, too shocked to deal, passed out again.

Bercilak caught him and eased him carefully to the ground. "I think this one is a little overwhelmed, sire!"

Kay gave Erik a sympathetic look and said, "Honestly? I think he took that pretty well. What do you think, Tiberius?"

"Hmmmmph," the dragon replied.

"Exactly what I was thinking," Kay deadpanned.

"Boy-king," Tiberius sang. "You're not armed. You should be armed."

It was true. Artie had Excalibur's scabbard strapped to his back, and Carnwennan hung from his belt, but he did look a little light.

"The dragon is right, my lord!" Bercilak exclaimed. "Strange things are afoot these past days. You should be more ready than you are."

"Care to help me pick out some new toys then, Bercilak?" Artie asked.

"Of course! Maybe we can find something for Erik the New too."

Bercilak led Artie back in to peruse his weapon racks. Kay joined them while Lance stayed behind with Erik. Bedevere went into the stables and let out his saber-toothed tiger, which was very happy to see his old master. They cuddled for a while, and then the tiger and the dragon started playing. Erik momentarily came around, but when he saw Tiberius pinning a white saber-toothed tiger to the ground he promptly passed out again.

A few minutes later Artie, Kay, and Bercilak emerged from the court, with Artie toting some new items.

"Whatcha get from the treasure trove, dude?" Lance asked.

"What's the spear called again?" Artie asked Bercilak.

"Rhongomyniad."

"Yeah, that," Artie said to Lance. "I have to learn to say it really well, because after I throw it, I can call it by name and it will zip back to my hand!"

"Cool!" Lance exclaimed.

Bedevere pointed at a small, cutlass-shaped sword that hung opposite Carnwennan on Artie's belt. "Is that Flixith, sire?"

"Sure is," Artie said.

"What can it do?" Lance asked.

"When he swings it around, it'll make him look like he's got four arms instead of two, which I guess is supposed to scare the cookies out of our enemies," Artie explained.

"Good," Thumb said seriously. "We have much work to do."

Artie nodded in agreement and motioned for everyone

to circle up near Tiberius. Lance carried Erik, who was coming back around again and moaning.

"Well, Tiberius? What's new in the Otherworld?" Artie asked.

Tiberius slowly blinked his magnificent, rainbow-colored eyes. "Hmmph," the dragon said. "The wizard's play was ill-conceived. He shouldn't've gone to Fenland. It has unsettled things more'n necessary. The witch's agents are on the hunt. She's unhappy. If Lord Numinae were well, I'd be more at ease."

"How is Numinae?" Artie asked.

"Hmmmph. Lord Numinae is better'n. He'll get back soon, in one form or another." No one bothered to ask what he meant by that. Erik, awake now, looked on silently.

"And Cassie?" Kay asked. She hadn't mentioned Cassie to anyone in the last few weeks, but she really wanted to know how—and where—her mom was.

"She is safe'n but not well. Her mind was poisoned fully by the witch. Lord Numinae will help her, young Kay, but some time will pass'n afore you see her again." Tiberius turned one of his long ears toward the woods beyond the stables. "Tell me, boy-king—can you call'n the wizard here?"

"Now?"

"Hmmph, now. He might be useful."

"I don't underst—"

Artie was cut short as a sound like a revving chain saw echoed through the surrounding trees. Bedevere's cat jumped up and eyed the woods.

"What was that, Tiberius?" Thumb asked, slightly alarmed.

"Hmmph. The witch's agents are on the hunt."

The buzzing resumed, and the trees to the east danced before being shredded to bits as a swarm of giant dragonflies burst through them.

Artie and his crew were surrounded in an instant. A rainbow of insects—hundreds of them, each around four feet long—blanketed the stable yard. Kay, Bedevere, Lance, and Thumb drew their weapons and swung or shot at them wildly. Kay had a lot of trouble getting close to any on account of Cleomede's special bug-repelling magic, but she still managed to down a few. Meanwhile, Bercilak leaped into action, hewing dragonflies with his double-edged ax. Lance managed to nock and shoot several arrows before resorting to using his bow as a hand weapon, swinging it around in wide arcs. Artie threw his spear directly overhead and impaled three dragonflies at once. He called it and it returned to him like a boomerang, driving into the ground at his feet. He drew Carnwennan and Flixith, pirouetting and flailing at the air. Flixith did indeed make it look like Artie had four arms, and at times even more, like a Hindu god. But the bugs didn't care.

They were bugs.

Their paperlike wings beat the knights on all sides, and the spiky barbs of their legs cut and scraped their skin.

The saber-toothed tiger killed so many dragonflies with such eager playfulness that, as far as it was concerned, the whole attack was a game.

Tiberius rose into the air, taking special care to protect Artie and Kay and Erik, the last of whom remained unarmed. The dragon used his long body to swat hordes of insects back into the woods and sprayed his acrid, crinkly breath selectively here and there, causing many bugs to fall to the ground half-encased in the dragon's black rock. These semi-frozen bugs buzzed and whined, and the desperate flapping of their wings grated on the ear.

But Tiberius remained calm. He didn't find the swarm to be incomprehensible or even much of a bother. He could see exactly how many insects there were, and while there were quite a few, the number wasn't unmanageable. They were only giant dragonflies, after all.

He swatted several more and saw that 518 were still alive and uninjured.

He looked down. Artie was a blur of arms. Dragonfly heads rolled at his feet.

Make that 514.

For all the expansive wonder of Tiberius's perception, though, he couldn't see everything. And at this particular moment he couldn't see that Erik Erikssen was being lifted by his shoulders into the air.

In fact no one noticed. But then Lance caught sight of Erik from the corner of his eye. "Artie, look!" Lance barked.

Erik was twenty feet above them. He was struck dumb with fear, but his face said it all.

"Lance!" Artie yelled.

"On it, dude!" replied Lance.

Lance let an arrow fly. It hit the dragonfly carrying Erik square in the eye.

The bug dropped him, and Erik's eyes bulged and his legs bicycled in the air. He seemed to be going a little crazy as he fell, his landing softened by a tall haystack. Fifty or sixty dragonflies swarmed to it immediately.

"Kay, come with me!" Artie said, and together they made their way toward the haystack.

But then it exploded. Half the dragonflies surrounding it were thrown off, while the other half darted up and around, jockeying for position as they tried to find a way to strike at Erik.

Or was that Erik? It was hard to tell. In place of the boy was a violent blur. A violent blur that had found something at the bottom of the haystack. Something that looked like a hammer.

"He's gone nuts!" Kay observed.

Erik felled the dragonflies so quickly, in every direction,

that they couldn't even touch him, let alone pick him up again.

Finally, after Erik had killed or maimed dozens of insects, they beat a retreat. Just as quickly as they'd arrived, the dragonflies regrouped and took to the sky.

The knights stared at Erik. His eyes were red with fury; his head whipped in every direction, looking for something to strike. It was like he was a cartoon character bursting with rage; Artie fully expected steam to spout from his ears.

Bedevere held out his sword and said, "Sir Erik, please, try to calm yourself."

Thumb mumbled, "A berserker . . ."

Artie knew what that was from all the fantasy games he'd played and books he'd read: someone who went into a savage frenzy in battle.

Erik began to calm. His movements became less erratic. His color returned.

"So, what, Erik's like a real Viking or something?" Kay asked.

"I—I guess," Artie said incredulously.

Why not? Really, with everything else that went on in their lives, why not?

Tiberius returned to the ground and settled behind them. Erik stared at the dragon with wonder, finally taking it in. Erik's arms and legs were limp and exhausted. His shoulders slumped. "Guys, *what* is going on around here?" he asked weakly.

Thumb stepped forward and said, "My boy, it's official. Welcome to the Otherworld."

IN WHICH A PLAN FORMS AND DRED HATES ON FAIRIES

𝕬fter 𝖜atc𝖍ing 𝕼𝖜on an𝖉 𝕾𝖍allot fight through the spy hole in his door, Dred gathered up Smash and went to report to Morgaine.

He wound through the castle and came to his mum's double doors. They were tall and curved at the top and had a fresh coat of bright-red paint. They had pewter knockers that were shaped like foxglove flowers. Dred stood still for a moment and then leaned forward, pressing an ear against one of the doors.

"Stop eavesdropping and come in!" Morgaine yelled, and the doors magically burst open.

How Dred wished she would teach him to do things like that. Despite all his pleas, she hadn't taught him even the simplest conjuration. He would never forgive her for that.

Morgaine sat at her vanity wearing a light-green cloak. All kinds of bottles and vials were arranged in front of her. Dred knew that some contained makeup, others held elixirs, and a precious few were filled with very strong potions.

She kept her back to him as she dabbed on some eye cream.

"How did it go? Qwon didn't see your face, did she?"

"It went okay. And no, she didn't see my face."

"Good. She mustn't."

"I *know*, Mum. They can't see my face. You've told me that a thousand times."

"Right. Now, tell me what happened."

Dred told his mother most, but not all, of the prisoners' meeting. He made sure to mention that Shallot had used her fairy scentlock ability to stun Qwon, but he intentionally left out the part about giving Qwon a staff, saying instead that Qwon had managed to break Shallot's staff in two and fought her off with one end.

Morgaine sighed. "Pity neither was killed. How I *wish* I could find the will to kill them myself." Dred said nothing as Morgaine wheeled around. Her cloak was clasped shut at the neck with a long pin shaped like a tree branch. A small fold of skin fell over the edge of the cloak. Dred thought this one small detail made her look so old. "Continue to watch them," she said, "and keep me apprised of their condition. Do not give them anything other than that weevil-infested porridge. Understood?"

"Understood, Mum," Dred said quietly.

"Now get out," Morgaine said, "before I turn you into a newt!"

Dred turned silently and loped out of his mother's chambers.

How he hated the person she'd become these last couple years. How he wished the old Morgaine would come back. Maybe when this whole thing was over—when Artie and Merlin were dead, and any open crossovers had been shuttered—she would go back to the way she used to be. Maybe.

Back in his bedroom he put Smash on a table and gave him a carrot. He moved to the door that led to the portico and slid open the little window that afforded a limited view of the courtyard. Qwon and Shallot were hunkered down in a patch of sunlight against the far wall. They talked casually, as if they were friends on a playground.

If he'd been within earshot, this is what Dred would have heard:

Qwon: So Artie is king of the Otherworld?

Shallot: Not yet, but he's getting closer.

QWON: Okay. But to become king he has to find these Seven Swords?

SHALLOT: Right. That's what the *Pretelling* says.

QWON: Crazy. So to help him we have to get the swords that are here—Excalibur and yours, The Anguish—and escape. How are we going to do that?

SHALLOT: Not exactly sure. But I think you should start by hitting me.

QWON: What?

SHALLOT: Hit me. Hard. The boy who brought you here is watching us through that door. Don't look.

QWON: Okay.

SHALLOT: In a few moments, act like I've insulted you—really insulted you. Then hit me.

QWON: What, then we fight again?

SHALLOT: No. Then I disappear. I can become nearly invisible. They won't be surprised if they can't see me—I've done it before. Meantime, you talk to Dred and try to get him to like you. Use the fact that he hates me as a conversation piece.

QWON: Why does he hate you?

SHALLOT: Fenlandians hate Leagonese, and vice versa. Also, I bit out a chunk of his ear when he captured me.

QWON: Oh.

SHALLOT: That's probably why he gave you that staff.

Anyway, convince him you hate me, try to bond with him over that, and maybe he'll open that door again. When he does, we make a run for it.

Qwon: I guess it's as good a plan as any. . . .

Shallot: It is. Listen—after I go invisible, I may torment you a little, just to keep up appearances. All right?

Qwon: Got it.

Shallot: Now hit me.

Dred strained as he watched the two captives conspire. How he hated the fairy! He hated the way she looked, the way she smelled, the way she disappeared for days at a time. He hated that she managed to survive.

And now he hated that these two seemed to be turning into friends.

But then! The odd-looking girl reared back and slapped the fairy across the cheek. The fairy was stunned. Clearly Qwon had been insulted. That wasn't very surprising—fairies *were* insulting. What *was* surprising was that the fairy wasn't striking back.

And then Qwon did something that made his heart leap! She reared back and slapped the fairy again—*with the back of her hand*! Man, did he wish he were the one knocking that creature around.

The fairy picked up her staff, and for a moment Dred's heart sank, as he was certain that Shallot le Fey would crush the girl's throat with it. But then the fairy sprayed her heady scentlock, and Qwon was thrown into frozen rapture. Shallot watched Qwon for a moment before tossing her long, pink hair and disappearing.

Dred had no idea how much time would pass before he saw her again. It could be hours. It could be weeks. He hated when she was invisible, and he figured Qwon wouldn't like it either. His spirits lifted a little as it dawned on him that these two prisoners were not going to be friends. They had begun their relationship by fighting, after all. What he mistook for friendship a few moments ago he now knew had been a ruse on the fairy's part. She probably wanted something from Qwon. She was probably trying to trick her in some way.

Fairies really were the worst.

Dred knew that Qwon would be stuck in her pungent dreamland for at least another half hour. He closed the spy hole and crossed his room. As he passed Smash, the animal leaped out of a running wheel and asked, "Dred play?"

"Not now, Smash," Dred said. He plopped into the chair at his writing desk and looked at a picture of him and his mom from a few years back when they'd gone on vacation to see the Towering Dunes of Sec. He looked like a child, and his mom, though still incredibly old, looked like a much younger woman.

Dred sighed. He put his elbows on the desk and cupped his chin in his hands. He looked at the wall, which had a mirror in a simple square frame on it. His reflection stared back.

A reflection that was the spitting image of Artie Kingfisher.

"**If the witch is that** active, then it's time to get this show on the road," Merlin said over a choppy video link on Artie's iPad. He'd left Kynder at the Library that afternoon to sequester himself in The Bunker.

"Totally," Artie said. "Not cool that she almost got another one of us with those freaky dragonflies."

Artie, Kay, Thumb, and Bercilak were gathered around the tablet inside the court-in-exile, and they'd just finished telling Merlin about the attack. Erik sat alone on the far side of the table, still recovering from his berserker rage, which he couldn't remember a thing about.

Bercilak leaned forward and said to Merlin, a little more loudly than necessary, "Tiberius and I have found her antics to be quite inconvenient of late! She's even been able to hit Sylvan with rolling blackouts!"

Merlin smiled. "Two can play at that game, Sir Bercilak."

"What do you mean?" Kay asked.

"Using some of my old tools here at The Bunker, I've devised a magical siphon that will tap Fenland's sangrealitic power lines," Merlin explained.

"Sangrealitic power isn't just for electricity, Artie," Thumb added. "It's also a major source of Morgaine's power. She has knowledge and magical skills on her own, of course, but without a steady supply of sangrealitic juice, her abilities will be greatly diminished."

"Sweet," Kay said.

"Quite sweet, my dear," Merlin said. "Opening crossovers will help curb her power as well, which you will do when you retrieve Gram. Speaking of Gram, I wonder how Master Erikssen is getting along? Is he ready to claim his sword?"

They turned to Erik, who held himself by the shoulders and rocked back and forth. When he realized they were staring at him, he blurted, "What?"

Bercilak said, "Wilt Chamberlain wants to know if you're ready to retrieve Gram."

The color drained from Erik's face as he said, "I guess. And why do you call . . . *Merlin*"—he was having trouble accepting the fact that there was a real Merlin—"Wilt Chamberlain?"

Kay chuckled as Bercilak turned to Artie and asked, "I can't remember. Can you, sire?"

"Nope," Artie said. "Just one of those things."

"Uh, all right," Erik said uncertainly. "Yeah, I guess I'm ready. I did see a dragon today. It can't be worse than that, can it?"

Merlin clapped his hands. "I hope not. I'll leave you to it then. So long, knights!"

Artie shook his head. "You're supposed to say, 'over and out,' Merlin."

"Aha." Merlin smiled. "Over and out!"

Bercilak rattled his armor and asked, "Over and out of what?" but no one bothered to explain as the video hiccupped and Merlin disappeared from the screen. "Truly, how does that work again?" Bercilak wondered, studying the iPad.

"I really don't know," Artie said. "Science. Lots of science."

"Fascinating," Bercilak uttered, shaking his empty helmet.

Artie elbowed Kay and pointed his chin at Erik. "Hey, Erikssen," Kay said gently. "Why don't you come over here?"

"Yes, why don't you?" Bercilak said, taking pains to sound super nice. "There's a very comfortable chair here. It's got pillows."

Erik shook his head. "Uh-uh."

"Suit yourself, lad," Thumb said, unwilling to treat Erik with kid gloves. "Bring up the sword app, Artie."

"All right." Artie reluctantly turned away from Erik and touched the sword app icon. The app popped up and revealed a stonework background with a banner across the top depicting Artie's coat of arms. Below the banner, in illuminated text, was the title *The Seven Swords*.

Below this, in smaller but still fancy type, were the names of the unique weapons: Excalibur, Cleomede, Gram, the Peace Sword, Kusanagi, Orgulus, and The Anguish. Behind each of these was a silhouette of the weapon in question.

Artie touched Gram and a block of text faded in next to two maps: One was of Sweden, with a red star in its northern region; the other was a detail of the starred location.

Artie read: "'In Old Norse, Gram simply means "wrath." It was forged at an unknown time by a mythological figure named Wayland the Smith.

"'In many ways, Gram is the Norse equivalent of Cleomede. Instead of a stone, it was stuck in an ancient tree—a tree that still stands, though in a very secret place (see map at right)—and like Cleomede, only one person could pull it out. In the case of Gram, this was the hero Sigmund.'"

At this, Erik leaned forward slightly.

"'It was eventually used by Sigmund's son, Sigurd, to kill the dragon Fafnir.'" Artie paused. "Good thing Tiberius didn't hear that."

"Please," Thumb said. "Each of these swords has slain at least one dragon."

"Quite true, sire," Bercilak added. "I half expect that's why Tiberius is so moody all the time. Not much fun being surrounded by dragon slayers—if you're a dragon."

Artie continued: "'Like most of the Seven Swords, Gram fell into obscurity, and eventually found its way back into the ancient tree. It is to the tree that you must go. It is called—'"

"Barnstokk," whispered Erik.

Artie's chair creaked as he turned to his friend. "That's right. You've heard of it?"

"My great-uncle used to tell my brother and me those stories about Sigmund and Sigurd," Erik recounted, trapped in reverie. "We loved them. He was a Minnesota wheat farmer. Big guy, long hair, a beard. Looked just like a Viking. We used to take turns pretending we were Sigurd.

His dog was always the dragon, Fafnir. Obviously we never killed the dog, but in our imaginations he died a thousand times."

Kay approached Erik and put a hand on his shoulder. He looked up at her. He was too exhausted and overwhelmed to be happy that Kay Kingfisher was actually *touching* him. Still, he smiled. She smiled back. "Welcome to the club, sport."

"So, what, I'm actually a Viking?" Erik asked.

"Not yet, I'd wager," Bercilak said. "You're quite scrawny."

"Erik, it was the same with me," Artie said, ignoring Bercilak's comment. "I couldn't believe any of this at first. But that started to change once I got Cleomede. And it *really* changed when I got Excalibur."

Erik stood. He was shorter than Artie, but outweighed him by about twenty pounds. He may have seemed scrawny to Bercilak, but he wasn't. He was strong.

"So," Erik said slowly, "if I go with you to find Gram— in Sweden—then maybe all this will make a little more sense?"

"Exactly," Artie and Kay answered together.

Erik looked around the great hall, eyeing the weapon racks at the far end. "Okay. But can I borrow some of those in the meantime? And maybe some armor? I mean, you guys look like you're ready for a pretty big tussle, and I look like I'm about to go to school."

"Of course!" Artie said, happy to hear that his friend was coming around.

Kay clapped him on the shoulder. "Come on, Erikssen, let's get you set up and then let's get our butts to Sweden."

𝕰rik chose a chain mail shirt, a thin but sturdy dagger, and a truly frightening war hammer as long as his leg. He figured he'd done well with the carpenter's hammer against the dragonflies, so he'd probably do even better with the kind that was meant for battle.

All the same, he was a little freaked out about the prospect of hitting something as hard as he could with a hammer.

While Artie and Thumb huddled over the iPad, studying the map of Sweden, Bedevere and Lance gave Erik some last-minute fighting tips (how to parry a thrust, how to duck a swipe, how to use the war hammer like a staff, and, most important, to remember that in hand-to-hand combat a fighter's first weapon was his feet—keep them moving at all times, and run if necessary). Kay sat next to her brother, coiling a long length of rope. They'd really needed rope when they were making their way down to Tiberius's cave a few weeks back, and they weren't going to forget it this time.

Thumb pointed at the map on the iPad. "For Gram, we have to start in the Otherworld land of Surmik, where we can open a crossover to northern Sweden. All we have to do is punch coordinates into this app and it will show us exactly where we need to go on this side."

Artie entered the Swedish coordinates, and a blue circle snapped to the middle of the screen as Sweden dissolved into a map of Surmik, the circle still intact.

"There it is!" Artie exclaimed.

"Looks like a pretty happening place," Kay said sarcastically, peering over Artie's shoulder at an icy, barren landscape.

"You're right that it isn't, Sir Kay," Thumb replied with a smirk. "It's big and cold. Lots of animals and very few people."

"Which I guess makes it a little like Sweden, huh?" Artie mused.

"Nah, Sweden's cool," Erik interjected, taking a break from swinging his war hammer. "We went there when I was eight. In the summer the sun never goes down, and in the winter it never comes up."

"For real?" Kay asked.

"For real," Erik said. "Since it's September, it should still be sunny most of the time."

"Cool," Kay said, putting the rope in the infinite backpack.

Artie smiled. "Definitely. Lance? Bedevere? You guys ready?"

"Yes, sire," Bedevere said.

"You know it," Lance boomed. "I need to see me some more of this Otherworld ASAP. I still can't believe I'm finally here!"

Artie turned to Thumb. "When will you and Tiberius leave for Leagon?"

"Right after you."

"Good. How long before you return?"

"Unsure, lad," Thumb said. "Dealing with fairies can be tricky."

"All right, but don't take long. We've got only nine days," Artie said despondently. He knew that they were going to be the hardest nine days of his young, regal life. Artie reached into his coat and pulled out the precious pommel. "Hey, Erik, you ready to go through your first moongate?" The other one didn't count since Erik had been knocked out.

"I guess I have to be, right?"

Lance clapped a hand on Erik's shoulder. "Stick with me, dude. You'll be fine."

The pommel warmed in Artie's hand. He closed his eyes.

"Here we go!" Kay barked.

"Good-bye, knights! Good luck! Don't lose any more extremities!" Bercilak said encouragingly, though Erik was about as far from encouraged by this advice as he could possibly be.

"Good luck, lads," Thumb intoned.

"*Lunae lumen!*" Artie exclaimed.

The moongate flickered open, and then just as quickly snapped shut around them.

Artie, Kay, Erik, Lance, and Bedevere found themselves in the middle of a vast, trough-shaped plain. A serpentine river flowed farther downhill. Rising in the distance were mountains shaped like upside-down bowls. Snow capped the peaks, and tendrils of white reached down their sides like crooked fingers. Across the river an ancient pine forest carpeted the land with millions of green, spear-shaped trees.

Not used to moongating, Erik fell onto his bottom as they materialized in Surmik. Feeling like he'd just been punched in the nose, he shook his head and said, "Whoa."

"Welcome to the King Artie Kingfisher Express," Kay said.

Erik rubbed his face. "Tell me you get used to that."

"You do, Sir Erik, you do," Bedevere consoled.

Lance was the only one facing uphill, and after he'd shaken off the moongate effect, he said, "Uh, guys, I think you should turn around."

They did.

About fifty yards away was a gigantic herd of bovine creatures. At well over six feet tall, they were easily twice the size of large bulls, and each had long, pointed horns. Most were bent to the ground eating grass, but a few had raised heads, their eyes trained on the knights.

"What the . . ." Kay trailed off.

"Aurochs," Artie said. "Basically cows that went extinct on our side. They used to roam all over Europe."

"And you know this how?" Erik asked.

"Excalibur taught me a lot about animals that have gone extinct on our side but that migrated to the Otherworld. Back when I had Excalibur . . . ," Artie said longingly before shaking it off. "Don't worry. I don't think they'll bother us. They're basically cows."

"Shall we look for the crossover markers, sire?" Bedevere asked, unimpressed by the aurochs. He *was* the proud owner of a saber-toothed tiger, after all.

"Yeah," Artie answered.

Artie, Kay, and Bedevere searched the ground for the pair of plate-sized rocks that would indicate the crossover. Lance watched the herd. Erik, still figuring it all out, barely moved an inch.

"Sire! Over here!" Bedevere finally announced, pointing his claymore at the ground.

"Good job," Artie said.

Just then thunder rolled underfoot. Artie and Kay each felt the other's heart sink, as they were briefly reminded of the earthen thumping that had announced the arrival of Twrch Trwyth, the horrible, divine boar.

"Guys?" Lance said urgently. "Hurry up."

Something had spooked the herd, causing it to shudder and move as dust swam in the air. The ground shook some more.

"What'd you do, Lance?" Kay asked plaintively.

"Nothing!"

Through the aurochs' chestnut-brown hides, something large and white could be seen moving in the distance.

"What's that?" Kay asked.

"Dunno," Artie said a little nervously.

But they didn't have much time to think about it because the three closest aurochs stamped their feet. Then the one in the middle took a few steps forward and made a series of gruff snorts. A silvery ball of snot shot from his nose, landing with a loud *splat* on the ground.

"Bedevere, you stand there," Artie said, indicating one of the crossover's disklike rocks. He moved to the other disk, pommel in hand.

The three closest aurochs jumped toward Lance. He stood his ground and nocked an arrow. "Hurry up, dude," he said.

"*Lunae lumen!*" Artie whispered fiercely.

The dark pommel swirled with a blue glow. It became very cold, and then a beam of light shot from it in two directions. One end passed through Artie's hand—which tickled a little—striking the ground a few feet behind him. The other arced through the air, bending down and hitting a spot the same distance behind Bedevere.

Half ovals of light spun like gyroscopes between these two points. The air around them shimmered, and a twinkling curtain fell into place. It hit the ground, and a shock wave of silence shot away in all directions, striking the knights' eardrums like a sudden drop in air pressure.

When this burst of silence hit the three aurochs, they shook their great, blocklike heads in confusion. When it reached the rest of the herd, it caused something like a mass panic. The beasts scattered in all directions, some of the larger ones awkwardly trampling over the smaller ones.

And that was when they finally saw the white creature. It was a regal-looking stag with at least thirty points on his rack of horns.

For a moment it surveyed the turmoil around it, like a general watching a field of battle. Then it looked at Bedevere, then Artie, then Bedevere again. And then, Artie swore, it realized what they were doing.

It recognized the crossover point.

The stag reared like a horse in an old western before taking off, driving a group of aurochs right toward the gate.

The knights had to get out of there.

Pronto.

Artie and Bedevere pivoted through the crossover gate. Next came Kay, followed quickly by Lance, who had Erik by the arm. Erik was looking over his shoulder, his face twisted and frantic.

And just like that, they were in Sweden, on another barren slope above a river. In the distance was an identical boreal pine forest.

They flanked the crossover point for a few seconds. No sign of the aurochs or the stag. No miniature thunder underfoot. No snotty snorting sounds. But then about a dozen of the animals burst through the gate and bolted past them. Bringing up the rear was the stag. It split the aurochs into two groups and continued full-bore downhill.

"Whoa!" Lance said.

"Should we let the aurochs cross, sire?" Bedevere wondered.

"I don't know," Artie admitted.

"We couldn't stop them if we wanted to," Erik observed. "I mean, they make cows look like calves! Besides, they seem right at home." The land around them was basically the same as Surmik, and the animals had trotted downhill a way, stopped, and begun to graze.

All this was fine by Artie. He wasn't concerned with the aurochs anymore. He was more interested in the white stag, now a speck moving at breakneck speed toward the river.

Erik, also dismissing the aurochs, stepped next to Artie and said, "That thing's fast."

"Yeah." Artie stuffed the pommel inside his shirt. The forest in the distance looked limitless and dark and more than a little spooky. Erik made a low humming sound and Artie asked, "What is it?"

"I've got a funny feeling, that's all," Erik said a little nervously.

Artie smiled. "Funny feelings are good."

Erik turned to Artie. "I'm not sure how," he said weakly, "but I know how to find Gram."

"We track that stag, right?"

"Right."

Artie bit some loose skin off his bottom lip and spit it at the ground. "Let's get tracking, then."

𝕬rtie kept it to himself, but he knew that a white stag had lived in the forest around Camelot back in the old King Arthur days and that the knights of the Round Table saw it quite a bit. It was so beautiful that, being knights, all they wanted was to kill it, stuff it, and put it on display in the court, but no matter how often they tried no one ever managed to catch it. Like a unicorn or a selkie, the white stag was magical in its ability to evade capture. This was because the white deer was more than just an animal; it was a symbol of the Otherworld itself.

Artie Kingfisher took this as a good sign. It was his turn to follow the white deer into the woods, his knights at his side. Unlike the knights of old, he didn't want to capture it and mount its head in his game room; he just wanted to follow its magical—even mythical—footprints.

Footprints that would lead them right to Gram.

It took the knights an hour to cover the distance that the stag had gone in about twenty minutes. When they finally reached the river's edge, Lance said, "Man, this river's a lot bigger than I thought."

Which was true. They'd watched the stag swim across it successfully but with effort. In crossing, it had been carried downriver about five hundred feet.

"No way we can do what that deer did," Erik said feebly.

Bedevere rolled his armless shoulder and eyed the churning water. "I don't think I could cross that with *two* arms."

They were silent for a moment. Artie leaned on his spear. The banks were littered with large rocks and much larger tree trunks. "Get out the rope, Kay. Let's see what my spear can do."

"You got it, Art," Kay said.

She swung the infinite backpack from her shoulders and dug out the rope. Artie tied some kind of crazy knot around the spear's shaft and cinched it tight. He said, "Beddy, Lance—I want you guys to stay here. We're going to set up a river crossing, and I don't want anything messing it up. Plus, we should keep an eye on that crossover. If Morgaine's power is so tied to them like Merlin said, she might send someone to check it out. If anyone bad-looking comes out of that thing, stop them."

"Roger that, dude," Lance said as Bedevere nodded.

Artie weighed his spear in his hand and eyed a tree trunk across the river. "Sis, take the free end of the rope and stand back there. When I launch the spear, let the rope uncoil, but don't let it go."

"Check," Kay said.

They gave Artie some room. He held the spear over his shoulder, turned sideways to the bank, and took a few jogs toward the target. When he had some momentum, he planted his left foot and let the spear fly with a grunt.

It absolutely flew out of his hand, true and on target. It crossed the river, and with a loud *thwack* Rhongomyniad drove deep into the tree trunk.

"Well done, sire!" Bedevere shouted.

Artie waved him off and took the free end of the rope from his sister. "Sis, can you use Cleomede to cut a hole in that rock?" He pointed at a large spur on the ground.

"Sure," Kay said eagerly.

"Wait—what?" Erik bleated.

Instead of answering, Kay pushed Cleomede into the rock and gave it a full turn. Crushed sand and pebbles fell from the hole on either side.

"Whoa," was all Erik could manage.

Kay shot Erik a smile and said, "Pretty neat, huh?"

"Is my sword going to be able to do that?"

Kay pulled Cleomede free and sheathed it. As Artie

threaded the rope through the hole, he said, "Only one way to find out!"

A look of wonder crossed Erik's face as Artie pulled the rope taut and tied it off with another fancy knot. Artie tested it, grabbed it with both hands, then swung underneath and flung a leg over the line, holding it in the bend of his knee. He pulled himself along hand over hand and moved over the river. The rope sagged heavily in the middle, but both ends held and he reached the other side safely.

Then Kay and Erik crossed, both without any hiccups. Once assembled, Artie, Kay, and Erik looked up the slope toward the towering wall of ancient trees and took off.

They'd been moving fast for about thirty minutes when Kay said, "I feel like we're in the second *Lord of the Rings* movie!"

Artie laughed and said, "Hey, at least we're not hunting orcs." He took a gulp of water from his canteen.

"You said it," Kay replied, winking at her brother.

Erik didn't say anything. Since dragons existed, orcs probably did too. He hadn't even *thought* of that. Erik didn't want to meet an orc. Ever.

The threesome kept trekking and eventually they crossed into the old forest. The woods were hushed and tranquil. All around them, towering firs and hemlocks reached up to a pale-blue evening sky that peeked through here and there.

Artie stayed in front, followed by Erik, who held his heavy hammer across his body with both hands, and Kay brought up the rear. The soft ground was clear of underbrush and carpeted with rust-colored needles.

Eventually they stopped in front of a massive fallen tree, its trunk at least ten feet in diameter. It smelled dank but pleasant. The deer's tracks went right up to the tree and disappeared.

"Looks like it walked *through* this thing, huh?" Kay said.

"Naw, I think he jumped it," Artie said. He pointed at the tracks behind him and added, "See here, how its tracks get farther apart, like it started to run?"

"You really think he could have cleared this?" Erik asked, slapping the tree's damp bark.

"Must've," Artie said. As he stopped speaking, the silence of the woods overcame them. The forest seemed endless and empty. Then a loud twang, like a giant guitar string had been plucked, echoed through the woods, followed by a high-pitched squeal.

A chill ran down Kay's spine, and Artie felt it. The Kingfishers locked eyes. Kay drew Cleomede, and Artie pulled Flixith halfway out of its sheath.

Erik, however, ignored the sounds and clambered over

the tree. "C'mon," he called. Artie and Kay followed and they dropped down the other side, landing behind a tangle of branches. Erik stepped forward and parted them like he was peeking at an audience from behind a curtain.

About a hundred yards away, the great deer hung in the air by one of its hind legs. It was alive, but its hip looked horribly out of joint.

It had been snared in a trap.

Kay whispered, "Poor guy," but Erik shushed her.

Emerging from the trees came a thing that looked like a reindeer walking on its hind legs. It had a reindeer's head, shaggy rack, and gray hide. But as it got closer, they saw boots. And gloves. And a belt.

And it was smoking a pipe.

It was the trapper. He walked under the deer and let out a long whistle, clearly impressed by his catch. Then he did a little jig and disappeared behind a tree.

The stag was lowered until its horns just touched the ground. The trapper reemerged and spoke to the animal with clicks and coos. He bound its front hooves. Then he tied a rope to the stag's horns and cinched this through the coil around the hooves, giving the animal a harsh crook in its neck. The man disappeared again and lowered the animal to the ground. Still talking to it, he gingerly relocated the stag's hip and tied its rear feet together.

Then he did something pretty incredible.

He picked the thing up and threw it over his shoulders, and started to walk back from where he came.

Artie, Kay, and Erik looked at each other in disbelief. The stag had to weigh at least a thousand pounds. The trapper was burly but didn't look *that* strong. They remained quiet until he was out of sight, and then Kay whispered, "Now what?"

Artie looked at Erik and said, "We follow him."

A short while later, the three found themselves hiding at the edge of a big bowl in the earth. Below was a camp with a single tepee-like tent, its flap thrown wide; a big stone fire pit; and lots of stacks of chopped wood. Bleached animal skulls of varying sizes were arranged all over the place. A little log storehouse at the far end of the bowl stood high off the ground on six tall posts.

The stag hung upside down from a spit. It looked strangely calm considering the trapper was not more than a dozen paces away sharpening some tools on a stone.

The most remarkable thing about the camp, though, was a gnarled beech tree at its center. It was only about forty feet high, but it had a huge, elephantine trunk and tons of crooked branches. Clearly, it was super old. Its leaves had turned to pale copper for the fall—or perhaps they were always this way, forever old, withering, and fragile.

Erik pointed his chin at it. Sticking out of the trunk on the side closest to them was a completely unremarkable-looking sword.

"There it is," Erik said with equal measures of awe and disbelief. "There's Gram."

"How the heck are we going to get it without that guy noticing?" Kay wondered.

"I don't know," Artie answered.

"We could wait for him to go to sleep," Erik suggested.

They watched as the trapper slid a long knife with a white bone handle over the sharpening stone.

"It doesn't look like that's going to happen anytime soon," Artie observed. "I think he's about to slaughter that deer."

Erik eyed Gram. "You sure I'm going to be able to pull that thing out?"

"Sure I'm sure," Artie said, trying to sound positive.

The woodsman stopped sharpening and cocked an ear in their direction, and they scootched out of sight, but as Erik slid back, he snapped a twig. They held their breaths and waited. Artie and Kay each had their weapons drawn fast in front of their faces.

They lay there frozen for several minutes. Finally Artie inched back to the edge of the camp and peeked in.

The man was gone.

The knife lay on a stump next to the sharpening stone.

The beech tree, Barnstokk, shed a few of its copper leaves.

Erik slid next to Artie, and again his eyes locked on the sword. They became freakishly wide and bloodshot. Artie put his hand on Erik's arm. Erik was beginning to shake furiously.

For some reason the sight of Erik's sword was sending him into a rage.

Before Artie could do anything, Erik stood and ran into the camp, making a beeline for Gram.

Kay yelped, "Fudge," as she jumped to her feet and followed, Artie right on her heels.

They dropped into the camp and Erik was almost to the deer when a pile of leaves exploded in front of him. The trapper had been hiding in a little trench in the ground, and now he was blocking their path to the tree.

Erik swung his war hammer at the stout man's head, but the trapper caught it with one hand and kicked something on the ground, and all of a sudden the three knights were whisked into the air in a jumble. Cleomede sliced deep into Artie's calf, which healed quickly thanks to the scabbard strapped to his back.

When the dust settled, they found themselves in a rope net about fifteen feet above the ground. Artie and Kay were ready to cut it to pieces when the trapper pulled hard on another line, cinching the webbing so tight around them that they could barely move.

"Erik!" Kay scolded, her arm twisted behind her uncomfortably. "That was *so* not cool!"

Erik, still coming down from his rage, just moaned.

Artie remained silent and eyed the woodsman intently.

The man was a shade over five feet tall with bright blue eyes and leathery skin. He had a beard that was more like a bird's nest, what with all the twigs and leaves in it. His expression was one of simple curiosity. He looked neither mean nor kind.

Artie, who was at the bottom of the snare, commanded, "Let us down right now!"

If the man understood, he didn't show it.

"I said, let us down!" Artie repeated.

The man still said nothing. He pushed his toes into the ground, where some of Artie's blood had fallen. He knelt, scooped some blood onto a filthy finger, and put it in his mouth. He stood, made a sucking sound, and considered Artie.

"What's going on down there?" Kay asked. She was on top and didn't have a good view of the ground. Erik whimpered from in between the Kingfishers.

Artie ignored Kay, looked their captor square in the eye, and said coolly, "I am Artie Kingfisher, and I demand that you release us. The longer you hold us like this, the worse it will be for you later."

That did it. The man's face snapped into an amused

smile, revealing a mouth with only a few crooked, yellow teeth. His eyes brightened. His nose turned red.

"I am Sami," the man said with a lilting Swedish accent as he jabbed Artie hard in the leg with Erik's hammer. "And *I* demand to know how you healed your leg, or it will get much, much worse for *you* right now."

Being a prisoner sucked.

After Qwon hit Shallot and Shallot disappeared, Qwon paced around the portico like a tiger in a cage. Since they wanted Dred to believe that she hated Shallot, Qwon liberally cursed the fairy. She punched her fist, whisked her staff through the air, and grunted. She also cursed Dred, since he had put her in there. And even Artie now and then, since he hadn't been able to stop Dred from kidnapping her in the first place.

After a while, she plopped down in the grass with her back to the birdbath and glowered at Dred's door, trying not to blink. Even though she and Shallot had a plan, she really couldn't believe all this was happening. Eventually she fell asleep and didn't wake until dawn.

Qwon had rolled onto her side in the night and was curled up like a cat as the sky turned from deep blue to gray. The birds outside the Castel began to greet the morning, and as she listened, Qwon shed a few quiet, genuine tears.

What is this Otherworld Place? And when will I get back home?

If only Qwon knew that at that exact moment Artie was back in Shadyside asking similar questions. This was the day that Merlin would materialize in the Kingfisher's backyard, but it hadn't happened yet, and all Artie could think about was when he'd be able to resume the quest to rescue his friend.

She clutched her stomach as a pang shot through it. She was hungry.

So, so hungry.

About an hour later a tiny door next to Dred's large door slid open, and two bowls and two cups were pushed onto the walkway.

Food!

Qwon ran to it as quickly as she could. Her mind raced as she thought of cereal and eggs and bacon and pancakes and muffins and burgers and pizza and fried chicken, even a veggie burger or tofu or plain rice, and, and, and . . .

Gruel. White, pasty gruel peppered with little, hard-backed weevils.

And no spoon.

Qwon sat cross-legged in front of the "food."

"Not much of a gourmet, are you, Dred?"

No answer came.

Qwon picked up the cup and found lukewarm water. She drank it all in three gulps.

She put the bowl in her lap and stared into it. She picked a dozen weevils out of one section and skimmed some of the porridge off the top with her fingers.

It didn't taste like anything, which, Qwon figured, was a lot better than it tasting like total crap.

Qwon continued removing the bugs and scooping up the food until it was gone. She was so hungry she even licked the bowl.

It wasn't a good meal, but it was filling.

She put the bowl back in front of the door and considered eating Shallot's too, but didn't.

After breakfast Qwon resigned herself to another day of pacing around. In the late morning a squall passed through, and Qwon tried to get clean, but it was no use. She was covered in grime and filth, and it wasn't going to come off with a little bit of rain and no soap.

Still, the water felt good.

As the day went on, she felt angrier and angrier. She yelled things like, "Shallot, where are you?" and, "Don't be a chicken!" and, "If you don't show up, then I'm going to eat your food, you dumb fairy!" and, "You stink!"

At one point an invisible Shallot whispered into her ear, "I already ate."

"What—how?" was all Qwon could manage. She went back to the door and saw that the second cup and bowl were empty and the little pile of weevils that Qwon had made was also gone. "You ate the bugs? Ew." This elicited a faint chuckle from behind Dred's door. She started pacing again and said to the unseen fairy, "So in addition to being rude, smelly, and mean, you're also a disgusting bug eater! Figures."

At which point a still-invisible Shallot smacked Qwon hard in the back of the head.

"Ugh!" Qwon blurted, rubbing her head and realizing that she actually did hate her fellow prisoner a tiny bit. "Coward!" she barked, brandishing her staff. Then she turned to Dred's door and said, "Can you believe that? What a sneak!"

No sound came from Dred's door this time, but Qwon had a strong feeling that he was still there, watching and waiting. For what, she wasn't sure.

The following morning Qwon was up before the sun. She went to Dred's door and sat in front of it. No food had come the night before, and hunger again twisted her stomach into knots. She wrapped her arms around her knees, pulled them to her chest, and waited for the little slot to open.

When it did, Qwon said, "Hey, Dred, can I have a spoon?"

No answer came. Just the bowls and cups, pushed out by a stick.

Qwon grabbed the stick. "I know you're there. C'mon, just a tiny spoon? Can't hurt, right? I mean, it's not like I can dig my way out of here."

Still nothing. Dred yanked the stick hard, pulling it from Qwon's grip. The little door slid shut with a bang.

Qwon crossed her arms and huffed. "Thanks a lot. You know, if it were the other way around, I would totally give you a spoon. Just a wooden spoon! I'm sure your crazy mom wouldn't like it, but who cares?"

Nothing.

"The silent treatment, huh? Suit yourself. But if you give me a spoon, I promise I won't share it with that darned fairy." Qwon paused for effect and said quietly, "Man, what a jerk she turned out to be."

Still nothing. She picked up the cup and took a few sips of water.

"You ever eat this stuff you're slinging, Dred?" she asked. "'Cause it's pretty awful. You should try it, just so you know what your prisoners are dealing with. Maybe it would make you, like, a better kidnapper or whatever."

Qwon picked up the bowl, stretched out her legs, and set it in her lap. She began to eat. At least it was warm. "Hey, Dred, you know what the best thing about it is? The bugs. They're really awesome. Thanks so much," she said sarcastically.

Qwon thought she heard something through the door. It might have been a giggle.

"Seriously, though. What I wouldn't give for a real home-cooked meal. Shoot, I'd even take a Happy Meal from Mickey D's. You Otherworld people eat hamburgers or lobster rolls or hot dogs? You ever drink a Coke? Or an orange soda? I might give up a big toe for an orange soda."

Qwon picked the weevils out of her food and made another pile as she spoke. It occurred to her that maybe she *should* eat the bugs, as a source of protein, but she wasn't ready to go that far yet.

She took another bite and spoke with her mouth full. "I wonder if the fairy thinks about food as much as I do," she said. "Who knows. She actually *likes* the bugs, so she's probably happy."

Qwon put down the bowl and had some more water.

"What's with that fairy, anyway? First she fights me, then she figures maybe we're pals, then she calls me something very unladylike that I'd rather not repeat, and then she disappears. Okay, so I hit her. Twice. But still. Why won't she talk to me? I mean, what's the point of being imprisoned with someone if you refuse to talk to them? I understand why *you* wouldn't want to talk to me, but why not her?"

She leaned closer to the door hoping to hear another laugh, or *anything*, but nothing came. How was she going to get through to him?

"So hey—since you're from this Otherworld place, does that make you some kind of fairy too?"

A loud thump came from the other side of the door, like maybe he'd fallen out of his chair.

Bingo.

She pretended not to hear it.

"Yeah, you must be. I mean, your mom looked human enough, but she did have a purple eye. That's not normal. And you wear that helmet all the time, so you must be hideously messed up in the face. Maybe you're like a troll fairy or something. Maybe your mouth is on your forehead and you don't have any eyes and you have a big pony-tail growing out of the middle of your face." She paused. "Whatever you are, you can't be as pretty as Shallot. I mean, she may be a jerk, but she is beautiful, you have to admit, even with that weird, lanky body and those teeth of hers."

Qwon thought she heard Smash yelp from behind the door.

She smiled wryly to herself.

"Oh, hey, one more thing before I head out and enjoy this lovely day—thanks for the staff. I mean it. I don't know why you gave it to me but, for what it's worth, I'll never forget that you did. But then, I'll also never forget that you kidnapped and drugged me and locked me up in here, so you still owe me. Just saying."

Qwon stood and walked away from the door, leaving Dred to ponder her words.

She woke the next morning, shaking, at the very same time Artie and his knights were preparing to leave for Sweden. It was cold. Way colder than the night before. Qwon stood and started running in place, trying to get her blood flowing. The sun rose, and again she heard the riot of morning birdsong beyond the Castel's walls.

Finally the air began to warm.

At breakfast time Qwon went to the door and sat in front of it.

"Blankets, Dred, blankets," she said quietly. "Tell your dumb mom that if she wants me to live until she can catch Artie, I'm going to need blankets."

No answer. She waited.

Finally the slot slid open and the bowls and cups were pushed out.

Qwon looked over. The water in one of the cups was

steaming! She grabbed the cup and laced her fingers around it. She blew on the water, and hot vapor coated her face. She took a sip, and it warmed her from the inside out.

It had a slight, minty aftertaste.

"Thanks, Dred," she said.

Then she noticed that one of the bowls of gruel was bug-free. She picked it up and held it to her face. It smelled different. It smelled sweet!

She dipped a couple fingers in and took a mouthful. It wasn't just sweet, it was salty too. Amazing!

Qwon forced herself to eat slowly. Food had never tasted so good.

When she was done, she let the bowl fall into her lap and closed her eyes. She drank her tea. "Dred, that was the best meal of my life. Seriously. I still basically hate you, but not as much."

She put her bowl back in front of the slot. And that's when she noticed a short wooden spoon. A little note was tied to it. She picked up the spoon. The note read, "Don't let her know you have it."

Qwon smiled and tucked the spoon into her shirt. No way was she going to share it with Shallot. Not until the fairy apologized for smacking her the day before, anyway.

A short while later, as Qwon paced the yard, it occurred to her that maybe it wasn't Shallot who Dred meant in his note. He could have meant Morgaine.

Qwon bit her bottom lip, suppressing a smile. If that was true, then maybe—just maybe—their plan was beginning to work.

𝔄𝔰 𝔔𝔴𝔬𝔫, 𝔣𝔞𝔯 𝔬𝔣𝔣 𝔦𝔫 Fenland, tucked the spoon into her shirt, Artie, Kay, and Erik swung uneasily in the snare in Sweden. Their captor, Sami, had just demanded that Artie tell him how he'd healed himself, but Artie said authoritatively, "The only way I tell you about my leg is if you let us out of here."

"I don't think so," Sami said.

"Think again," Kay said from the top of the trap. "If you let us go now, Artie won't hurt you."

A resonant belly laugh rose from deep within Sami. As he wiped tears from his eyes, he looked at Artie and said, "*You* hurt *me?*"

Artie just nodded while Kay said, "Heck yeah, dude!"

"Let me show you something," Sami said, turning from his catch. He sauntered over to a gigantic tree stump. "You see this?"

"Yeah," Artie said.

"What do you think it weighs?"

"I dunno. A couple thousand pounds?"

"Probably. Watch."

Sami bent and hugged the stump. His arms didn't even make it halfway around, but it didn't matter. He stood with hardly any effort, lifting the stump as if he were picking up a bag of leaves, and walked it closer to his tools. He set it down with a *thump* and disappeared.

"So? Big whoop," Artie yelled after him. "You should see some of the things I can do!" No response came. It was kind of a bluff, anyway. Without Excalibur, Artie wasn't sure *what* he could do.

Erik asked in a whisper, "How *are* you healing yourself, Artie?"

"Excalibur's scabbard!" Artie hissed.

"Wow," Erik said. "That's pretty cool."

"You want to know what's not cool, Erik? You bum-rushing this guy's camp and getting us caught in this net," Kay said, still upset.

Erik sighed. "Sorry, guys. But seeing that sword kind of messed me up. I guess that means it's really mine, huh?"

"Sh!" Artie said. "Don't say anything else, either of you. I have a plan. Also, can you move your knee, Erik? It's really digging into my shoulder." Erik tried but just made it worse. "Ow! Never mind."

"Not much fun being caught in a snare, is it?" Sami boasted as he waltzed into Artie's field of vision carrying the largest, sharpest-looking ax Artie had ever seen.

"Nice ax. I've got a friend who'd like that," he said, thinking of Bercilak. "Maybe one day I'll bring him here so he can take it from you."

"Ha!" Sami chortled. Then he walked over to the huge stump, raised the ax over his head, and brought it down with a deafening *smack.*

"What was that?" Kay demanded.

"Nothing," Artie said as he looked at what the woodsman had done. The stump was cleanly split in two. "You're quite the show-off, Sami," Artie said. "Let me ask you something—how long have you lived here?"

"My whole life. I am Sami—it's not just my name but my people. We go back thousands of years, back to the ancient world. The world of magic."

Artie believed it. This guy was like some Otherworld missing link. "Is that why you're so strong?" Artie asked. "Because of magic?"

"I am strong because of my people. Plus, I eat a lot of protein. And I *am* a woodsman," Sami said with a wink.

Artie winked back. "Tell me, Sami the magic strong-man, do you get a lot of visitors?"

"Well, no."

"Then don't you think it's a little strange that now you've got three American kids caught in a net?"

"I guess," Sami said, shrugging.

"Not the sharpest knife in the drawer, is he?" asked Kay.

"No, he's smart, Kay." Artie hoped a little flattery might help. "He just doesn't know what to do with us. Do you, Sami?"

"Ha! There's where you're wrong, boy." He walked back to the sharpening stone and picked up the long knife he'd been working on earlier. He moved to the stag and whispered some words to it. With his free hand he stroked its head between the horns. Artie could see the animal's breath quicken. It was scared.

The edge of the woodsman's knife threw off a glint of light. A few more coppery leaves fell from the beech tree.

"You ever go hunting, Artie?" Sami asked, saying Artie's name for the first time.

"Only for dragons," Artie answered as his stomach started to turn.

Sami shot Artie a dubious glance and said, "One thing you learn when hunting is that it's important to do certain things quickly." And then, without hesitation, Sami moved the knife into place and opened the deer's throat. "I don't know who you are or how you got here or why you're carrying the kinds of weapons you are," Sami said, moving closer to them. "All I know is that you are going to tell me how you did that thing with your leg, one way or another."

"You don't know who you're messing with," Artie said, sticking to his guns.

"Ha! I don't really care."

With that, Sami cut Artie across the forearm. The blade was so sharp that it hardly hurt. Some blood dripped out, but in an instant the wound sealed and any trace of it faded away.

Sami jumped back. "You're a witch!"

"That's right," Artie said, his mind racing.

Sami looked at his knife and back at Artie. Then, just to make sure, he quickly sliced Artie again.

Artie wasn't ready for this one. "Hey!" he yelped. This cut was deeper and painful, and blood gushed momentarily before the wound shut itself.

Sami was quiet for a moment and then he said, "You're from the magic world, aren't you?"

"Maybe," Artie said. "But enough about me. Why don't you tell me about the sword."

"What sword? I'm a woodsman. I have axes and knives, not swords."

"You have that sword over there," Artie said. "The one in the tree."

"Ha! That's not a sword, it's a branch. It's been stuck there for as long as I can remember and a lot longer than that, I'll tell you what."

"Are you saying that *you* can't pull that sword out of the tree?" Artie asked doubtfully.

"No, I can't," Sami huffed. This was obviously a sore point with the woodsman.

"So you've tried?"

"A hundred times. A thousand. It won't budge. I've tried cutting down the tree, burning it, poisoning it. I've tried heating the blade, oiling it, freezing it. It's no use. That tree has a lot of magic, and the sword even more."

"Well, *we* have enough magic to get it out."

"You lie."

"I don't," Artie said with conviction. "And I'll tell you something else. We're not alone. We brought friends."

"What do you mean?"

"There are two more of us near the river outside the forest. One of them is an archer—a very good archer. They'll come looking for us if we don't return soon. When they do, our archer will shoot you before you even see him."

"You're bluffing."

"I'm not."

"Well, these are my woods. No one can sneak up on my camp."

"That's a chance you can choose to take, of course. Or, you can let us go and I'll *give* you the thing that heals me. Then, if you happen to get run through the neck with a giant hunting arrow, you'll probably be all right, although I have to tell you I've never put it to that kind of a test."

The woodsman said, "So you're not a witch? It's something you carry that does this magic to you?"

"Exactamundo."

"And you would just give it to me?"

"Yep, in exchange for our freedom." Artie paused for effect before saying, "But . . ."

"I knew it," Sami said, rolling his eyes. "There's always a *but*."

"But—if one of us can pull the sword from the tree, then you have to return my healing thing and let us go. If you do, then I promise you won't get hurt."

Sami flashed a big smile. There wasn't a man alive—let alone a child—who could pull the sword from the ancient tree. He spit in one of his palms and rubbed his hands together. "All right. You have a deal."

He swiped his knife at the rope that held the net. Artie, Kay, and Erik fell to the ground in a painful crash. They stood and untangled themselves from the webbing, their bodies sore.

But not so sore that Kay wasn't going to try to kill Sami!

Less than ten feet separated them, and she erased this

distance in a flash, Cleomede leading the way. She didn't want this guy to get Artie's scabbard, and she wasn't at all happy about being trapped.

But just as Cleomede's blade was about to run through Sami's barrel chest, he clapped his hands around it. The sound echoed into the boreal canopy. The sword, and Kay behind it, came to a screeching halt.

Holding the blade flat between his leathery hands, Sami leaned to one side and twisted Cleomede out of Kay's grip. She cried out as her wrists turned. Sami took the sword and tucked it under one of his arms.

"Kay!" Artie exclaimed angrily.

As she rubbed her wrists, she said, "What? You know I don't let bullies get away with being jerks."

Artie looked at Sami. "I'm sorry about my sister. She's pretty hotheaded."

"I understand," Sami said, eyeing Kay with a look of bemusement.

"You have no idea," Erik said. "I've watched her beat up boys twice her weight!"

"Thank you, Erik," Kay said as if Artie wasn't being appreciative enough. She turned to Sami. "When we get the sword in the tree, then you have to give me my sword back too, all right?"

Sami gave her a nod. "Sure—all I care about is the healing talisman."

"Right," Artie said. He unbuckled the leather straps crisscrossing his chest and lifted the empty scabbard over his head. Then he held it out with both hands, offering it to Sami.

Sami inspected the scabbard and asked, "Where's the blade that goes with this?"

"I lost it," Artie said curtly.

"That's fitting. You're going to lose this too," Sami said. "How does it work?"

"You just wear it, you freak," Kay said wearily.

Sami gave Artie a questioning look as he strapped it on and then placed the blade of his knife along the back of his forearm. He pressed down and drew it across his flesh.

Sami barely winced as blood instantly coursed around his arm, and then just as quickly stopped. Sami dropped the knife and wiped the blood away. With widened eyes, he searched for the cut.

But it was gone.

"Wow!" Erik said, also having witnessed the scabbard's healing power for the first time.

Artie shrugged. "See? Nothing to it."

"Amazing," Sami said.

Artie stepped forward. "I've kept my side of the bargain. Will you keep yours?"

"Of course. I am a man of my word," Sami said, leading them to the tree.

As they got closer to Gram, they saw that the sword was buried nearly to the hilt in the thick trunk. It looked to be in pretty bad shape. The exposed part was weatherworn and rusted and covered in several layers of calcified muck and splotchy lichens.

Sami slapped the hilt and it didn't move. Then he grabbed it in both hands and pulled on it as hard as he could, even going so far as to plant both feet on the trunk so he could push away from it like someone rappelling down a rock face.

It didn't budge.

"Give it your best shot," Sami said, stepping aside.

Artie looked at Kay and Kay looked at Erik and Erik looked at the ground.

"Kay, why don't you try first?" Artie suggested

Kay shot her brother a look. "What, me?"

"Yes, you." Artie liked the idea of working up to Erik's big moment.

"Fine," Kay said.

Kay went to the sword and pulled at it halfheartedly, making a very fake grunting sound. As she stepped away she mumbled, "Yep, it sure is stuck."

Sami laughed quietly.

"Great; thanks for trying, Kay. Way to put your back into it," Artie said sarcastically. "My turn."

"Have at it."

Artie stepped up to Gram and took it with both hands. Before he pulled, he thought about Cleomede and how it had been stuck in the stone and how he, Artie Kingfisher, had freed it. He started to pull. He pulled harder and harder. He got up on the tree like Sami had and pulled with all his might. Finally he stopped and took a deep breath. He looked at the sword. Nothing.

Artie walked to Erik and put a hand on his shoulder. "You can do this," Artie quietly insisted.

Erik looked at Artie nervously. His eyes asked, *But what if I can't?* Artie squeezed Erik's shoulder and smiled.

"Go on," Artie said.

"All right," Erik whispered.

He marched to the tree. There was no way. Still, he reached out and wrapped his hand around the hilt, closed his eyes, and pulled.

And nothing happened.

"Ha! I told you," Sami exclaimed.

"Try again; use both hands!" Artie suggested, his heart pounding.

Erik did. And then his body started to jitter. This grew to a shake. This amplified to a vibration that made the edges of Erik's body blur. The energy coursed through the hilt, to the blade, and into the tree. In a matter of seconds, every branch and leaf began to tremble and flutter. For an instant Erik was joined to the tree and vice versa, the sword their conduit.

Then he stepped back and twisted his shoulders, and with him came the legendary dragon slayer Gram. The part of the blade that had been embedded in the tree was bright and silver and sharp. He stepped away from Barnstokk and uttered a proclamation in Swedish that he didn't even understand. It was like the sword was speaking through him.

Artie beamed and Kay yelped, "Woo-hoo!" while Sami fell to his knees and bleated, "I can't— How?"

Energy continued to run through Erik's body like a freight train, rising from his feet, through his legs and chest, around his head, and then back down through his arms and finally out through Gram. The weapon shook so violently that Artie couldn't understand how Erik managed to keep hold of it. Finally the blade lit up with a red glow, and a stream of light flew up and away from its tip. As the beam passed the tree, its branches shook one last time and then, all at once, it dropped all of its leaves save the highest one.

Erik stood there, panting, in a shower of copper beech leaves. The forest was quiet, as if the trees themselves were staring down in wonder.

Sami gathered himself enough to ask, "How did you do that?"

Erik looked down on the woodsman, his nervousness gone, replaced by confidence and knowledge. Artie knew that Erik had just experienced something similar to what he had when he'd finally gotten Excalibur.

Man, how Artie missed his own legendary sword. . . .

"I did it because it's mine," Erik said, striding toward Sami. "And now I think you owe us some things," he added.

"Erik Erikssen!" Kay exclaimed, brimming with excitement and even, she hated to admit it, a little bit of admiration. "Wow . . . just, wow."

Erik flashed Kay the easy smile of a school-yard crush. Gram had given him confidence in many areas, and he was glad for it. Super glad.

Artie clapped Erik on the shoulder as Kay spun to Sami and said, "How do you like us now, strongman? I'll be taking this back, thank you very much!" She snatched Cleomede from the ground and sheathed it.

Artie stepped next to Kay and held out his hand. "I'll take my scabbard too, if you don't mind," he said calmly. Sami wordlessly unbuckled the scabbard and passed it to Artie, his eyes never leaving Gram. As Artie retrieved it, a wave of relief washed through him. "I told you I wasn't lying," he said

"I . . . I'm sorry. I'm sorry I cut you like I did. I'm sorry I doubted you."

"Don't sweat it," Artie said graciously.

"If I can ever make it up to you, please, let me know."

"I doubt we'll ever be coming this way again, Sami, but if we do, you can count on it," Kay said for Artie.

Artie glanced at Erik, who'd moved back to Barnstokk. Gram rested easily in one hand, and his other pressed against the bark of the tree. Very quietly he said, "Thank you for keeping this."

The tree shuddered and shed its final leaf. It drifted down, cradling back and forth through the air, and landed gently on the flat of Gram's gleaming blade.

Erik turned to the others and said, "What a trip."

"Cool, right?" Artie asked. "Getting Excalibur was a major rush for me too."

"Yeah, it's cool," Erik confirmed. "A little overwhelming, but cool."

Sami's voice wavered as he said, "Did you just say 'Excalibur'?"

"Yes, I did," Artie said confidently. And then he asked, "You ready to go, Erik?"

Erik stared at his friend, his classmate, his neighbor. The whole experience of visiting the Otherworld—and meeting a dragon, and going berserk—had been like a dream. But now he had woken up. He understood. He might return to school one day, or he might not, but he knew that his life would never be the same. He was ready for everything. For anything. Erik nodded. "I sure am."

Kay joined them. Before they left, Artie said, "So long, Sami of Sweden. Next time consider being nicer to strangers."

"Okay," Sami said weakly. Then Artie, Kay, and Erik

started walking out of the camp. "But wait!" Sami called, jumping to his feet. "Who are you?"

Without turning around, Artie said, "I'm King Artie Kingfisher, and I'm no longer at your service."

"𝔐oooor-dreeeed!" 𝔐orgaine screamed over an intercom into his room.

Man, Dred really hated hearing his mum say his name like that.

He had given Qwon the spoon that morning and now he was beginning to regret it. Not so much because he thought Qwon didn't deserve it—in truth, he kind of liked her—but because if his mum ever found out, she would probably kill him.

Literally.

So it was with heavy feet that Dred dragged himself to Morgaine's room. Dred pushed the doors to her chamber open and trudged in. He looked around and didn't see any sign of his mother.

"Mum?" he asked.

She rose like a shot from behind a stack of books and magic knickknacks littering her desk. "What took you so long?" she wailed. A scarlet-tufted jaybird flapped excitedly around her head.

"I came as soon as—"

"Come and look at this, snookums," Morgaine interrupted. "You must see it."

Dred approached the desk and found a messy contraption of wires and transistors and colored glass surrounding a thin sheet of sangrealite. On the sheet was a picture of a vast plain dotted with aurochs.

"Nice snap of Surmik, Mum," Dred said, relieved that it wasn't a picture of Qwon eating porridge with her spoon.

Morgaine slapped him hard on the back of the head.

"Hey!" Dred blurted. "That hurt."

"Look closer. Did I not raise you to pay attention?"

Dred rubbed his head and leaned forward. Nothing seemed out of the ordinary to him. But then one of the aurochs loped across the image, only to disappear into thin air!

Dred jumped back. "Is that a crossover point? One that's just been *left* open?" Dred said with a sinking feeling.

"Yes," Morgaine said. The scarlet-tufted jaybird then landed on the table next to the picture machine. He had a small green gem affixed to the front of his neck, which Dred knew allowed him to gate around the Otherworld.

"This is Eekan," Morgaine said. "He was attached to a dragonfly regiment on Sylvan. A *decimated* dragonfly regiment."

The jay made a guttural click and bowed his head. His plumage, mostly dark purple and black, was streaked on the wings and crown of his head with bright red. Dred knew that Eekan was a spy.

"What happened?" Dred asked earnestly. He might have been sick of his mum, but he still believed that the Otherworld's sister world had to remain closed off under all circumstances.

The jaybird explained (every Fenlandian boy and girl learned Jaybird in school) what had happened to the dragonflies when they'd tried to capture one of the special knights in Sylvan. As the dragonflies were beaten, Eekan hid in the forest, carefully avoiding the keen eyes of Tiberius, and waited. He surreptitiously followed the boy-king and four others, including the boy-king's sister, through a moongate to Surmik. He then hid in a herd of aurochs and watched as the group found and opened an ancient crossover point—and went through.

"So it's as you feared, isn't it?" Dred asked when the bird was finished.

Morgaine stared hard at the image on the sangrealite screen. "It is. And what's worse, I can tell that the sword Gram has been retrieved. The boy-king is moving."

"How are you feeling, Mum?" Dred asked, knowing that open crossover points were bad for her power.

"It's just one crossover. So long as the King's Gate stays shut, I'll be fine."

"Good," Dred said. Then he asked, "Where does that crossover let out?"

"I checked the ancient maps. Some place called Sweden. Surely it's awful," Morgaine said. "Mordred, we must redouble our efforts."

"Is the wizard with them?"

"No."

"Then we should go and meet them. We can try to stop them as they cross back."

Morgaine frowned. "Mordred, my child, there's hope for you yet. Gather thirty men and leave at once. Don't harm the boy-king. Kill the others. Bring me Gram and the sword carried by the girl."

"Yes, Mum."

"Now go!" Morgaine ordered. "Eekan will show you the way!"

The jaybird took off. Dred followed him down to the barracks, and then onward as they gated to the barren slopes of Surmik.

Lance and Bedevere were relieved when Artie, Kay, and Erik finally emerged from the boreal forest.

"How'd it go?" Lance asked after they'd shimmied across the rope bridge.

"And how does it feel to have *that*?" Bedevere asked, pointing at Gram.

Erik turned his new ancient sword in his hand and said, "Weird. Really weird. After I got it out of the tree, it, like, downloaded a bunch of stuff into my head."

"Such as?" Lance wondered.

"Well, it taught me how to control myself when I'm in one of those berserker rages. I also think I can determine when I go berserk, although I could be wrong about that. I may still fly off the handle without warning."

"Time will tell, I guess," Lance said.

"What else did it teach you?" Bedevere asked.

"A bunch of swordsmanship stuff and Norse mythology. It also taught me a ton about the Otherworld. I don't think I'll be so freaked out there anymore."

Artie pointed up the slope toward the crossover and asked, "Anything happen up there?"

"Negative. A few more aurochs wandered through is all," Lance said.

Artie called his spear, which flew across the river and landed at his feet, and untied the rope. Kay coiled it and packed it up, and then they headed back up the hill to the crossover.

When they got there, Artie inspected the portal and proclaimed, "Looks good. I think it's here to stay." Then he walked through to the Otherworld.

He led the knights up the hill toward the herd of aurochs, wanting to get away from the crossover a little before opening a moongate to the court-in-exile. As he ambled along he noticed that one of his shoelaces was untied. He bent to tie it, and when he did something zipped through the air, narrowly missing his head!

"What was that?" Kay exclaimed.

Lance dropped to the ground. "A crossbow bolt!"

Whoosh! Whoosh! Whoosh!

More crossbow bolts.

A lot more.

Everyone took cover. As Artie dropped into the grass, one ricocheted off his spear, nearly knocking it from his hand.

Lance and Kay crawled next to Artie. "Where're they coming from?" Kay asked.

"The aurochs," Lance said.

"There must be someone hiding in the herd," Artie said.

"Ya think?" Kay blurted.

"I'll take care of it," Lance said with a wink. He drew two arrows that had bulky cylinders where the arrowheads should have been. He nocked them, propped himself up, and let them fly. As he dropped back into cover, he ordered, "Heads down, folks!"

The arrows hit the ground between the feet of the first line of aurochs and exploded with a bright flash and loud *bang*!

Lance pumped his fist. Artie and Kay looked at him quizzically. "Flashbang grenades," he explained. "Awesome, right? I made those arrows special. Got some other tricks in my quiver too."

But they didn't have time to discuss any of that, because the explosions had set the herd in motion.

Big-time.

Lance stood defiantly as a contingent of the giant animals barreled toward them. He shot another arrow at the ground twenty feet in front of them. When it struck, a large fireball lit the plain, creating a wall that diverted the herd. Lance motioned for Artie and the knights to join him closer to the blaze. Not only did the fire prevent them from being trampled to death, it also prevented whoever had shot at them from being able to see them very well. Everyone moved up and took a knee, forming a little circle.

"Holy sugar, Lance! What're you, some kind of level-twenty-seven ranger or something?" Kay exclaimed, sounding more like a Dr Pepper head than she would've liked.

"You weren't kidding about those other tricks in your quiver, were you?" Artie asked with a lot less irony.

Lance, all business, said, "No, I wasn't. What now, dude?"

Artie had momentarily forgotten that he was the one in charge. "If they're Fenlandian, we should try to stop them, otherwise they might try to shut the crossover. Kay and I'll go left; Bedevere, you take Erik to the right."

"Got it," Erik said.

"Lance, you have more of those fireballers?" Artie asked.

"Three," Lance said.

"Good. Put two in the middle of the stampede, fifty feet apart. Save one for an emergency. *Bercilak* will be our go word. If you hear me say it, repeat it as loud as possible, and rendezvous back here so we can moongate out."

They nodded as Artie felt a surge of power and pride run through him.

"Should I try to go berserk?" Erik asked.

"I don't see why not!" Artie exclaimed. "All right. On

three. One. Two. Three!"

They split around the fire wall, Lance momentarily joining Artie and Kay. He quickly shot two arrows—*swoosh*, *swoosh*—into empty spots in the stampede. Two more fireballs blossomed on the plain. Then he knelt and got ready to cover his friends.

The knights moved out.

Into utter chaos.

Before they'd gone twenty feet, Artie and Kay had dodged five charging aurochs, jumped over a wayward calf, and ducked a few more crossbow bolts.

Kay spun and yelled, "Over there!" Artie looked and saw a large man in dark-green leather armor lying on the ground. He appeared to be unconscious, a crossbow on the ground a few feet away. They moved toward him and saw that he'd been trampled.

"Ugh," Kay said, looking at his bloodied face and his caved-in chest.

"Yeah," Artie agreed.

An arrow screamed inches above their heads as they turned to see another man, also in green leather armor, falling to the ground clutching his chest.

Another of Lance's shots zipped by Kay's shoulder, but the soldier it targeted swiped his mace through the air just as he was about to be hit, knocking it down. In another instant he was upon Kay, swinging at her head.

Kay stepped back and parried with Cleomede. The man brought the mace low and grabbed it with both hands, unleashing a backhanded swing at Kay's stomach. She jumped back again and brought her sword across the mace, cutting it cleanly in two.

"Don't mess with me, dude!" Kay shouted, but the man moved very quickly, drew a knife, and stepped right up to her. He was preparing to push the blade between her ribs when he was run through the side with Artie's spear and collapsed in a heap.

Artie called for Rhongomyniad and the spear lifted out of the wounded man's body and returned to Artie's hand.

Artie and Kay spotted more enemies about fifty feet to their right, locked in battle with Bedevere and Erik. Erik had followed Artie's advice and flown into a berserker rage. In just a few seconds he knocked down at least six assailants. Bedevere wasn't much worse. His claymore swept through the air like a whirligig, knocking down one, then two, then three attackers.

Over the thumping of the stampede Artie heard someone yell, "Remember—do not kill the boy-king!"

Artie spun in the direction of the voice. The guy giving orders was up the hill a short distance, behind more soldiers and a few straggling aurochs. He was about Artie's height, had a medium-sized bird perched on his shoulder, and over his armor he wore a purple-and-white tunic that had a large double-headed, golden bird stitched onto it. A helmet obscured his face, and on top of this helmet were two short and crooked stag's horns: one red, one blue.

Artie didn't recognize the coat of arms, but he knew that helmet.

He turned to Kay and shouted, "That's the guy who nabbed Qwon! He's wearing the same helmet!" and bolted toward the kidnapper. A large aurochs crossed in front of him and he jumped over it like a track-and-field star, using the spear like a vaulting pole.

About a dozen soldiers stood between Artie and his target. Three arrows zoomed past Artie, each hitting a different mark. What a shot Lance was!

Artie threw his spear, and it impaled two more soldiers through their thighs like they were shish kebab. The men fell to the ground wailing.

Artie drew Flixith and Carnwennan.

A pair of soldiers was next in line. They each had long swords and plate shields. Artie spun Flixith wildly, and to the soldiers it appeared as though Artie spawned four, then six, then eight arms—all wielding swords!

The trick bought Artie a fraction of a second. He used this moment to move between the soldiers and slice behind their knees with Carnwennan and Flixith, dropping them to the ground in useless, moaning heaps.

Kay, ostensibly covering Artie's flank, couldn't believe how driven her brother was.

Four soldiers were left. Two of these were armed with really evil-looking flails made of reinforced sticks and chains and spiky steel balls. The other two were snapping silver-roped whips.

The kidnapper stood behind them holding a common-looking broadsword.

"You're not getting away this time!" Artie yelled as Kay skidded next to him.

Dred looked down the slope past his remaining soldiers. The archer was occupied by half a dozen Fenlandian foot soldiers; the rest of Dred's men were not faring well against the Black Knight and the one that wielded Gram. No matter. If Dred could capture the boy-king and the girl's sword, it would still be a successful raid. He could get Gram later.

Dred eyed Artie. He looked kind of familiar, but Dred couldn't place him, and his features wouldn't come into focus for some reason. Dred shook his head and said, "Drop your weapons, there's no point in resisting further." The bird on his shoulder flapped its wings and screeched.

"Ha! As if, loser!" Kay yelled. Then she stepped forward

and took on the two bruisers with the flails.

The soldiers tried to land a series of crushing blows on Kay's rail-thin body, but before they knew what hit them, Kay had used Cleomede to cut the flails' chains like butter. The shocked men stood there for a moment staring at nothing more than a couple of sticks.

Kay was about to dispatch these guys and go after the ones with the whips—what idiot brought a whip to a sword fight?—when something caught her around the feet.

As she fell, she saw a silver strand wrapping around her thighs and body, swiftly encasing her like a bug caught by a spider in its web.

Oh. They were *magic* whips.

Bummer.

In a matter of seconds she was completely covered, her sword pressed flat against her cheek. And when she rolled over she saw that the same thing had happened to Artie!

Artie couldn't believe it. He looked from his sister to the guy with the horned helmet. "Where's Qwon? What did you do with her?" Even though they were in pretty deep doo-doo, this was all Artie could think about.

"Qwon? She's fine. But she's not very important right now," Dred said. Artie's face was still strangely obscured. It briefly occurred to Dred that if Morgaine didn't want Artie to see him, then perhaps for some reason she also didn't want Dred to get a clear look at Artie. Maybe she'd enchanted his helmet to do just that. He'd have to ask her about it later.

Artie, ignorant of all this, said forcefully, "I'm going to get you for taking her."

Dred chuckled. "I doubt that, but you might get to see her again. Because you're coming with me."

Kay growled, "Not if I can help it, you son of a—"

"Shut up!" Dred interrupted, and when he did, his voice cracked, just like Artie's sometimes did.

"Hey—are you a kid?" Kay asked doubtfully.

"I said, shut up!" Dred repeated, intentionally deepening his voice. "We're leaving. Now." He prepared to open a gate back to Fenland—but something downhill caught his eye. It was almost like the wall of fire had spawned a small, mobile fireball that was moving toward them.

Quickly.

This movement also distracted the two remaining soldiers fighting Lance, and he took advantage. He slammed their heads together, knocking them out cold, then turned and watched the moving fireball too.

It jumped quickly up the hill and took cover behind one of the aurochs' huge bodies. But then the fireball creature picked up the aurochs and threw it!

The beast struck the two soldiers Kay had disarmed,

the impact making an awful noise as their bones crunched and shattered.

Artie rolled over as a second aurochs sailed above him, taking out his whip man.

Dred moved toward Artie as an electrical gate opened, filling the air with the smell of ozone. The jaybird immediately took wing and darted through it.

An arrow shot up the hill, catching the last soldier in the shoulder. He started running for the open gate, but another arrow caught him in the leg and he went down hard.

Dred sheathed his sword and grabbed Artie by the ankles. He ducked through the portal and was on the other side when Kay said, "Hey, buddy, you better look out!"

But Dred wouldn't look. He had to get Artie and salvage some part of this mission. He concentrated on pulling Artie through while Artie writhed and yelled, "Let me go! Let me go!"

The fireball creature drew closer, and finally Artie got a good look at it as it shed its conflagrated clothing.

"Sami?" he yelped.

There was no doubt. The guy they'd just duped was here, trying to save him. And he was about to tackle Dred and jump through the gate!

Which meant Sami was going to end up in Fenland!

"Wait!" Artie yelled, but Sami was already airborne.

Sami's broad shoulder barreled into Dred's chest, knocking the wind out of him as the gate snapped shut, taking their enemy and their savior all at once.

"Shoot!" Artie shouted at the top of his lungs.

Qwon's kidnapper had gotten away.

Again.

CONCERNING A BUNCH OF STUFF, INCLUDING A SURPRISE FOR KYNDER

𝕶𝖞𝖓𝖉𝖊𝖗 𝖜𝖆𝖘 𝖘𝖑𝖊𝖊𝖕𝖎𝖓𝖌, 𝖘𝖑𝖚𝖒𝖕𝖊𝖉 𝖔𝖛𝖊𝖗 a great oak desk in the Library's main reading room, when his iPad began to make a noise.

It took him more than a minute to come to and figure out what the sound was, and then another half a minute to unearth the thing from the books stacked haphazardly all around. When he found it he folded back its cover and accepted an incoming call from Artie.

After a few seconds his kids' faces filled the screen. They were back at the court-in-exile. "Arthur, Kay! I'm so glad to see you guys."

"Hey, Kynder!" his kids said together.

"How ya doing?" Kay asked, a big smile on her face.

Kynder rubbed the sleep from his eyes and said, "Good.

I've been worried sick about you two of course, but what's new?" Over the last few months, it seemed like all Kynder did was worry. "How'd the Gram quest go? Did you find Erik's sword?"

At that moment it struck Kynder how ridiculous it all sounded. He was used to asking his kids about their exploits in school and sports and video games, but as exciting as those could be, they weren't life-and-death. *They were school and sports and video games.* This was something else. Artie and Kay weren't innocents anymore. They weren't students or athletes or gamers. They were—Kynder could hardly believe it—real-life heroes who'd been told that nothing less than the fate of the world would be determined by the success of their quests.

"We got Gram all right!" Artie said, swinging the iPad's camera to Erik, who stood in the background holding his sword proudly.

"Cool! Was it hard?" Kynder asked.

"Eh, not really," Kay said convincingly. Artie knew he wouldn't have been able to lie so well. They'd decided not to tell Kynder how close they'd come to getting captured by Morgaine's forces because they didn't want to freak him out any more than he already was.

"What about you?" Artie asked. "Any luck figuring out who's got the Peace Sword?"

"No, but I'm homing in on some good leads, I think,"

which was a lie since all Kinder had really been doing was trying to discover why Excalibur wanted Merlin dead. It was the first time in a long time that Kynder could remember lying to his children, and it made him feel awful. Also, the secret that Merlin had told him—that Artie was made by none other than Morgaine—gnawed relentlessly at him. How could he justify keeping this knowledge from his son? It felt so important, if not for Artie's kingly missions, then at least for Artie's peace of mind.

Kynder *had* to tell him. And now was as good a time as any. He swallowed hard and tried to speak.

But nothing came.

Kay leaned forward and said, "You all right, Kynder? You're turning red."

Kynder brought his fist to his mouth and coughed several times. When he was done, he said, "Yeah. I'm fine. Sorry." With his other hand he was clutching Merlin's magic stone as hard as he could.

Kay gave Kynder a comforting smile. "Take it easy, Dad. We'll be fine."

Kynder smiled back. His heart warmed when Kay called him Dad. "I know. I just wish I were there with you guys."

"Me too, Dad," Artie said. There it was again. Kay put her arm around her brother and gave him a little hug.

Man, being a parent was tough sometimes.

Artie asked, "Have you learned anything else interesting?

Maybe about the witch, or something that might help us get to Qwon?"

"Come across anything about Mom?" Kay wondered. Cassie was always at the back of Kay's mind, even though she tried hard not to think about her.

Artie squeezed his sister's knee as Kynder said, "I'm sorry, but no. Nothing on your mom, sweetie. Come to think of it, I haven't seen anything on Merlin, either, which is pretty strange. Although a ton of this stuff is in languages I don't know. . . ." Kynder trailed off, rubbing his forehead. It had only been one day, but he looked pooped.

Artie was about to suggest that his dad take a break when two more video chat chimes interrupted him, one from Merlin, the other from Thumb.

Merlin, reporting from The Bunker, had baggy eyes and pale skin. His tattoos looked faded and blurry around the edges. In the corner of his video feed they could make out the top of a can of Mountain Dew.

Kay pointed and said, "Hey, where'd you get that?"

Merlin looked at the can before saying, "Special delivery. I have to say, Kay Kingfisher, that even though this stuff is probably poisonous, it *is* delicious."

"Soda hoarder," Kay said bitterly. "You need to special-delivery some of that over here."

Merlin grinned and said, "Is that okay with you, Kynder?"

Kynder rolled his eyes at Kay. "Why not."

"Sweet! Thanks, Kynder," Kay exclaimed.

Merlin changed the subject, asking about Gram.

"We got it. It wasn't that hard," Kay said, lying again.

"Kay Kingfisher, please. Don't downplay anything. You quested to get one of the Seven. It can't have been easy," Merlin scolded mildly.

"Were you guys holding out on me?" Kynder asked.

"Maybe a little," Artie said sheepishly.

"Arthur, Kay," Kynder said in his best I'm-your-dad-and-I'm-disappointed-in-you voice, "tell us everything."

Artie sighed and fessed up, giving all the details. Kynder was not happy that they'd gotten in a huge fight trying to escape from Surmik, but what could he do? Fighting was part of the deal.

When Artie finished, Kynder said, "Well, I'm glad Lance and Bedevere were with you."

"Yes," Merlin seconded. "And thank the trees for this Sami!"

"I remember people like him from the old days," Thumb yelled over his iPad. He was outside in a really windy place. "They were powerful hunters and beast masters. Surely his heritage is what allowed him to cross."

"Agreed. I remember them too," Merlin said. "I hope he's not treated too roughly in Fenland, though I imagine he will be."

"I think Sami'll be fine," Artie replied. "He was crazy strong."

"Yeah," Kay added. "I think he can look after himself."

"We shall see," Merlin said.

"Merlin, who *was* that guy Sami saved me from? I'm certain he's the same guy who took Qwon."

Merlin held his chin in his hand and said thoughtfully, "Well, the coat of arms you described—the white-and-purple field with a golden double-headed bird—belongs to Mordred, the witch's son."

Kay frowned. "The same Mordred who killed Arthur the First with the Peace Sword?" she wondered.

"No," Kynder answered for Merlin. "The history books say that the original Mordred died a long time ago."

"Correct," Merlin said. "This is a new Mordred, just like you are a new Arthur."

Kynder's ears perked up at this. Was Merlin trying to tell him something?

Artie shrugged. "Whoever he is, I'm going to take care of him next time. No way he escapes again."

Thumb said loudly, "If you're thinking of killing him, I wouldn't, lad. A good king shows restraint, and Mordred will know much that we do not."

Merlin nodded gravely. "Yes, he could be quite useful if captured."

Artie silently conceded that they had a point while Kay

asked, "Tommy, where the heck are you? A wind tunnel?"

"Not exactly. I'm flying." He flipped the camera around so they could see the back of Tiberius's gigantic head framed by puffy white clouds. Thumb turned the camera back and said, "I'm glad things went well in Sweden, because I'm afraid there's bad news from Leagon."

"Lord Tol wouldn't agree to give us a spy?" Merlin asked anxiously.

"No. He was eager to gift us the spy Bors le Fey. He's the best. He can go completely invisible, which, needless to say, is a keen skill for a spy to have. The bad news is that Shallot le Fey and The Anguish were taken by the witch as well. Shallot has been imprisoned at the Castel for over a month."

"Oh, dear!" Merlin exclaimed.

"We'll have to try and free her too when we go for Qwon," Thumb yelled over the wind.

Artie said, "I guess on the plus side, we know where two of the Seven Swords are now. Excalibur and The Anguish are together, right?"

"I'd think so," Merlin said. "Hopefully Bors will be able to find out for certain."

"Where is this Bors dude?" Kay asked, eager to see an actual fairy.

Thumb held his iPad high over his shoulder. Beyond Tiberius's long tail was *another* dragon. A golden one. Riding on its neck was a lanky teenager with pink-and-black hair. Thumb brought his iPad back down and said, "The dragon is called Fallown. Tol loaned us him too. The lord of Leagon is not at all happy with Morgaine."

"*Two* dragons!" Artie exclaimed.

"Aye, lad," Thumb said knowingly. "The plan is to fly high over the witch's castle and air-drop Bors. We should get there in the next twenty-four hours, leaving us eight days until the new moon. Bors has a scrambled radio texter that he'll use to send regular updates."

"Nice! Someone behind enemy lines!" Kay exclaimed.

"That's right, lass," Thumb confirmed.

Merlin clasped his hands and said, "I should be able to help you with the airdrop, Mr. Thumb. The magical siphon that will produce the sangrealitic blackouts of Fenland is nearly ready. Another day should be sufficient to get it going. Wait until the dead of night, and Bors will be able to drop into a Fenland completely deprived of electrical—and magical—power. They won't see him coming at all."

"Smashing, Merlin," Thumb said. "We won't move until Fenland goes dark. Now if you don't mind, I'm going to sign off. The connection on my end is atrocious."

"Fine, Mr. Thumb," Merlin said.

"Yeah, fine," Artie added for good measure. Wasn't he the one who was supposed to say it was okay? He was the king, after all.

"Cheerio, lads," Thumb said to Artie and Kay. "Good

luck, Kynder," he added before terminating his feed.

Merlin tented his fingers and asked, "Well, what's left?"

"Uh, the next of the Seven Swords?" Kay said bluntly. "We only have nine days to go!"

"Of course!" Merlin said. "How ridiculously forgetful of me! The sword app will have more details, but Orgulus is in a very strange place called Mont-Saint-Michel."

"Yeah," Kay said. "Didn't you say something about it being in both our world and the Otherworld at the same time?"

"That's exactly right, Kay," Merlin said.

Kynder said, "If you mean the Mont-Saint-Michel in France, I went there before you guys were born. It's pretty spectacular."

"That's the one," Merlin confirmed.

"And in the Otherworld?" Artie wondered. "What's it like there?"

"Let's just say it's not at all spectacular," Merlin said seriously.

"Wonderful," Artie said.

"Wait," Kynder interjected. "I read a story about Mont-Saint-Michel a couple weeks ago while we were waiting for you, Merlin. Didn't the first Arthur go there? To defeat someone who was terrorizing the French countryside?"

"Yes," Merlin said, "but not some*one*. Some*thing*. A giant. A nasty, ravaging, homicidal giant who liked to make his clothing out of the beards of men. Arthur the First cut off his head with Carnwennan. For a while the beast's offspring surreptitiously lived in the castle in France. But now—"

"Let me guess," Kay interrupted, "they moved to the Otherworld."

"Precisely," Merlin confirmed. "They had to. Giants were banished from your side not long after Arthur the First died."

Artie said, "No problem. We'll just stay in the French one to get Orgulus. Should be easy!"

Merlin frowned and said, "I'm sorry, but it doesn't work that way. Mont-Saint-Michel has a special quality it shares with only a few other places. You see, there aren't two castles built on two islands in two different worlds. There's only one castle and one island; it's just that in the Otherworld it appears one way, and in your world it appears another. But for you, because you are King Arthur, I'm afraid the castle will not be very reliable."

"What are you trying to say, Merlin?" Artie asked.

"That while there, you will randomly switch back and forth between the two Mont-Saint-Michels without warning."

"So one second we could be in the French one, with tourists and whatever, and the next we could be in some nasty giant's castle?" Artie tried to clarify.

"Right, and then back again," Merlin said. "And then repeat," he added apologetically.

"Sounds fun," Kay said sarcastically.

"It may not be, but we have to get Orgulus," said Artie.

"Right, my boy," Merlin said proudly. "I think that's it then. I'm going to sign off. By this time tomorrow Bors should be ready to drop into Fenland and, with any luck, you'll be on your way back with the legendary rapier. See you, guys. Merlin out!" And before anyone could say good-bye, Merlin was gone.

After a few moments Kynder raised his eyebrows and said, "Be careful, guys."

"We will," Kay said.

"Check in with me as soon as you're back."

"Will do," Artie said.

Kynder reached out for his kids. "Okay, bye!"

"Bye!"

"Love you! Bye," Kynder said one last time, but his kids had already gone.

He leaned forward and buried his face in his hands.

What had they gotten into? It was all too much, and as special as his kids were, he couldn't shake the fact that they were still kids. Wasn't he supposed to be protecting them? But how could he at this point?

Kynder stood, shook out his limbs, and tried to gather his wits. He knew how to help them. Forget trying to find out why Excalibur wanted Merlin dead. He was going to switch gears and find out anything he could about this Peace Sword, and the person who had it, and Qwon's kidnapper, Mordred.

Kynder looked around the huge and Byzantine reading room. There were probably a hundred thousand books in the Library that would be useful in some way. He needed months to review them all, not days.

He needed help.

And it was at that exact moment that a bell rang.

At first Kynder thought it was the iPad again. But it wasn't. It was the doorbell.

Kynder grabbed an electric lantern and made his way into the hallway.

It took him a while to get to the main entrance. He passed door after mysterious door along the Library's long hallway—the same hallway down which Lavery had led Artie and his knights several weeks back. But Lavery was gone now—Kynder had watched as Merlin angrily shrank the wood elf to the size of a grasshopper and then stepped on him—and Kynder was totally alone.

Finally he reached the entrance. He hung the lantern on a peg and peered through a peephole. Sylvan was regarded as pretty safe, and with Lavery gone the Library was very safe, but Kynder didn't want to let any monsters in. That would just be foolish.

Luckily for him, the visitor outside the door looked pretty harmless.

To be sure, Kynder pushed a button on a staticky intercom and asked, "Who's that?"

The little creature said, "Evening, sir. Name's Clive, sir."

"What do you want, Clive?"

"Are you Kynder Kingfisher?"

"I am," Kynder said, a little taken aback.

"I want to help you," Clive rattled. "My lord Numinae sent me as his emissary. I am at your service."

Kynder leaned away from the peephole. Could he be so lucky? Help was exactly what he needed. Since he didn't have the luxury of time, he figured he had to take a chance. He pushed the button again and said, "One second, Clive."

He grabbed a giant ring of keys, threw the locks, and heaved the door open.

"Hallo, sir," Clive said in a raspy voice.

"Hello," Kynder returned, bending low to shake the little man's hand. "Numinae, you said?"

"Yessir. My lord thought it bad manners to leave you alone in his Library."

"Well, your timing's impeccable, I'll give you that." Clive had a slight hunchback on his left side, his eyes were uneven, and his wiry beard grew in splotches. His brownish skin was awful—riddled with pockmarks and scars—and while it was hard to tell, Kynder was pretty sure that his hair was dark green. "If you don't mind my asking, what are you?"

Clive lowered his gaze, letting it come to rest just above Kynder's knees. "Mostly gnome, some wood dwarf and troll. All unlucky," he explained while gesturing at his gnarled body.

"Ah, well, it's a pleasure to meet you, Mr. Clive."

"Just Clive, if you please, sir," he said.

"Not a problem, Clive. And it's just Kynder for me. The only person who ever called me 'sir' was my granddaddy."

Clive smiled. "Understood, Kynder."

"Tell me, Clive, what kind of help did Numinae think I needed?"

"Well," Clive rasped, "he figured you might be needing some help finding things. I'm not sure what you're looking for, but I do know a fair amount about the Otherworld."

"Do you read any of the Otherworld languages?"

"Most passably. More than two dozen fluently," Clive said with a knowing smile.

A wave of relief surged in Kynder's chest. "And how do I know that I can trust you?" he asked.

Clive winced. "You don't. I can only give you my word that whatever I help you with will stay between you and me. I won't even tell the wizard, if you wish it." Kynder couldn't fathom why, but he felt a little uneasy at the mention of Merlin. "My lord and I also know that the witch made your son," the gnome said conspiratorially.

Kynder straightened. "Go on."

"We know something else that perhaps you don't. I'd like to share it with you, as a token of good faith."

"What's that, Clive?" Kynder liked this little creature.

"The witch—she's made others too," Clive said deeply.

That did it. "Please, come in," Kynder said. "Come in and make yourself at home."

𝕿𝖍𝖊 𝖌𝖆𝖙𝖊 𝖋𝖎𝖟𝖟𝖑𝖊𝖉 𝖘𝖍𝖚𝖙 𝖆𝖘 Dred and Sami crashed through it, landing hard on the barracks' earthen floor at Castel Deorc Wæters. As they materialized in the room, a group of off-duty soldiers hooted and clambered to grab their weapons.

Dred felt like snot. He'd had the wind knocked out of him and had probably broken a few of his ribs.

Worse, Dred had come *this close* to capturing that Artie kid, but no.

Epic fail.

Which meant that Morgaine was going to be pretty miffed.

But Dred couldn't think about that just yet. He had Sami to deal with first.

Immediately after they'd come to a stop, Sami pushed up and straddled Dred, grabbing him roughly by the shoulders. "You leave that boy alone!" Sami shouted in a mysterious accent.

Apparently he hadn't noticed the change of scenery.

"Seize this fool!" Dred wheezed to the soldiers in the barracks as he tried to regain his breath.

A dozen soldiers descended on Sami. He let go of Dred and flung the first few men away like he was shooing flies. It was then that it dawned on him that he'd been transported to a place he didn't recognize.

Dred slid out of the melee and stood. He watched as the strange man's expression went from one of unmitigated fury to one of stark confusion.

The soldiers took advantage of Sami's disorientation and attacked him with maces, staffs, and whips. They knocked him furiously on the head and shoulders, where welts and bruises popped up like giant goose bumps. Two soldiers managed to get the ends of their magical whips looped around his ankles.

These were about to coil themselves around Sami when his instincts replaced his confusion. Ignoring the flurry of weapons, Sami reached down and tore the silver strands from his legs like they were made of straw. Then he whipped his arm through the air and with a single haymaker laid out five men.

Dred drew his sword. The remaining soldiers drew theirs too.

"Show no mercy!" Dred commanded.

Sami crouched and bounded across the room on all fours, bowling over half a dozen men. He headed for a huge anvil that hadn't been moved in a hundred years. He jumped over it, turned, and then picked it up with ease, brandishing it like a shield. As the remaining soldiers attacked, their swords hit the anvil uselessly. Without letting go of it, Sami pushed the anvil into the chests of a pair of men, knocking them on their butts, and then he mercilessly dropped it on the feet of two more. They cried out in pain.

Only five able soldiers remained.

"Morgaine!" Dred yelled.

But she was already there. The jaybird, Eekan, flapped wildly on her shoulder as she stood in the entryway between Sami and Dred. Beside her were a couple of their fierce short-faced war bears.

The animals—one brown, the other black with a few gray spots—sprang forward. They were huge, bigger than sabertooths or aurochs by an order of magnitude. Aside from dragons and a handful of other mythical beasts, Dred knew that they were the largest land predators in all of the Otherworld.

The bears landed a few feet from Sami and growled. The Swede squinted and lowered into a defensive position.

They attacked simultaneously. Both scored hits, drawing deep gashes in Sami's arms with their sharpened claws, but the blood didn't faze him. Sami counterattacked, smacking the bears hard on their heads with his open hands, hitting the brown one so forcefully that its legs buckled. Sami quickly grabbed this bear around the neck and squeezed. A great snapping sound filled the low-ceilinged room, and the bear collapsed. Sami effortlessly swung the ursine body at its partner, knocking it back a dozen feet.

Then Sami screamed.

No.

He roared.

The remaining bear understood and took a step back and sat on his haunches, like a dog brought to heel.

"A beast master," Morgaine hissed lowly.

Sami's rabid gaze swung to the witch.

"Enough!" she wailed, as Sami hoisted the dead bear and hurled it at her.

Morgaine calmly held up her hand. Her form flickered, and so did Sami's, and in an instant they switched places, causing the bear to come crashing into Sami instead.

Dred saw the look of surprise on Sami's face as he was violently knocked back by the very animal he'd just thrown!

Morgaine raised a bejeweled staff. Her form flickered again, and suddenly she was standing above Sami. She brought the point of her staff down on his forehead. His eyeballs bulged and spittle sprayed from his lips as he was shot through with thousands and thousands of volts of electricity. The dead bear, lying on top of him, convulsed reflexively, and some of its thick, musky fur began to singe.

The fight was over. A few guards emerged from the margins and made their way closer to the witch.

"Take this filth to the tower!" she barked at a gigantic soldier. "I'll be there shortly to cast a dragon's bubble on him. Tell the jailer no food or water. I want this man broken."

"Yes, ma'am," the soldier barked.

He rolled the bear's smoking body over, and heaved Sami onto his shoulder with a bunch of grunting. Then he slowly made his way to the tower.

Morgaine wheeled on Dred and said, "Where is Cleomede? Where is the boy-king?" She banged the ground with her staff, and a spine-tingling screech rang out from the impact.

"Mum, I tried, but you saw what I had to deal with," Dred explained, waving his hand at Sami. "And it wasn't just him. The boy's knights—and the boy-king himself—they're excellent fighters."

"How many were there?"

Dred tried to remember. "Six, I think. I almost had

the boy, Mum. I almost did!"

Morgaine huffed. "*Six?* My sweet boy, are you joking? And what difference does it make that you 'almost' had him, hmm? I *need* him! I don't 'almost' need him!"

Dred stepped closer to Morgaine. "Please, Mum, give me another chance. Let me use his own sword against him!"

Morgaine's eyes went wide. "Use Excalibur? You? I wouldn't let you within fifty feet of that sword now. Besides, how smart do you think that would be, letting him get so close to *his* weapon? He'd take it from you, and you'd be in pieces before you could count to two."

Dred slumped. "All right, maybe you're right. But give me another chance. Please," he pleaded.

Morgaine spun away in disgust. "Proxies!" she spit.

"What's that, Mum?" Dred asked.

"Lavery, Twrch Trwyth—neither could stop him. My tornadoes nearly had him, but that damned Sylvanian dragon had to whisk him away. Now you—who were raised to be his equal!—you can't stop him either."

"His equal?" Dred asked. This was the first time he'd ever heard anything like that. "Mum, I'm sorry, but—"

"Oh—never mind," Morgaine said, shaking her head like she was trying to rid her mind of unwanted thoughts. She waved her staff through the air in front of her son. "I'm just mad. Forget it," she said softly.

Dred felt a little queasy, and quite suddenly did forget

what she'd just said about proxies and Lavery and monsters. And being the king's equal.

"You're too dim to understand anyway," Morgaine added in a dulcet tone.

Dred stepped back, confusion covering his face. He remembered saying that he'd almost captured Artie, but . . . then what? Still angry, Dred clenched his teeth and said, "I'm so sorry I couldn't get him, Mum. I didn't want to let you down."

Which was true.

Morgaine said, "It's okay, dear. So long as we have his sword and The Anguish, he can't get to Avalon. Eventually, he will have to come to us. Now it's clear *I* must be ready. *You* will never be. Come. Tell me what happened. It will be helpful," Morgaine said, squeezing his arm.

Dred hesitated but then followed her and told the story of how he'd fought and nearly captured King Artie Kingfisher. Morgaine didn't say a word, and her silence made him angry. He couldn't put his finger on it, but he felt like she was toying with his feelings. Literally.

Sometimes parents were really a pain in the butt.

He finished as they came to her room. Morgaine turned to Dred and he could tell that he wasn't going to be let in. He gathered his strength and said, "Can I ask a question, Mum?"

"Of course, dear," she said.

"What's wrong with Artie's face? Is there a spell on my helmet that prevents me from seeing it?"

Morgaine lowered her eyes. "Don't concern yourself with that, pet. I mean it."

Dred wanted to ask more, but couldn't. He knew when his mother was finished talking about something.

"Leave me now, child. Go check on the prisoners."

"They need blankets," Dred said quietly, remembering Qwon's request. "It *has* been cold at night."

"Fine," Morgaine said. "Give them blankets, but not tonight. I only need them for nine more nights anyway. Now go. I'm done with you for today." She turned away, and then added, "I don't need you anymore."

Dred stood there as his mother disappeared into her room, her final words ringing in his ears.

As evening descended, a jarring screech reverberated around the portico.

Qwon sat up quickly and was mildly startled when Shallot's disembodied voice whispered in her ear, "Something's happened."

After a few minutes of silence, Qwon lay back on the grass. The sun was down, but an army of great, puffy clouds could still be seen as they marched across the twilit sky. She played that game of looking for shapes in them. She tried to force herself to see animals or famous buildings or cars or boats, but all she really saw was food: a fried egg, onion rings, a banana, a bunch of grapes.

Man, she missed food.

It was getting cold. She moved and huddled in a corner, pulling her knees to her chest. She really, really wanted a blanket.

But Dred still hadn't brought one.

Breakfast was late the next morning. For whatever reason, the little door had remained shut, and no tray with porridge or water had appeared.

Qwon waited in a patch of warm sun, letting the night's cold melt away. Her eyes were closed and the sunlight made the inside of her eyelids glow like embers.

Embers that could be used to grill hamburgers, zucchini, or hot dogs.

Man, she missed food!

Finally the door slid open. She lifted her head and looked down the length of her body as the tray was being pushed out.

Something was different. Previously, Dred had used a stick to push the tray out. Today, he used his hand. His fingers lingered on the edge of the tray and even turned it a little bit, as if to put it in place.

Qwon got up. And when she got close to the tray, Dred's hand bent up and gave her a little wave!

Qwon plopped onto her knees and said, "Hey."

Dred rested his hand back down, and then, as though he realized that he'd made a mistake, pulled it back quickly and shut the little door.

"No, wait!" Qwon said, lunging forward. But it was too late.

Not like she knew what she would have done with it, anyway. Was she going to hold it? That would've been weird. Slap it? No. Pull it toward her? Also no.

Maybe she *did* want to hold it.

Whatever. Being alone was doing funny things to her.

She picked up the cup. Something was different with it too. It wasn't tea. Something brown was floating on top of it. She brought it to her nose.

It was apple cider! Hot apple cider!

With cinnamon!

Qwon slurped the liquid. It burned the tip of her tongue, but it was like a revelation. Memories of Christmas and ski trips to the Poconos crashed over her. She remembered her mom and dad when they were still together, and her grandfather and grandmother on vacation from Hawaii (she never could understand why someone would leave Hawaii to come to Pittsburgh in the winter, but they did). She remembered her grandfather's strange and amazing stories of their ancestors.

"Thanks, Dred. This is amazing."

And to her surprise, a muffled "You're welcome" came through the wooden door.

Bingo.

The food door cracked open again. Qwon leaned over but couldn't see anything on the other side.

"There's something under the porridge too," Dred said. His voice was clearer, and Qwon could tell that he had lain down on the floor and put his mouth near the slot.

It instantly occurred to Qwon how stupid Dred was being. If Shallot had wanted, she could have reappeared and thrust her staff quickly and violently through the little crack, crushing Dred's face. Qwon desperately hoped Shallot wouldn't do anything like that, because it would ruin whatever was happening.

"What is it?" Qwon asked, picking up the bowl. She cautiously pulled the small spoon from inside her shirt.

"Just look," Dred said.

Qwon pushed the porridge around and found two absolute treasures: a thick mass of melted chocolate and a soggy but well-cooked strip of bacon.

She looked over her shoulder, as if Shallot might try to steal her treats. Then she dug into the bottom of the bowl, breaking the meat into smaller pieces, and scooped up a spoonful of chocolaty bacon.

Ahhhhhh.

That was more like it.

She took another bite. And another. And another.

"You like it?" Dred asked quietly.

"Oh my god," Qwon said with her mouth full. "I love it. Thank you."

"Slow down. Others watch you guys from time to time too."

Oh, right. In her excitement Qwon had momentarily forgotten she was a prisoner.

She turned and slumped against the wall and faked nonchalance, even disgust. She covered the treats with porridge and ate slower.

Qwon finished her cider and then everything in her bowl. She desperately wanted to lick it clean, like she had on her first day there, but thought that might draw attention.

Finally she asked, "What was that awful noise I heard last night?"

Dred didn't answer. Instead he slid out another cup. It was full of water, and it even had an ice cube in it. The food door slid most of the way shut again.

Qwon could barely believe it. "Dred," she asked wryly, "are you going to ask me on a date or something?"

Dred chuckled, but then he sighed. "I shouldn't be doing this."

Qwon took a full sip of water. It was crisp and cold. "No kidding," she said, and drank the rest greedily. Neither of them said anything for a while.

"Have you seen that accursed fairy?" Dred finally asked.

"No. She whispers insults to me now and then, and I smell her occasionally, but I never see her. You?"

"No. They're awful things, those fairies."

"Yeah," Qwon pretended to agree. "I hope I never see her again."

More silence. Then, "That sound was my mother."

Qwon swallowed hard. "*That* was Morgaine?"

"Uh-huh," Dred said. "Or her sorceress's staff at least."

"Wow. Was she pissed or something?"

Dred didn't answer and Qwon didn't press him. She realized that as strange as this Otherworld place was, kids still probably fought with their parents.

His silence persisted. A breeze pushed through the portico. Shallot, still invisible, whispered in her ear, "Ask about the king."

After a few moments Qwon whispered, "Dred, have you heard anything about Artie?"

Dred hissed and said, "I'd rather not talk about him."

"So you *have* heard something?" Qwon asked a little too eagerly.

Dred's strange answer came almost too quickly: "By the fens, I hate her!"

Then he slammed the little door shut.

Qwon didn't understand why, but she knew perfectly

well who he was talking about.

"Sorry if your mom's bugging you," she said, wondering if Dred was still there. "And thanks again."

She licked the spoon clean and slid it into her shirt. Then she stood and stretched and walked to the patch of sunlight that was now creeping across the inner yard of the portico.

Free from hunger, she looked to the clouds again. And this time she saw a snake, a skyscraper, a motorcycle, even a perfect unicorn in midjump.

That evening before bed, the food door slid open and Dred wordlessly pushed out a stack of blankets. Qwon stared at them for a few minutes before going to get them.

While she did this, Shallot whispered from somewhere behind her, "It's working. With luck we'll be out of here before the new moon rises."

Qwon hoped Shallot was right.

𝔚𝔥𝔦𝔩𝔢 𝔔𝔴𝔬𝔫 𝔴𝔞𝔰 𝔢𝔫𝔧𝔬𝔶𝔦𝔫𝔤 𝔥𝔢𝔯 surprise breakfast of porridge, bacon, and chocolate, Bercilak clanked through the great hall of the court-in-exile carrying a large wooden box. Everyone was at the round table having a big breakfast before heading off to Mont-Saint-Michel. Bercilak joined them and plopped the box down.

"By the trees, Master Merlin packs a heavy crate. This just arrived for you, sire," the green knight boomed.

"Mind opening it, Bercy?" Artie asked.

"Not at all." He pulled his giant battle-ax over his shoulder, took a step back, and with a single swing cleanly took the top off the box. Bercilak stowed his weapon and began digging in the container, throwing a mixture of packing peanuts and wood shavings to the floor. A lot of the peanuts stuck to his hands and arms, charged by static electricity.

"My, how I hate these silly things," Bercilak said. "Such a pain to clean up."

"What's in there, Bercy?" Kay asked.

"Oh, of course. Let's see." He reached into the box and pulled out a case of Mountain Dew.

"A case! No way! No one tell Kynder," Kay whispered excitedly.

"It's cold too," Bercilak said. "Don't know how he did that. . . ."

"Magic, right?" Erik asked.

"Right," Artie confirmed.

"Ah, but look at this!" Bercilak said, heaving out a second case.

"Two! Oh, man." Kay sighed. "I *love* that Merlin. Bercy, toss a cold one over here, please."

Bercilak peeled open one of the cases and threw a can to Kay. Then he passed cans to everyone else and kept one for himself. He watched as they drank, all *ahhh*ing with delight. Bercilak opened his, held it directly over his helmet, and poured in the entire contents.

"Hmm," he said. "I have to admit, it's quite good. Tell me, Artie, from which mountain is this dew collected?"

"Mount Pepsi, I think," Artie answered seriously as Kay shot him a wink of approval.

"Well, if I ever have the pleasure of visiting your side,

I hope to visit Mount Pepsi and sample its dew alfresco," Bercilak intoned.

"That'd be great, Bercy. I'll join you," Artie said. "Anything else in there?"

"Hmm . . . yes! A tube for Sir Lance, a small box for Sir Bedevere, and a soft paper package with a tag on it that says, 'All.'"

Bercilak handed out the packages. Lance opened his first. "Let's see . . . three arrows and some kind of necklace with a nasty yellow tooth on it." He turned the tube upside down and a tiny tag fell into his hand. He squinted at it and said, "Man, Merlin sure can write small."

"What's it say?" Kay asked.

"'Three limitless arrows. Will travel any distance and always hit their mark. Use wisely.' Wow," Lance said as he tickled one of the arrows' feather fletchings. He continued to read. "'Tooth on necklace belonged to Sir Geoffrey Mallory, last rightful bearer of Orgulus. Wear this talisman and Orgulus will be yours.' Sweet!" he said, and pulled the necklace over his head.

"Sir Geoffrey Mallory, did you say?" Bercilak said.

"Yeah. You know him?"

"I know *of* him. He was an inveterate rapscallion in his day. Got into tons of trouble. Master swordsman, of course, and a fairly able writer, if I recall."

"Cool," Artie said. "What's in yours, Beddy?"

Bedevere tore open his package and pulled out a plain copper ring about seven inches across. Tied to this was another minute note. He read, "'I present your phantom limb, Sir Bedevere. Will magically fit your stump. When activated ("Phantoma!"), it will conjure a superstrong, ghostlike arm that will last two minutes. Needs an hour to fully recharge, and will do so on its own.' A phantom arm . . . ," Bedevere wondered.

"That's awesome! Try it out!" Artie said.

Bedevere rolled up his sleeve and pushed the ring onto his stump. As promised, it was a perfect fit. He moved what was left of his arm around, looking at the ring, and finally said, "Phantoma!"

A hazy, barely visible appendage grew from his stump. Bedevere moved it through the air, turning it over. He ran his real hand over it and then swiped right through it. "Amazing," Bedevere said.

"Can you feel it?" Erik asked, his mouth full of eggs and bacon.

"I can. It's kind of like . . . like my old arm," Bedevere lamented.

"Sorry, Beddy," Artie said.

"Don't worry about it, sire. Besides, it doesn't feel *exactly* like my old arm. This one feels better. And it can't be chopped off!"

Bedevere grabbed the edge of the round table with

the phantom limb—*and then lifted the table clear off the ground!*

"By the trees!" Bercilak exclaimed. "I had to move that last year, and it took me a full hour to drag it ten feet! What a wonder! Wilt Chamberlain sure is a fancy wizard!"

"So that leaves one more package, Art," Erik said. "What's in it?"

Artie took the remaining gift from the table and tore it open as Kay peered over his shoulder.

"Shirts?" she asked dubiously as she stared at the package's contents.

Artie picked up the tiny note that sat on top of the clothes and read, "'Special armored shirts depicting your respective coats of arms. Each contains three million bonded sheets of graphene, an experimental lattice of carbon that will not tear. Wonderful stuff. Try it!'"

Kay passed them out. Blazoned across the front and back of each was a large, shield-shaped coat of arms. Artie's was blue with three golden crowns; Bedevere's was black with a red castle; Erik's was blue with a yellow tree; Lance's was red-and-white diagonal stripes crossed by a pair of black arrows; and Kay's was blue with two white keys. There was one more, adorned by a white field with a red fist sticking up its thumb, which was for Thumb.

They pulled the graphene shirts over whatever they were already wearing. Each fit perfectly. More magic, no doubt. They smoothed them over their bodies and checked each other out.

"We look like a motley soccer team or something," Artie said.

"Who's gonna try one?" Kay asked.

Erik shrugged. "I will. Bercilak, would you do the honors?"

"I'd be delighted to!" Bercilak said, removing his ax from his shoulder again.

Erik held out the front of his shirt like he was going to catch something in it. Bercilak tried to cut it with the edge of his ax, but nothing happened. "Go ahead, give it a whack," Erik said as he steadied himself.

Bercilak held up his ax and brought it down hard. Erik teetered but didn't fall as the shirt was knocked out of his hands. Then he held it up again and examined it.

Nothing.

Artie took his dagger and tried to punch a hole in his own shirt with its point.

Also nothing.

"Sweet," Kay said.

"I'll say," Artie agreed. "I might never take mine off!"

Kay stuffed Thumb's shirt into the infinite backpack and said, "Thank goodness for Merlin."

"Amen to that," Lance said.

"Kay, can you grab the iPad?" Artie asked. "I want to

see what it says about Orgulus. Plus we need to get a bead on this Mont-Saint-Michel place so we can gate there."

"Roger that," Kay said as she handed the tablet to her brother.

Artie fired up the sword app and touched the Orgulus icon. The screen went dark before fading in on a twirling animation of a long, thin rapier. Artie read the words that appeared below the picture:

"'The name Orgulus comes from an Old French word meaning "pride," and this blade is certainly full of it. Of the Seven Swords, it is by far the youngest. Forged from a sangrealitic alloy by a heretic Christian monk and black-smith on Mont-Saint-Michel in 1440, it was indisputably the first weapon of its kind. The monk, Emmanuel del Espada de Loja, was a direct forebear of its last rightful owner, Geoffrey Mallory. Orgulus has never lost a duel. It is blindingly quick, and can bend like a reed in the wind but never break. The ornate cage protecting the hand can punch through anything.'"

"Cool," Kay said. "Cooler than Cleomede's bug-shooing power, anyway."

Artie gave his sister a small smile.

"All right, let's see. 'Orgulus is hidden in the bowels of the Mont-Saint-Michel abbey in an ancient crypt. The crypt is guarded by strong magic, so you will have to gate to a cistern in the lower section and work your way up.

When you are done, you must exit the castle through a large drainage tunnel, located in the same cistern. This leads to the woods on the northern side of the island. Make sure to open the crossover in these woods before returning to the court-in-exile.'"

Artie held up the iPad so everyone could see as he flicked through the screens showing the floor plan of the abbey and a map of the oval-shaped island. It was almost completely covered with a huge castle/church, a dark patch of woods blanketing its northern section. Finally a picture popped up. The castle was massive. It had everything a castle ever wanted, from a snaking curtain wall to dozens of turrets to countless archways to a high, reach-for-the-heavens spire set right in the middle. Everything about it looked grand and foreboding. No wonder it was such a tourist trap.

"Man," Kay said. "Now, *that* is a castle."

The others agreed as Artie flipped back to the Orgulus entry. He finished, "'Don't forget to mind the giant. Avoid it if possible. It is a cunning and mischievous brute.'" Artie put the iPad on the table and leaned back in his chair.

"Aw, it'll be fine, dudes," Lance added. "What's one giant against the five of us?"

"*Five* of you? Am I to stay here again, King Artie?" Bercilak asked.

"Yeah, I think you should," Artie said apologetically. "We have to know that we can come back here whenever we need to, and you're so good at keeping it safe, Bercy."

Bercilak bowed and said, "Of course."

Kay pointed at the Mountain Dew and added, "Keep that safe too."

"Why, Sir Kay! I'll guard the dew of the mountain with my life!"

Artie stood and slapped both hands on the table. "Well, guys, let's get out of here as soon as possible. We've got to keep going. Qwon is counting on us."

"Lunae lumen!"

The knights found themselves in a pitch-black room. The air was cool and damp.

"Kay, can you get our headlamps?" Artie asked, his voice bouncing off the walls.

"Sure." Kay fumbled in the infinite backpack and pulled out the lights. She turned one on and passed out the others. They put them on, and beams of light shot from their heads like horns.

They were in a windowless stone room. A small metal door was set high on one wall, and across from it was a round opening about five feet wide.

Artie pointed at the door. "The map showed that leading to the hall that would go up to the crypt." He swung around and indicated the opening. "And that's the drain that lets out into the woods. So if we—"

"Oh my god!" Kay interrupted, brandishing Cleomede in front of her.

"What?" Erik asked, standing next to her.

Kay repositioned her light and said breathlessly, "I swear that wall was just covered with, like, a million bloody handprints."

Artie stepped forward, but the wall was blank. "Looks fine to me," he said.

"You know I wouldn't lie about something like that."

"Yeah, I know, but . . ."

A grating sound echoed through the room and silenced Artie.

"Sire, I think we should get out of here," Bedevere said as they became aware of a low, persistent hiss.

"Totally," Artie agreed. "Beddy, open that door. Lance, give him a hand."

"Got it," Lance said. He moved into position so Bedevere could climb onto his shoulders. While they worked on the door, Artie noticed a line of small holes surrounding the top of the cistern; the hissing sound seemed to be coming from these, but what was making it?

And that was when the sound became extremely loud and morphed from a hiss into a thousand little squeals.

All of their headlamps flickered briefly as Kay said

frantically, "Artie, look!"

"Rats!" Erik cried.

Artie joined his light with Kay's, and sure enough, dozens of gray rats were falling from the holes into the room. Artie gagged and closed his eyes.

He hated rats.

"Oh god, Beddy, hurry up!" Kay implored. Her light now lit the floor, which was quickly coming to life with furry gray rodents.

Kay hated rats too.

But not Erik. Using the flat side of Gram, he hit any rat that came near him like a golf ball. Some exploded on impact; others sailed to the wall and smacked into it with a sickening *splat*!

Artie and Kay moved next to Lance and Bedevere as Erik went to town on the rodents. "Beddy, please open that thing!" Kay begged again.

The rats started crawling over their feet, and Lance began stomping, trying to shake them off.

"Hey, stay still," Bedevere ordered.

"You want to switch?" Lance shot back.

Just then, four plump, musky rodents plopped directly onto Kay's head, getting immediately tangled in her long red hair. She screeched as their claws dug into her scalp.

"Oh, forget this," Bedevere said, abandoning his effort to open the door's lock. He reared back and said,

"Phantoma!" The magical arm shot to life, and he grabbed the iron ring in the middle of the door and simply pulled it off its hinges.

He threw the door to the floor and offered Kay his real arm. "Grab ahold, Sir Kay!" he said. Kay spastically batted the rats from her head and grabbed Bedevere's hand, and he hoisted her through the doorway. Bedevere vaulted forward, following her.

"You're next, kid," Lance said. Artie climbed onto his archer's shoulders and jumped through to safety. Erik followed.

Lance was the only one left.

Rats poured from every hole. As Artie scanned the room, he realized that most of the little creatures had red eyes, and that their teeth were stained with blood. He also noticed that the walls were indeed covered with hundreds and hundreds of bloody handprints, just like Kay had said.

Now he understood. For a few minutes they had been in the French Mont-Saint-Michel, but now they were in the Otherworld version.

Bedevere was about to reach down and grab Lance when all their headlamps flickered again, and suddenly Lance was alone in the stone cistern. No rats. Not a single one. And no bloody handprints all over the walls.

"You all right?" Artie asked.

Lance huffed and said, "Shoot, I'm not afraid of a few rodents. Beddy, get me out of here."

Bedevere helped Lance with his superstrong arm and then deactivated it.

"I guess that was that switching thing Merlin warned us about, huh?" Kay asked as they regrouped.

"Yup," Artie said. "The rats and the bloody handprints were part of the Otherworld castle, but now—"

"We're in the nice French version," Erik finished for him.

Artie nodded as Kay said, "Let's hope it stays this way. I *do not like rats*!"

Artie noticed Lance standing silently, holding his hand over his chest, where the tooth of Geoffrey Mallory hung on its necklace. "What's up, Lance?" Artie asked.

Lance peered toward the stairs at the end of the hall. "I think this dead guy's tooth is giving me a bead on Orgulus. The crypt's up there."

"Great," Artie said. "Lead the way."

They went up the stairs and were surprised when they ran into a lean Frenchman in crisp slacks and a button-down shirt at the top of the first flight. Judging by his expression, he was pretty surprised too.

His eyes widened as he exclaimed, "*Eh! Qu'est-ce que vous faites?*"

Artie stepped around Lance and held out his hands,

which probably wasn't the smartest idea since one hand contained Flixith.

"*Attendez!*" the Frenchman said, backpedaling

"English? Do. You. Speak. English?" Kay said slowly.

"*Anglais?*" the man said before adding nervously, "*Non. Je ne parle que français.*"

What Kay didn't know was that Artie could speak French. He'd taken a year of it at Shadyside Middle School, but really he had Excalibur to thank for his fluency. He cleared his throat and said, "*Nous sommes désolés, monsieur. Mes amis et moi, nous recherchons pour une crypte. Savez-vous s'il y a une crypte près d'ici?*"

Kay shot her brother a look, and he waved her off as the man said, "*O-oui. I-il y a une crypte juste en haut,*" he said, pointing his thumb over his shoulder.

"He says there's a crypt right up there," Artie translated. "*Bien, très bien. Maintenant, monsieur,*" he said, but then, right before their eyes, the man shimmered and disappeared!

And the stairway they were in got a *lot* spookier.

They were back in the Otherworld Mont-Saint-Michel.

"Well, this is going to be quite interesting, isn't it?" Bedevere said from the rear.

Artie frowned and said, "Let's move. Lead the way again, Lance. We need to find this thing and get out of here ASAP."

"Hoo-ah," Lance seconded, moving back to the front.

They ascended two more flights and found a heavy wooden door flanked by a pair of twinkling fluorescent lightbulbs. On the door was a worn brass plaque with some writing in French. Artie read, "'*Sire chevalier, parlez doux, pour là-bas est un diable, et s'il vous entend, il viendra vous détruire.*' It means we have to keep it down because there's a devil in there that wants to tear us to pieces!"

"Great," Kay said.

Artie put his ear on the door. "I don't hear anything," he said quietly. He carefully lifted the latch and pushed the door slightly ajar. He turned to his friends and gave them a look that asked whether he should open it.

They nodded and he did.

And the darned thing squeaked the whole way.

Artie winced. Lance quickly nocked three arrows and hoisted his bow, waiting for the devil to pounce.

But nothing happened.

Artie stepped into the crypt and checked the corners. It appeared to be all clear.

The crypt was a large chamber with a vaulted Gothic ceiling supported by dozens of stone pillars. A cool, putrid draft wafted through the air. The ground was wet with a thin sheen of water. Weak lights were placed in the arches of the ceiling here and there.

Lance stepped next to Artie. "No giant?"

"Not yet," Artie whispered, peering deeper into the cavernous room.

They stepped all the way in and took a closer look. The door they'd just come through was set in a long semicircle of columns. About a dozen feet farther in was another semicircle of columns. This served to divide the crypt into an outer section, in which they stood, and an inner section. All of the columns were extremely thick; two very tall men couldn't have joined hands around one. From where the knights stood, they couldn't see into the inner chamber.

"Crypts are for dead people, right?" Erik asked.

"Last I checked," Lance whispered, poking his nose into the air like a dog following a scent. "Orgulus is in there somewhere," he said, pointing his chin toward the inner chamber. "You guys ready?"

"You bet," Artie said. "Beddy, you and Erik watch the door. If we flicker back to the French version of this place, close it. I don't want to deal with any P-Oed guards or confused tourists."

"Got it," Erik said as Bedevere nodded.

Artie, Kay, and Lance walked toward the middle of the crypt as quietly as they could, which because of all their stuff and the acoustics in the place was hardly quiet at all.

But still, no sign of the giant.

"Maybe this whole monster thing is bunk, right, Art?"

Kay whispered hopefully as they entered the central chamber of the crypt.

"Uh, I don't think so," was all Artie said as he came to a stop.

The crypt's inner chamber opened up before them. A large archway on their right led into a darkened hallway. Immediately in front of them a hot cauldron hung from a tripod of iron rods over an extinguished gas burner. It seemed as though someone—or something—had just been there.

Three piles of white bones were arranged in the room. Two of the piles were small and looked to be made up of foot or hand bones.

But the third was very large. It rose to the ceiling and dominated the room.

"Oh, shitake mushrooms," Kay said.

"Are those *leg* bones?" Lance asked.

"Yeah," Artie said in a sinking tone.

Kay flipped her headlamp on. "Call me crazy, but are the pillars covered in blood?"

"Yeah," Artie said again.

"And . . . are those *beards*?" Kay asked, pointing at the far wall.

It was hard to tell, but it certainly looked like five different-colored beards—very much separated from their owners' faces—were pegged to the wall.

"Looks like it," Artie said gravely. "Remember what

Merlin said about how the old giant used beards to make his clothing? I guess this one does too."

"Wow," was all Lance could manage. He had a nice little five-o'clock shadow going and did not want to lose it—or his face—to some beard-clad monster.

Kay turned off her headlamp. "All right, Lance, let's get this Orgulus and skedat. Like, now."

"Roger that," Lance whispered, and moved toward the far wall. He sidled along it, moving his hands up and down, pausing a couple of times before shaking his head and continuing on. "It's behind here somewhere. I can feel it." He lowered his hands to the base of the wall. "Here."

"Kay," Artie said, "can you cut us a hole, please?"

"On it." Kay knelt and began carving away the stone with Cleomede. It was easy enough but, unfortunately, it was also pretty loud. Finally she exclaimed, "There!" and pried a chunk of granite away from the wall.

The threesome leaned forward, and sure enough, in a little recess in the rock was the ornate handguard of a sword!

"Nice work! Now grab it, Lance, and let's get out of here," Artie ordered.

Lance got down on his knees and asked, "Where's the rest of it?"

"You know how it goes, Lance," Kay said easily. "All of these things are stuck in something or being watched over by some chick in a lake or whatever. You've got that guy's tooth, so I'm sure you can just yank it out."

"Yeah, give it a shot," Artie said.

But before Lance could do anything, a loud *clang* reverberated through the room, followed by a faint, far-off huffing, like a thing out of breath.

"Come on, Lance, you've got this," Artie said encouragingly, trying to ignore the noise.

Lance slid his hand into the hole and grabbed the hilt, giving it a hard pull. Nothing happened. He leaned back with all his weight, but still nothing.

A sound that was half roar and half wail echoed through the room. Artie looked at the big archway and said, "You're going to have to cut it out, Kay. Quick!"

Kay pushed her sword farther into the rock and jiggled it. Half the stone encasing the rapier turned to gravel and sand. She pulled Cleomede out and said, "Try again."

Lance tried. "Still stuck!"

They began to hear the slap of bare feet smacking on stone. The giant was moving fast.

Kay hastily cut away more rock as a loud "Arrgh!" echoed outside the archway to their right.

This time when Kay yanked Cleomede free, she pulled Orgulus with it a little. Lance knelt and was finally able to pull it out the rest of the way. He expected some kind of revelation like Artie had gotten from Excalibur and Erik from Gram, but there was nothing. It was just a sword, caked here and there with some calcified granite.

Sure, it looked pretty cool, but still, it was kind of a bummer.

Lance didn't have time to be too disappointed, though, because just then the giant crashed through the archway.

And he looked none too happy.

Kay made a shocked sound halfway between "Oh" and "Ugh" as the giant came to a stop in the archway.

He was around twelve feet tall and nearly as wide, with green, oily skin that was covered in boils and pockmarks. His flat, four-toed feet were bare, but his torso was covered with a furry smock embellished with hundreds of sparkling jewels. His head was squat and brick-shaped, his eyes milky and saucer-sized; a few strands of wiry black hair stuck out of his otherwise bald pate like pins in a pincushion. In his gargantuan hand the giant held a wooden club with a spiked metal ball lashed to its end.

He took a loping step into the room, picked up one of the leg bones from the pile, and hurled it at Lance, who dodged it expertly.

Artie threw his spear at the giant's neck, and it was on target to strike, but at the last moment the creature swiped the air with his club, knocking Rhongomyniad to the floor with a clatter.

Since Orgulus hadn't taught Lance any cool tricks, he wasn't going to fight with it. As Artie called back his spear, Lance stuck the sword through his belt, unslung his American-themed bow from his shoulder, nocked a trio of arrows, and fired. One glanced off the giant's temple, one struck his cheek, and the other embedded in the thick skin above one of his eyes.

The giant flicked away the arrow in its forehead and tore the other one from its cheek. He spit a wad of black blood on the ground, then threw the arrow back at Lance like a dart. Lance dodged again and the arrowhead struck the granite of the closest pillar.

Lance and Artie shared a glance.

They were in trouble.

The giant pointed its club at the rapier in Lance's belt and said with a rumbling, gravely voice, "*C'est le mien!*"

No one needed a translator to know that he had just said, "That's mine!"

"No it isn't!" Lance barked. "It's mine now!"

The giant didn't like this. He smashed his club on the ground, shaking the entire room. He was about to charge Lance when Bedevere slipped into the crypt's inner chamber, said, "Phantoma!" and grabbed the giant with his magical arm, stopping him dead in his tracks.

The monster twisted and roared and tried to pull away but went nowhere. He swiped at the invisible arm to no effect. If anything, the strength of Bedevere's grasp just got stronger.

"Way to go, Beddy!" Kay barked.

"It's not fully charged," Bedevere yelled desperately. "We've got about thirty seconds! Run, sire!"

Artie, Kay, and Lance kicked into high gear, but as they skirted the giant, he swung violently with his club and caught Artie and Kay across their chests.

Their new graphene shirts saved them from being killed by the club's spikes, but they still went flying and it still hurt like all get-out. They hit the back wall, and both slid to the floor in a heap. Several of Artie's ribs broke but were instantly mended by Excalibur's scabbard. He looked at his sister; she was breathing but totally knocked out. He grabbed Cleomede and Rhongomyniad and called Lance over to help with Kay. Artie quickly removed the scabbard from his back and strapped it onto her, just to be safe.

The giant turned again to Bedevere, who could tell from the look in the giant's eyes that he'd had about enough of the Black Knight and his fancy ghost arm.

Bedevere let go, deactivated the arm, and was about to jump out of harm's way when the giant grabbed his stump and squeezed. The magical metal ring that contained the phantom arm was all that prevented his stump from being crushed like a wad of paper. The giant pulled his club to his side and then thrust it forward, its thick, rusty spikes headed right for Bedevere, who reflexively shut his eyes.

This was it.

But then the lights flickered. Bedevere cautiously opened his eyes and found himself face-to-face with Artie, the shiny point of Rhongomyniad parked right over Bedevere's chest. Artie's face was gnarled with wrath, and he was putting his full weight on the spear, which was doing nothing to Bedevere's graphene T-shirt.

Realizing they'd switched back to the nice Mont-Saint-Michel in France, Artie recoiled and said, "Oh! Sorry, Beddy!"

Bedevere pushed Rhongomyniad off his chest and said, "No worries, sire. Thank you for coming to my rescue."

"Uh, Artie?" Lance called, Kay slumped over his shoulder. "We have some new friends."

The giant was gone, but in the main chamber of the crypt there were now several people speaking loudly in French.

Not just people.

Cops.

Artie lowered the points of Cleomede and Rhongomy-niad and told the cops that everything was okay, that he and his friends were just leaving.

But the cops weren't having any of it.

While this was going on, Bedevere ushered the others to the door that led to the stairs back to the cistern. They were just about to sneak through it when Bedevere said, "Oh!" and stopped cold.

Three more policemen, holding pistols, blocked the way.

More shouting in French. The policemen were scared, and very confused, by what they were faced with.

Artie repeated as calmly as he could that they just wanted to leave.

Kay moaned as the police moved closer, boxing them in even more.

The youngest-looking cop, who also happened to be the largest, was very upset. His face was red and agitated, and he stepped forward brandishing his pistol, demanding in French that they put down their weapons.

Lance understood perfectly. He'd been in plenty of tense situations on both ends of a gun and knew that the best path was the one of least resistance. "Artie," he advised, "let's just put our things down and do what they say."

"Screw that!" Erik cried, shaking Gram in the air for emphasis.

Which wasn't smart.

The nervous cop jumped back and fired three deafening shots. Two missed, but the third hit Bedevere in the chest. The graphene shirt and the armor underneath stopped the bullet, but it still knocked him down. He hit his head on the wall and collapsed in the doorway, out cold.

Artie again tried to calm the police, but since he was still armed with a broadsword and a spear, it wasn't very convincing. The two police officers nearest Artie raised their guns and prepared to fire.

Artie had to do something. Against his better judgment, Artie lunged forward and sliced the muzzle off the nearest gun with Cleomede. But he couldn't reach the next one quickly enough. The cop fired, and the bullet headed right for Erik Erikssen's head.

He would have died had the lights not flickered and the cops disappeared.

Artie and crew had shifted back to the bad Mont-Saint-Michel.

Considering how crappy things were going at the *good* Mont-Saint-Michel, this was actually an improvement.

Artie held his finger to his lips. Lance froze. Erik,

realizing that he wasn't about to be shot, relaxed.

"Agh!" the giant exclaimed from the inner chamber of the crypt. *"Où? Où? Où est l'épée? Où vont-ils?"*

"He wants to know where we are," Artie mouthed.

Using hand signals, he got Erik to take Kay from Lance. Erik was a little embarrassed to be carrying Kay Kingfisher, but he had to. Lance then quietly hoisted Bedevere over his shoulders. Artie slid Cleomede into Excalibur's sheath on Kay's back and picked up the Black Knight's claymore.

They heard the giant's club drag across the floor, and then he popped his gruesome head through the nearest set of pillars and screamed, *"Je vais vous manger!"*

Artie didn't want to be eaten. "Go!" he yelled to his knights.

They took off as fast as they could, making it down one flight of stairs before they heard the giant say, *"Je vous entends!"*

"It can hear us," Artie translated as they stumbled onto the landing that led to the cistern.

Which, it turned out, was now literally overflowing with rats. Artie kicked a few rats to the side as he scooted next to Erik and peered into the little room. The drain that led to the forest, and their escape, was only ten feet away.

All they had to do was walk across a floor made of rodents.

Artie took a deep breath and closed his eyes. He stepped into the cistern and sank to his knees. Innumerable rats nibbled at his shins and calves. He fought back a wave of nausea and ushered his friends across the rat floor. First Erik and Kay, then Lance and Bedevere.

The giant's huge, rank face came into view in the hall just as Artie headed for the drain.

Erik and Kay were in. Lance had put Bedevere in and was pushing him along. Artie leaped next to the drain as the giant's hand strained forward through the doorway; it swung back and forth and grasped at the air blindly.

"Get in here, kid!" Lance screamed. Artie clambered into the drain just as the giant obliterated the doorway with his club. Then the giant vaulted into the cistern and crashed into the pool of rats like a huge kid landing in a ball pit, sending rats flying in every direction.

Artie and Lance were struggling to pull Bedevere to safety when the giant rammed his head into the drain and caught Bedevere's leg in his mouth. He bit down just as Lance and Artie gave Bedevere's shoulders a hard pull.

A horrible tearing and crunching sound came, as Artie wailed, "No!" He couldn't bear it: the Black Knight had just lost another limb in service to Artie Kingfisher!

"C'mon, dude!" Lance yelled as he finally yanked the bleeding Bedevere to safety. Then he unslung his bow and nocked an arrow. "Here's to a short life!" he yelled, and let it fly. It went into the giant's mouth and struck deep in the back of his throat.

The giant's eyes bugged out of his head. Artie ordered everyone down and out of the drain. Before leaving, Artie turned and faced the horrible creature as it sputtered and let out a last gurgle of air. Finally something that passed for silence filled Artie's ears.

The giant was dead.

The group hastily pushed down the damp stone tube, Artie and Lance taking extra care with Bedevere, not wanting to injure him further. They emerged from the drain, which was set in a high stone wall, in a copse of poplars. Artie grabbed the backpack from Kay, who was coming around, and dropped next to a moaning Bedevere, who lay across the ground, his head cradled in Lance's lap.

"His femoral artery is shot," Lance said desperately.

"W-what's happening?" Kay asked, her arm draped over Erik's shoulders.

"Bedevere's hurt," Erik said in shock. Gram had prepared him to fight, but not to see such a grievous wound.

Lance leaned over the leg stump. "He's gonna bleed out, dude!"

"No he's not!" Artie said defiantly. He rooted through the infinite backpack and grabbed the rope, a warming elixir, and a healing potion. He pulled the scabbard off Kay's back and tied it to Bedevere's side. Then Artie poured the potions down the Black Knight's throat.

They waited a few moments.

"Why isn't the scabbard working?" Erik asked desperately. "I thought it was supposed to heal anything!"

Artie didn't look up as he said, "I don't know. Maybe if he'd been wearing it when the giant bit him, it would have been better."

"Look!" Kay said.

Some of Bedevere's torn flesh began to stretch and seal, and the blood stopped flowing. The color in Bedevere's face returned. His breathing became less shallow.

"Is he going to be all right?" Kay asked, showing no ill effects from being knocked out.

"I think so," Artie said, "but we need Merlin to work on him. Let's find this crossover point, open it, and get the heck out of here. Erik, go look down there," he said, pointing past the poplars toward the sea. "Kay, help me look over here. Lance, you stay with Beddy, all right?"

"Got it," Lance said.

They fanned out and searched the ground, poking the soil with the ends of their weapons. As they left the group of trees, the sea came into view. It smelled putrid and rank. Merlin had said this was a forest, but he'd been wrong. It was a barren wasteland, ravaged by axes and fire.

"This place is awful," Erik yelled from down the hill.

"Any sign of the crossover stone?" Artie asked, silently acknowledging that it was pretty hellhole-ish.

"Not yet," Erik said.

"Whoa," Kay breathed.

Artie turned to his sister. She was looking up, not down. He followed her gaze, and his heart skipped a beat.

Soaring above them was the castle they'd seen in the picture—kind of. This wasn't the lovely-if-imposing French tourist attraction, but a forbidding horror-story fortress rooted in a dark recess of the Otherworld. It had the same arches and towers and spires as the one in the photo, but its gray stone was blackened by years of neglect. A large fire burned at the wall's highest point, and a murder of crows took off in front of this, silhouetted against the blaze like dark confetti.

Artie let out a whistle. Erik, coming up behind them, was just as impressed. "Seriously. That thing's no joke."

Artie looked back to the ground. "Enough. We've gotta get out of here."

A bank of dark clouds rolled in, carpeting the sky overhead as they resumed searching. Five, ten, fifteen minutes passed.

Finally Artie stopped next to a large boulder and said a little uncertainly, "Kay—you ever feel like Merlin's holding out on us?"

"Huh?" Kay said absently.

"I think it's weird he doesn't come with us on these quests. It's not like he's trapped in the invisible tower anymore. He would be a big help on these things, right? Being a wizard and all? I guess what I'm asking is, do you think we're, like, expendable to him?"

Kay frowned. Artie pushed some pebbles around with the end of his spear. "You're not saying we shouldn't trust him, are you?" Kay asked.

"I don't know. I mean, Tom agrees with him—goes along with everything he says—and I trust Tom completely."

"Me too," Kay said.

"But Merlin is supposed to be *my* wizard, right? I know I'm just a kid, but I'm the top dog here. I feel like we're the ones helping him, not the other way around. I don't know. Sometimes I feel like we're being taken advantage of—Bedevere just lost a freaking leg—and it's starting to piss me off!"

Kay had never seen Artie like this before. "All right," she

said soothingly, "we'll talk to him when we get back. I'm with you, Art."

A loud and unexpected clap of thunder rocked the air. Artie jumped and his spear fell to the ground. When he bent to pick it up, he said, "Well, lookie here." Kay leaned over Artie's shoulder and saw one of the crossover stones lying in the dirt.

Artie called the other knights and they gathered around. He located the other stone and got out the pommel. This time Kay anchored one side while Artie did his thing on the other.

"*Lunae lumen!*" he commanded.

As before, the pommel swirled with a blue glow, and a beam of light shot from it, arcing over and into the crossover stones. Then a gossamer curtain dropped down, and when it touched the ground, a shock wave of silence shot out in all directions. They'd opened the crossover of Mont-Saint-Michel.

Artie stepped away from the portal. "I'm not going to bother going through. It's open and that's good enough for me." He looked at Lance, the moaning Bedevere slung over his shoulder, and said, "You ready to go to the court-in-exile?"

The archer nodded.

"*Lunae lumen,*" Artie said wearily to the pommel, and

a moongate slid open. Lance hustled through, carrying their fallen knight. Erik followed. Artie took a deep breath as Kay slumped against her brother. "We're never coming back here," he said definitively.

"Good," she said, resting her head on his shoulder.

Side by side, they stepped through and were gone.

𝕷ance carefully placed 𝕭edevere on the round table. Bercilak ordered the court-in-exile's three servant trolls to fetch warm water, linens, and bandages. Artie put an emergency call in to Merlin.

He paced as the iPad rang and rang. No answer. He disconnected and tried again. Nothing. He disconnected and tried *again*. Third time had to be the charm.

After two minutes Merlin finally accepted, and his tattooed face flickered onto the screen. "What is it?" he asked impatiently. Pushed onto his forehead was a silver eye mask with the words *Let Sleeping Wizards Lie* embroidered on it in a purple, flowing script.

Artie lost it. He flipped to the iPad's other camera so Merlin could see Bedevere. "*That's* what it is, Merlin.

Bedevere's lost *another* limb." Then Artie caught Merlin rolling his eyes. "Merlin—did you just roll your eyes at me?"

"What? Of course not, sire."

"Yes you did," Artie said loudly as the other knights turned in his direction. "Don't ever let me catch you doing that again," he ordered, sounding more like an adult than he ever had in his life.

"Now wait one minute. I am Merlin; I won't be spoken to like that by a . . . a . . ."

"A child?" Artie asked, finishing the wizard's obvious train of thought.

"Well . . . "

Artie seethed. "You're the one who brought us here, Merlin. You're the one who keeps telling me I'm king. You're the one we *helped*, for Pete's sake. You—Merlin, the greatest wizard ever—are the one who sent us into that horrible giant's lair, and you are the one who is going to haul his butt over here right now and fix up my friend."

"I will not be spoken to—"

"Yes you will. I am your king. Start acting like it."

Everyone was speechless—except for Bercilak, who said so quietly that only they could hear, "You tell that Wilt Chamberlain!"

Merlin pulled the sleep mask from his head and said, "Yes, sire. Of course, sire. Right away, sire."

"Good," Artie said. "And don't patronize me either." He

slid his finger across the screen and ended the chat without saying good-bye.

He stared at the iPad for a few moments. "Can you believe the nerve of that guy?" Artie asked his knights, who still looked startled by his outburst.

"No," Kay said after a pause. "He was being a real turd."

"No kidding." Artie walked up to the table. "How you doing, Beddy?" he asked.

"I'm fine, sire," Bedevere answered bravely.

"He's stable," Lance said. "But he needs blood."

"Or some of Merlin's magic healing," Kay said. "I hope you didn't make him *too* mad, Art. We still need him, you know?"

"Well, he needs us too, last I checked," Artie said. "I'm getting tired of putting our necks on the line for him. Seriously, when's *he* going to fight? Aren't wizards supposed to, like, throw down every now and then? Like in video games?"

Before they could discuss it anymore, a moongate opened and Merlin stepped into the court-in-exile carrying his plain canvas bag, which held all his gear, and his owl-headed cane. He was hunched over, and his stride was a little creaky as he made his way to Bedevere.

An awkward silence descended on the group as the wizard inspected Bedevere's latest wound. Finally he turned to

Artie and said wearily, "I'm sorry, Artie. Making the black-outs for Fenland has been very taxing. That's why I was sleeping while you were at Mont-Saint-Michel." He paused before saying, "It's so important that I defeat Morgaine. . . ."

He seemed to mean it, but Artie couldn't help but wonder: Weren't they fighting for so much more than that? I mean, hello, Qwon! And the Seven Swords! Not to mention the whole thing about sangrealite being a form of clean energy and all!

But Bedevere was all that mattered at the moment. Artie waved his hand through the air as if to push those other thoughts aside and asked, "Can you fix him, Merlin?"

"Yes. But please, I need some room."

The knights retreated several feet and watched as Merlin took his cane with both hands and started to chant. His feet lifted from the ground, and his baggy linen pants began to billow. His tattoos swirled across the surface of his skin.

"Dude," Erik said quietly, in awe of the scene in front of him.

The closed eye of the owl's-head cane opened, and a beam of white light shot out of it and into Bedevere's mouth. The Black Knight's chest heaved, his back arched, and his body began to convulse. Kay took a step forward, but Artie held out an arm to stop her. "Let him work," he whispered.

Then the light from the cane got very bright. The fabric of Merlin's pants flapped like a flag in a gale. Bedevere's body calmed before lifting a few inches off the table. Excalibur's scabbard, which was still lashed to his side, began to glow and vibrate and throw off heat. The light's intensity grew so much that the knights had to close their eyes against it.

When they were able to reopen them, Bedevere was wrapped in a white robe, his head resting on a pillow. Merlin bent over him, cradling Bedevere's face in his wizened hands. The cane and the scabbard leaned against the edge of the table. "Thank the trees the witch didn't also get the scabbard when she stole Excalibur," Merlin said.

"Amen to that," Artie said.

"So he's okay?" Erik asked, his voice shaking a little. Merlin's healing act was pretty impressive.

Merlin turned, and they were shocked to see that he looked kind of horrible. His tattoos were faded and his skin ashen. "Bedevere will be fine, but I need some things from the invisible tower. An IV bag, type AB blood, and a prosthesis."

"You keep fake legs just lying around your old basement?" Kay asked.

"Yes, Kay Kingfisher. In a jet-black armoire with a red circle painted on it." Something about his tone suggested that she not ask why he kept fake legs lying around.

"I'll go," Artie said. "I know my way around and I can get in and out."

Merlin gave Artie a weary look and said, "While you're on your side, you need to get a trinket—a monocle—from Qwon's house. The pommel will show you where it is. This monocle will enable you to find the crossover in Japan that leads directly to the katana Kusanagi."

"Okay," Artie said. "Lance, come with me. You can bring back the medical stuff while I gate to Shadyside."

"Roger that, dude."

"The rest of you chill out here. After tonight, we've only got seven days until the new moon." Then Artie pulled out the pommel and opened a gate to the basement under the Invisible Tower.

The moongate dropped them in one of Merlin's old living rooms. It had red brick walls, a deep chair, and a TV mounted to the wall.

Artie peered in both directions. "I can't remember where the medical stuff is, Lance. You go that way, I'll head this way, and we'll meet back here."

"Cool," Lance said.

Artie soon found the IV bags and the blood, but no fake legs. He went all the way to the back room looking for the black armoire. He paused and found himself next to Mrs. Thresher, the little wooden door he'd traveled through the first time he entered the Otherworld, to get Cleomede from the stone. It seemed like so long ago, and even with all that had happened, he could still hardly believe the things he'd seen and done. Everything had been so strange, and difficult, and uncertain.

And also kind of wonderful.

Artie doubled back, putting the IV bag, blood, and an ice pack in a Styrofoam cooler, and stopped in the living room. Lance hadn't returned, so Artie sat down in the comfy chair and turned on the TV.

It was tuned to CNN, and Artie wasn't prepared for what he saw.

It was an aerial shot of the Swedish plain they'd been to. Grazing on the cold, scraggly field was a sizable herd of giant cows—the aurochs.

A little box wedged into a lower corner of the screen contained the talking heads of an interview. The confused male reporter asked, "So these aurochs—you're saying they're extinct?"

"Yes. Well, they *were*," a woman answered. A subtitle said she was a zoologist.

"So they're *not* extinct?"

"I guess not," the zoologist said, shaking her head in disbelief. "We were certain that there hadn't been aurochs anywhere on earth for over four hundred years."

The reporter made a Very Serious face. "So where did these aurochs come from?"

"No one knows."

"Could they have been living in the wild up there and no one knew about it?"

"That can't be ruled out, but it's very unlikely. Remember, Bob, this isn't the only instance of extinct animals showing up. There were those passenger pigeons in Ohio last month. And then there were those strange red-tufted jaybirds in Pittsburgh a week ago, which as far as anyone can tell is a new species altogether. A new bird hasn't been found in such a heavily populated area in a very long time."

The reporter shook his head and said, "Fascinating. Just incredible stuff. Thanks for your time, Beth." The reporter switched cameras. "There you have it. Is it a new era of animals returning from extinction? Where do they come from? And could all this have anything to do with the strange weather occurring in Ohio, Pennsylvania, and now northern France?" He turned to yet another camera. "When we return, more on the unsubstantiated reports of a band of armed children roaming the bowels of the abbey of Mont-Saint-Michel. Stay right here with CNN."

Artie muted the commercials. Lance had come back to the room during the newscast and stood behind Artie. "Whoa."

"Yeah," Artie said, standing up. "Looks like opening the crossovers is having some side effects."

Lance shrugged. "The worlds haven't been joined in a long time. I suppose there's bound to be an adjustment period."

"I guess," Artie said, his brow furrowed. "Opening the crossovers was supposed to be good for the two worlds, but right now it just feels like one huge mess." Artie pointed at something under Lance's arm. "You found it?"

"Yup," Lance said as he held out a thing that looked a little like a huge boomerang.

"That's it?" Artie asked.

"Yeah. It's called a parabolic leg. This is some state-of-the-art stuff. Couple buddies of mine from Iraq got ones like this. You can run in them. Really fast. The curve in the plastic kind of acts like a spring."

"Cool," Artie said. He handed Lance the cooler with the IV bags and the blood and said, "Take this stuff and look after Beddy." Then he got out the pommel and opened a gate back to the court-in-exile. Before Lance stepped through, Artie said, "Don't mention that news report to anyone. I want to talk to Merlin about it first. The more things happen, the more questions I have. . . ."

Lance smirked. "I can pretty much guarantee that it's all part of being king—sire." It was the first time Artie could remember Lance calling him that. But before he could comment on it, Lance stepped through and disappeared, the moongate shutting behind him.

Artie stood in silence and thought. *What am I doing?*

He was bringing extinct animals back to life. He was apparently responsible for strange weather. He was helping a wizard get even with a witch. He was angry with the same wizard for having a crummy attitude. He was waiting to hear from a fairy spy that would soon be air-dropped into Fenland. He was trying to get to Avalon so he could become King Arthur.

He was putting himself, his sister, his friends, and his father in danger.

He was doing these things, when all he really wanted to do was go and save Qwon.

And then a surprising—almost horrifying—realization came to him: when Qwon was safe, Artie Kingfisher wanted to go back to school. He wanted to go back home. To Shadyside.

Not the Otherworld.

He looked at the pommel and made a decision. Before doing anything, he would wait to hear from their spy, Bors le Fey. Then he would get Kusanagi. Not because Merlin had ordered him to, but because it belonged to Qwon.

And then, he would go and free his friend.

Artie wrapped his fingers around the pommel and pictured Qwon's house.

"*Lunae lumen,*" he said, and the gate whisked him away from Merlin's lonely basement.

HOW BORS IS DELIVERED

19

Late that night, Tiberius circled high over Fenland as Thumb peered through the mottled clouds below. Fallown, the golden Leagonese dragon that carried their spy, Bors le Fey, flew several hundred feet above.

They were waiting for Merlin's blackout as they turned wheels in the sky.

"Hmmph. Wizards," Tiberius cooed scornfully.

"He's doing the best he can, Tiberius," Thumb countered.

The flat, low-lying island of Fenland sprawled out below them. It was shaped like a plump lizard perched on a tree branch. Castel Deorc Wæters was located on the island's highest point in the middle of the lizard's head, right where its eye would be.

The stars were bright and plentiful. Fenland was also constellated with twinkling lights, as little towns and thoroughfares and the Castel itself were lit up. The sea surrounding the island was black as pitch.

"We've'n't much time," the dragon said. "Two minutes. Otherwise Scarm'll notice us and give chase."

Thumb had never encountered Scarm, the Fenlandian dragon, but he knew all about her. She was younger than both Tiberius and Fallown, and renowned for a quick temper. Her coloring was a deep, iridescent purple. Of all the dragons she had the biggest wings, and, unlike any of her kinfolks', these were covered in green feathers. Her breath attack was a scalding-hot stream of black oil.

"Merlin will come through," Thumb said quietly, hoping he was right.

The dragon just said, "Hmmph."

Two minutes passed. Nothing happened. Tiberius snapped his tail, signaling to Fallown that they would have to leave. Even though Bors could turn invisible, they wouldn't drop him without the blackout in effect. Light wasn't the issue—magic was. With the sangrealitic power out, most of the Castel's warning enchantments would be on the fritz.

The dragons turned east and prepared to kick it into high gear. But then Bors, who was a mute and couldn't yell, split the air with a loud whistle.

"Hmmmph!" Tiberius exclaimed, displeased with the unnecessary noise.

"Look!" Thumb said.

The island's lights flashed and then snuffed out.

The dragons pointed their heads to the earth and dived. Thumb suppressed a gleeful yelp and dug his fingers into Tiberius's skin as the wind screamed around him.

They dropped a thousand feet in seconds. Tiberius leveled off as Fallown descended another five hundred feet. He hovered there for a few seconds before beating his wings to rejoin Tiberius. When he pulled alongside Tiberius and Thumb, they saw that Bors was gone.

Tiberius said, "Hold'n on tight, Jester Thumb."

Thumb lowered his chest onto the dragon's neck and waited for the kick.

The dragons winked at each other and accelerated to jet speed in an instant.

It was such a rush that Tom Thumb couldn't help but laugh.

"𝔐ordred!" 𝔐orgaine crackled over a walkie-talkie as the lights went out again. "Come here!"

Bors had been dropped the night before, and over the past twenty-four hours the entire island of Fenland had been suffering intermittent blackouts. Most of them only lasted a few minutes, but two had gone on for more than an hour. It was a development that had angered Morgaine to no end, since they not only shrouded the island in darkness, but also dampened the primary source of her strongest magic.

Morgaine was positive that Merlin was behind these machinations. She wanted the wizard dead so badly, and she knew that he wanted the same for her. After all, she had led the coven of witches that had imprisoned him in the invisible tower, and he would never forgive her for it.

Of course she would never forgive him either. So many centuries ago he had helped deny her rightful ascent to power.

Back then Merlin had sided with Arthur the First, her nauseating, righteous half brother. Arthur the pure, the chaste, the noble. Morgaine had hated that Arthur with all her heart. Why had Nyneve, that loathsome Lady of the Lake, chosen *him* for Excalibur? He was nothing but a hypocrite, a sheepish bore who was all too ready to follow the wizard's orders. He was the glove to Merlin's hand. The first Mordred, Arthur's son *and* nephew, and the apple of Morgaine's eye, was the person who *should* have been chosen as king. Mordred the brave, the right, the bold! Morgaine's coven had tried to oust Arthur and replace him with Mordred, but they had failed. It was true that Mordred dealt that old Arthur his fatal blow with the Peace Sword, but not before suffering his own dying wound.

Her sweet, sweet Mordred. This new "son" of hers was nothing next to him.

How she missed him.

And how she hated the wizard.

Morgaine wasted no time in dispatching hundreds of soldiers across Fenland, tasked with finding out how the wizard had managed to tap into their sangrealite grid, and with finding a way to stop it.

Because of these orders, Castel Deorc Wæters was operating on a skeleton crew.

It was a condition that Dred found to be a pain in the butt. Without soldiers to run around for Morgaine, *he* had to pick up the slack. Just in the last day, he'd made eight trips to the basement to flip the circuit breakers. Now it sounded like his mother wanted him to do it again.

"Moooor-dreeeed!" she repeated.

Dred, who was talking through the door with Qwon, rolled his eyes and said, "Jeez. I guess I'll see you later."

"Okay. Let me know how it goes," Qwon said.

Dred slid the little door shut. He grabbed Smash and headed to his mum's chambers.

Qwon rolled onto her back and watched the sky turn from purple to pink as the sun set in the west.

She was nervous. Things were happening fast. Early that morning, well before sunrise, an ecstatic Shallot had appeared at Qwon's side and shaken her awake. "Whassup?" Qwon asked groggily, surprised to actually see the fairy after so many days.

Shallot whispered, "Another fairy has joined us!"

"Another prisoner?" Qwon asked confusedly.

"No. My cousin Bors le Fey arrived during the blackout in the middle of the night. He's here on behalf of my clan and King Artie Kingfisher. He's going to help us escape!"

"Wow!" Qwon said. "How do you know this?"

"His smell told me, of course. We fairies can communicate through our odors."

"Oh," Qwon said. "So, what—we're out of here then?"

"Soon, Qwon from Pennsylvania! Be ready!"

"I will," Qwon said a little unenthusiastically.

"What is it?" Shallot asked.

"I don't know. . . . It's just . . . Has the plan changed at all? Since we have help now?"

"What do you mean?" Shallot asked.

"Are we still planning on . . . taking care of Dred?"

The fairy huffed. "Don't go soft on me now, Qwon. We have to escape, and I plan on doing whatever it takes to get out of here."

"I know, I know. But . . . let's try to go easy on him, okay?"

Shallot spit out an exasperated "Ha!" and promptly disappeared, leaving a heady trace of her sweet smell that stunned Qwon for a few moments.

When the mini scentlock passed, Qwon's mind raced. In seven days the new moon would rise. At any moment their escape would begin. But what if it didn't work? What if they got caught? Or what if it *did* work? Morgaine would blame Dred for their escape. Qwon didn't want Dred to bear the brunt of Morgaine's anger. It wouldn't be pretty. She also didn't want Shallot to hurt—or worse, kill—Dred out of spite. Qwon had come to like Dred and she decided that when the time came, she would do what she could to protect him.

Meanwhile, Dred slowly made his way to Morgaine's chambers, Smash perched atop his shoulder. And as it happened, he was thinking of Qwon.

Not just thinking of her, but thinking of releasing her. Morgaine had Excalibur and The Anguish. Wasn't that enough to lure King Artie? Did they really need this innocent girl too? The simple truth was that over the past few days Dred had come to like Qwon, and he didn't want her to get hurt.

Dred came to a stop and rapped on Morgaine's door, trying to force these thoughts from his mind before his mother could detect them.

"Come in!" his mother said in her singsong voice.

Dred entered. Her room was lit with candles and small, battery-powered lanterns.

"You called?" he asked, walking toward her.

Morgaine was slumped at her vanity, her green hooded cloak draped over her body. She answered, "Yes, dear boy." Her voice was strong but it had a shake to it that he'd never heard before.

"Mum, are you all right?"

"All right? No, of course I'm not all right." She turned

away as he got closer, but she didn't realize that Dred could see her in her mirror's reflection.

The face he saw there was his mother's, but it was very different. She had aged thirty years in the last twelve hours. Her cheeks were gaunt, and her chin pointed. Her mouth gaped a little every time she drew a breath.

"Mum!" Dred exclaimed. "What happened to you?" Smash, also startled, nuzzled in his master's neck.

"The wizard is toying with me!" Morgaine said as she faced him. "If the power was up, you'd see me as you know me, but when it goes down . . . I look like this."

"I'm sorry, Mum," Dred said, and he meant it.

"I don't want your sympathy, boy. I'm still strong, so don't get any ideas."

Dred, worried that his mother could see his nascent thoughts about freeing Qwon, tried once more to strike his mind clean. "What ideas, Mum?"

"'What ideas, Mum?'" Morgaine mimicked, sounding exactly like Dred, which was super creepy. "Ideas. I don't know, you're practically a teenager. You've all sorts of ideas, I'm sure."

"Mum, I don't know what you're talking about," Dred said pretty unconvincingly.

"Fine. Be a dear then and take your empty head to the basement and flip all the breakers. Start with the main feeds and work your way down."

"I know, I know," Dred said, already turning around. "Just like last time."

Morgaine spun back to her mirror. "Yes, pet, just like last time."

Dred left and wound his way around the Castel to the modern glass structure in the middle of the compound. It was new, but the sublevels below it were some of Castel Deorc Wæters' oldest.

He descended several flights of stone stairs and finally came to a low hall a hundred feet underground. The breaker room was housed in what used to be a formal dungeon, replete with ancient iron maidens and racks to prove it.

Dred walked down the hall with his flashlight, counting the doors. When he reached the seventh one, he froze.

He'd stepped into an unexpected scentlock, and at the last second Smash screamed, "Fairy!"

But this was unlike any scentlock Dred had ever experienced. It wasn't flowers, or sea air, or pine needles, or dew. It wasn't anything. It was like the aromatic equivalent of total silence.

Only Dred's eyes would move. He frantically glanced around the hall, but saw nothing.

And then Smash squealed in agony, and Dred felt him tumble off his shoulder and land with a muted *thump* at his feet. The invisible fairy's hot breath fell on the nape of Dred's neck. He was grabbed by the shoulders and forced around to face the right-hand wall.

The fairy drew a word on Dred's back with its finger, but Dred didn't catch it. Dred made a sound like "again" in the bottom of his throat.

The unseen fairy wrote the word out two more times before Dred understood: *There.*

What did it mean? The only thing in front of him was one of the many recesses that were used to hold lamps and torches in the old days.

Dred sensed the fairy circle around him. Then a stone in the nearest recess moved, and a low grating sound filled the hall as the wall in front of him swung inward.

A secret passage.

The fairy slid behind Dred again and traced another word on his back: *Look.*

Two beats later, the fairy was gone, and the scentlock was lifted.

Dred wheeled and drew his sword in a single motion. He swiped furiously at the air in every direction, but his blade met no resistance. Whoever it was that had stopped him—and killed his pet—was gone.

Dred sighed, sheathed his weapon, and bent to pick up Smash's body. A little yellow card lay on the creature. He picked up both, slipped Smash into his shirt, and looked at the card. It said, in a full, flowing script:

Sorry. It would have told her.

Dred stared at the note, and he knew it was true. He'd suspected as much, even though he had always hoped that Smash was his friend in spite of his allegiance to Morgaine.

Dred was about to crumple the note when the corner farthest from his fingers spontaneously caught fire. He dropped the card and watched it burn. After a few seconds, nothing was left but some black curls of ash.

He let these go and stamped them into the floor. Then he turned to the secret doorway and stepped through.

What was this place? He would have sworn that he knew every nook and cranny of Castel Deorc Wæters, but he'd never been here before. His heart raced as he walked through a long tunnel supported by wooden beams. It sloped downward, and the soft surfaces of the passageway snuffed out all sound.

The tunnel terminated after several hundred feet at a large, perfectly round door. In the middle of the door was a brass ring the size of a dinner plate.

Dred considered knocking, thought better of it, and placed a hand flat on the wood. He took a deep breath and pushed. The door swung inward a few inches. He quietly drew his sword, and then nudged the door all the way open.

Dred stepped into a large room with high ceilings cut out of the bedrock. He shone his light around. The room appeared to be a laboratory of some kind. It had endless rows of metal gurneys and glass cabinets full of all kinds of instruments and vials and packages. But it also had wooden shelves stuffed with musty, dusty books and scrolls. On the wall to his left were hundreds of vials containing dried herbs and multicolored powders. Next to this was a cabinet of various wands, staffs, and bracers. An old black velvet cloak he vaguely remembered Morgaine wearing long ago hung on a peg.

He walked deeper in. After the gurneys came row upon row upon row of tall glass cylinders filled with a slightly cloudy liquid. And suspended in these giant bottles were . . . *things*.

Some were the size of a fist, others were so big that they pushed fleshily against the glass. Some had arms, some didn't. Some had heads, some didn't. Some had eyes, some had five eyes, some had eye sockets but no eyes. Some had webbed fingers and toes, some had no fingers or toes. Some had dark, purply skin; others had white skin; others still had no skin at all.

Some looked half human. Most looked like monsters.

Dazed, Dred walked on. The farther down the line of cylinders he went, the more fully formed the things became. They began to have hair and features. Some were very young, others looked like ten-year-old children.

They all appeared to be boys.

The next several rows contained older children—teenagers—and even a few men. Something was horribly wrong with each of these specimens. Ears on their necks, no noses, feet for hands, skeletons on the outside.

The last row, however, contained boys that looked completely normal. They were about Dred's height and, despite being dead, looked healthy.

He stepped right up to the last one and shone his light on its face. Dred stopped breathing when he realized . . . *that he was looking at himself!*

The boy in the cylinder suddenly opened his eyes and looked directly at the light.

Dred stumbled backward and dropped his flashlight and sword, which made an awful racket as they fell to the ground.

His heart pounded out of his chest as he struggled to regain his breath. Dred counted to ten, and then back to one, and then leaned over and picked up the light, sweeping its beam over the boy-thing again. Other than the eyes, which were closed now, it hadn't moved at all. Dred took a deep breath and let the light rest on his double's face again.

And again, after a few seconds, the eyes opened and turned in their sockets to look directly into the light.

Dred forced himself to take full breaths. He moved the light away, waited, then shone it on the creature once more. Again it opened its eyes after a pause.

It wasn't alive. It was just light sensitive. The eye thing was a nervous reaction or something.

Satisfied that he wasn't going to be attacked by a bunch of zombie doppelgangers, Dred gathered himself. Turning from the hundreds of glass tubes, he continued to the back of the room.

There he found two final metal gurneys, an array of medical and magical instruments—tubes, beakers, potion mixers, burners, crystals—and a floor-to-ceiling bookshelf with a little altar built into it.

And in front of this were two baby's cribs.

Dred's stomach churned as he stepped up to them and looked inside. The cribs were empty.

Of babies, at any rate.

But what he found instead was nearly as disturbing. Each crib had a blanket, and on each blanket was a coat of arms. One was blue with three golden crowns: Arthur's. The other was purple and white with a golden, double-headed eagle.

His.

Dred's knees trembled and he had to put his sword's tip on the ground to use as a crutch. His mind raced.

What had he discovered?

Correction: What had he been shown? By a fairy, of all creatures!

Dred took a deep breath. There was one more thing he had to look at. On weak legs, he made his way to the altar set in the bookshelf. Before it was a podium supporting a gigantic, ancient, leather-bound tome with brass fittings. He flipped through it. It was full of drawings and notes and formulas.

He glanced at the altar and found two bell-shaped glass containers, each etched with silver lettering. One said "Uther" and contained a small bone fragment of some kind. The other, which contained a lock of wavy reddish hair, said "Igraine."

Dred knew these names. Everyone who knew anything about Arthur knew these names. They were the first Arthur's parents.

He looked back to the book and slammed it shut. The noise bounced around the room. He ran his fingers over the metal plate riveted to the book's cover. He leaned in and read:

THE ARTHUR PROJECT

He reopened the book and frantically turned to the final entries, scanning the pages for a date.

Finally he found it:

August 23. Arthur trial attempt 1,298. As with previous 147 attempts, twins, though for the first time they are identical. Both live.

The second I shall call Mordred.

At that very moment Morgaine's voice crackled over the walkie-talkie. "Where *are* you, boy?"

Dred scrambled to his feet and rushed back, telling Morgaine over the walkie that he was nearly done. He closed the secret door, and stopped in the breaker room to throw the power switches. Thankfully, the power hummed back on. Then he made his way up to Morgaine's room, his mind racing.

A twin! *That* was why Morgaine didn't want he and Artie to see each other! Because they had the same face! *That* was why Morgaine had enchanted his helmet and given him a spy as a pet! What else had she done? What other secrets lay in that grotesque lab under Castel Deorc Wæters?

For the first time in his life, Dred truly and irrevocably hated his mother.

He finally reached her room. He pushed the door open and walked in. Morgaine stood at a counter, tapping her fingers on its surface. "What took you so long, pet?" The word *pet* sent chills down Dred's spine.

She looked younger. Not all the way younger, but still.

"Nothing, Mum. I just had to give it a couple tries is all." The lie was well delivered, and Dred was pleased.

Morgaine studied him. Her fingers made a rhythmic *di-di-di-dit* on the countertop. "You know, Dred, this whole blackout thing has me in a state. An absolute state!"

"Of course, Mum," Dred said. "It's a drag."

"Completely. The worst thing isn't the blackouts themselves, but the fact that Merlin is behind them. Merlin! Which also means that this new Arthur is involved!"

"I'm sorry again that I couldn't—"

"Tut-tut. Don't worry," Morgaine said cheerfully. "Such is war. Win some, lose some."

"Of course."

"But because Merlin has been able to get to us, I've been racking my brain for ways to get back at him. I've come up with a couple new ideas. One involves one of our esteemed prisoners."

Dred's stomach knotted. "You've finally decided to deal with the fairy?" he asked.

Morgaine laughed. "The fairy? Of course not the fairy, muddleheaded child. She can at least be used to blackmail the lord of Leagon. The other one, I've realized, is less useful. The strange-looking girl."

"Who—Qwon?" Dred said, his voice cracking slightly.

"Yes, Qwon. You don't think we should kill her?"

"I-I don't see why we would," he stammered.

Morgaine looked disappointed. "This Artie cares for her, right?"

"It seemed so, yes." *We are talking about my brother,* Dred realized for the first time.

"Then let's give him a bit of a pause. Let's *scare* him."

Dred fought back a growing fear. "But won't it make him angrier?"

"Of course it will," Morgaine said, turning from the countertop. "Angry adversaries are the best. They're predictable. And much easier to manipulate. We shall deliver her head to him, and once we do, you'll see how quickly he'll come."

Dred knew his mother was right, and it made him sick.

But what made him sicker was what he'd seen in the basement. What he'd learned about himself—and his brother.

Dred made a little bow and said coolly, "As you wish. When?"

"Three days from now, midmorning. I want her to suffer a bit more."

"Very well. I'll order an executioner from the barracks."

Dred turned and headed for the door.

As he pulled it open, his mother said, "That won't be necessary, snookums. The Castel is thin on staff as it is. You can do it. And no need for one of those ridiculous axes. Just use your own blade. Just use the Peace Sword."

𝕶𝖞𝖓𝖉𝖊𝖗 𝖈𝖔𝖚𝖑𝖉𝖓'𝖙 𝖜𝖔𝖗𝖐. 𝕳𝖎𝖘 𝖒𝖎𝖓𝖉 was in overdrive because he couldn't stop thinking about the events of the last thirty-six hours.

First: Even with the help of Clive, his exemplary if odd research assistant, Kynder could not find one jot of information about the person who wielded the Peace Sword.

Second: He'd spoken with Artie very early that morning and learned that Bedevere had nearly died on the Orgulus quest. It didn't take much for Kynder to imagine one of his own kids losing a limb—or worse—and it made him sick.

Third: After his one-on-one with Artie, they conferenced with Merlin, who was obsessing over the fact that they had only six days left, and insisted that Artie and his knights leave immediately to retrieve Kusanagi. But Artie wanted to wait for Bors's report. He said they were tired of hunting down swords for Merlin, and that he wanted to start focusing on rescuing Qwon. The call ended with Artie saying, "You know what, Merlin? Why don't *you* go and get Kusanagi, and we'll take it easy and wait for *you* for a change."

Merlin didn't like that. He disconnected in protest and no one had heard from him all morning. Thumb apologized for Merlin, but it wasn't enough to satisfy Artie—or Kynder, for that matter.

Fourth: Bors's report, which had arrived only a little after the Merlin tiff, basically sucked:

Witch very unpredictable—Q to be executed day after tomorrow. Wants Mordred to do it. Unsure if he will comply.

Advise for escape tomorrow, predawn. Have found good route out of Castel. Require big blackout for cover.

Will not be able to acquire Excal. or Anguish prior to escape. It is impossible. Morgaine sleeps with them. After escape Morgaine will give chase and try to take Artie, retrieve the pommel and the rest of the Seven Swords, and kill the knights. Advise that we meet at predetermined rendezvous, allow Morgaine to follow, and quickly gate back to empty Castel to retrieve weapons. Then, to Avalon.

TTYS,

B. le F.

PS: Map of Castel encls'd.

PPS: Location of seaside rendezvous encls'd.

PPPS: Mord. has Peace Sword! Need to confront him directly.

Fifth: Mordred had the Peace Sword!

At least that took care of Kynder's first problem.

But, thanks to Clive, Kynder also knew that Mordred was another one of Morgaine's genetically engineered experiments. Something about this didn't add up for Kynder. He didn't know why exactly, but Kynder Kingfisher couldn't shake the feeling that Mordred was not their enemy but their friend.

Kynder checked his watch. It was ten in the morning. The escape from Castel Deorc Wæters was to occur in less than twenty-four hours. If the escape failed, then Qwon Onakea, a girl he now felt achingly responsible for, would be killed in forty-eight hours.

Kynder decided to talk with Artie again. He couldn't reveal Merlin's secret, but he could reveal his Mordred theory. Kynder grabbed his iPad, pinged Artie, and made his way to the reading room.

After a minute Artie accepted and, just like that, they were face-to-face.

"Hey, Arthur," Kynder said.

"Hey, Kynder."

Kynder smiled. "Your sister around?"

"Course she is," Artie said, and wearily called for Kay. Artie looked so worn down. No kid should have to bear what Artie did.

A peppier-looking Kay popped up next to her brother and said, "Hey, Kynder."

Kynder paused.

"Whassup, Kynder?" Artie asked.

"Ummmm. I've got this hunch. It's kind of a whopper."

"What is it?" Kay asked.

"I think . . . or rather I *don't* think . . . I don't think Mordred is your enemy."

"*What?*" Artie exclaimed as Kay's jaw dropped.

"I know it sounds crazy, but I can't shake the feeling that he's the key to getting the rest of the Seven Swords. It's just this overwhelming gut feeling I have."

"I don't understand," Artie said, overcome with confusion and a tiny bit of anger.

Kynder clutched his chest, not realizing that he was also clutching his shirt pocket, which held the stone Merlin had given him. "I can't tell you, Son," he said.

"Give it a try, Pop?" Kay encouraged. She could see her dad struggling and didn't like it.

Kynder swallowed hard. He felt sick. What was wrong with him? "I can't. I'm sorry. I'm pretty sure, though, that the next time you see Mordred, something will tell you I'm right."

Artie was shocked. He didn't know what to say. He hated Mordred even more than Morgaine. The fact that he was the one with the Peace Sword made it even worse. "I . . . I don't know what to—"

But then they were cut off.

Kynder tried desperately to reconnect with his kids, but it was no use. The network had shut down. He hoped—even expected—Artie and Kay to *lunae lumen* over to the Library to finish their conversation, but they didn't come.

Kynder collapsed onto the table. He felt awful. After a few moments Clive appeared next to him holding two cups of coffee. He put one down next to Kynder. "You told them about Mordred, eh?"

"Yeah," Kynder said into the crook of his arm.

"Did you tell them why?"

"I wanted to but I couldn't," Kynder whispered, full of shame. He picked his head up and said, "It was almost like an invisible hand was stopping me."

Clive slurped his coffee. For several moments that was

the only sound. Finally he said, "Can I ask you something?"

"Sure."

"What do you know about this Merlin?"

Kynder thought. "I don't know . . . that he was imprisoned in Cincinnati, that he knows Morgaine made Arthur, that he's the same guy from all the old stories, that he and the witch hate each other. Sure, he can be bossy in his own way, but he seems like a generally stand-up guy. That's why Artie—"

Clive cut him off with a brisk wave of his hand. "That's all fine. But have you come across his name in any of these books?"

No, Kynder hadn't. Merlin's name was impossible to find. It could have been because so many of the books were in strange languages, but even now with Clive translating, Kynder still had no recollection of seeing Merlin in the research. Perhaps, it dawned on him, this was why he couldn't find out anything about Excalibur and why it wanted Merlin dead.

Kynder started to say as much when his chest shot through with pain. He wrenched forward and realized for the first time that he'd been clutching the stone the whole time he'd been talking to his kids.

"May I see it?" Clive asked.

"See what?" Kynder asked with wild eyes.

"The thing he gave you?"

"Oh. Uh, sure." Kynder slowly pulled the dark pebble from his pocket, holding it in a fist. It took a lot of effort, but he managed to open his hand for Clive to see.

The gnarled man leaned forward but kept his distance. "Ah, that's a beaut. I haven't seen one like that in a long time."

"One what?"

"Kynder, did the wizard tell you what this does?"

"Of course. It enables me to be in the Otherworld."

Clive winced. "Bollocks," he chirped. "You don't need this to be here. Why do you think they picked you to raise Artie? You've got a lot of magic in you, Kynder, just like your son. Just like your daughter. Just like your ex-wife."

"You mean I don't need this to cross?" Kynder asked, unconsciously wrapping his fingers around the rock again.

Clive nodded at Kynder's fist. "That, my friend, is what's called a keeper stone. They're used to 'keep' people from doing certain things. For instance, I've seen plenty of mentions of Merlin in these books, but this stone has prevented you from seeing the same. I've even mentioned them to you, but the stone made it so you couldn't hear."

"So it keeps me from learning anything about Merlin!" Kynder said in a revelatory voice.

Clive nodded.

Kynder was in shock. "So this stone—" he began, but then the muscles in his hand cramped up and he yelled out in pain.

Clive yanked a small black box out of the inside of his shirt, flipped its top, and put it on the table. Then he took Kynder's fist and tried to open it, but it wouldn't budge.

Clive said, "I'm sorry. This is going to hurt."

Kynder looked down in fear. Clive shook his free hand and to Kynder's astonishment it appeared to be made of wood instead of flesh and bone!

Clive slid a long, skinny digit into Kynder's fist and began to pry his fingers away from his palm. And then—*snap! snap-snap!*—the index, middle, and ring fingers of Kynder's hand broke backward at disturbing angles. The stone was revealed. A blue light shot from it, sweeping in desperation this way and that.

Clive tried to pick up the stone, but it was stuck, melded to the flesh of Kynder's palm. Still using his long wooden finger, Clive dug into Kynder's skin and popped the pebble out with a *smack*! He slid it into the box and hastily shut the lid.

Kynder, breathing hard, looked at his hand. It was a mess. His broken fingers were useless, and a bloody divot had been scooped from the center of his palm.

He looked at Clive, full of shock and awe, relief and disgust.

He could finally feel that the pebble, even though the size of a marble, had been a great burden. "Thank you," Kynder breathed.

"Don't mention it."

"He won't know?" Kynder asked nervously.

"Perhaps, but he won't risk coming here to find out."

"Why not?"

Clive ignored this question and said gently, "Shall I set your fingers?"

Kynder clenched his jaw. "Sure." Then Clive carefully worked each one back into place. It hurt, but Kynder didn't make a sound. When Clive was done, he excused himself to get some bandages.

Kynder let his hand fall to the table. His mind was overrun. Why had Merlin done this to him? Was the wizard afraid of Kynder? Or did he just not trust him? What other enchantments had Merlin cast over him?

And then, as Clive returned, the worst occurred to Kynder. "Are my children safe?" he demanded.

Clive sighed. "The wizard is . . . complicated. I think the answer to this question is yes, but to be truthful, Kynder, I don't know."

Kynder stood, alarmed at the implications.

"Kynder," Clive said soothingly, "they're fine for now. Merlin still needs them. I could arrange transport to them for you, but I think it would be more helpful if you stayed here."

Kynder couldn't believe what he was hearing. "But my children could be in danger!"

"Your children *have* been in danger ever since they met Merlin, haven't they?"

Kynder sank back to his chair. He felt like a total failure as a father. "Yes . . . ," he murmured.

"I think you should stay here and find out as much as you can about Merlin, now that the spell is broken. It won't take you long."

Kynder considered this advice as Clive wrapped his wounded hand. "Okay. But only till this evening. If I haven't spoken to them by dinnertime, then we go to them."

"Sounds reasonable."

"Thank you, Clive. For everything."

"Don't mention it." He took a sip of coffee. "Now, I'll go and get you some books."

Clive stood and gave Kynder a sidelong glance. "The wizard won't risk coming here because of me. I'm not all the way better yet, but I will be soon."

Kynder frowned. "Because of you? What do you mean? Who are you?"

"From now on, please, call me Numinae."

𝔄rtie and 𝔎ay tried to reconnect with Kynder on the iPad for about ten minutes, but it was pointless. Apparently the network at the Library was down. They didn't know what to do, but a short while later the iPad chimed, and Kay rushed to it.

"Is it Kynder?" Artie asked.

"Naw. It's Merlin," Kay said unenthusiastically.

Artie stepped next to her and took the tablet. He swiped it on and accepted the chat invite.

"Merlin, I don't—" Artie began.

"Wait," Merlin said, holding up a hand. "Before you get mad at me again, let me speak. I want to apologize for the way I've behaved. I can see that you are devoted to Qwon, and committed to saving her, even, it seems, at the expense of reaching Avalon."

Artie frowned. "Go on."

"Being a king is hard, isn't it, Artie?" Merlin asked.

"You can say that again."

"All people with responsibilities like yours face the same problem at one time or another," Merlin continued. "Sometimes you have to choose between what's right and what's smart."

Artie considered this for a moment.

"What's he talking about, Art?" Kay asked.

Artie looked at Kay. "I want to save Qwon. I *have* to save Qwon. That's the right thing to do. But going to Avalon is the *smart* thing to do." Artie let out a long sigh. "I mean, the fate of the worlds hinges on my getting there! Is Qwon really more important than that? Should I want to save her more than I want to go to Avalon? More than I want to become king?"

Kay blew out her cheeks. "Man, I never thought of it that way."

"I think I can help, Artie," Merlin consoled him. "There's a word—one I'd forgotten and that used to be very closely associated with the first King Arthur—that perfectly describes your desire to save your friend."

"What is it?" Artie asked.

"Noble," Merlin said with an air of gravitas.

Noble. Artie liked that.

"Like kingly," Kay observed.

"Yes, Kay, like kingly. But it's more than that. It means honorable, moral, principled. Only the best kings are noble in both rank and in spirit. You, young Artie Kingfisher, in spite of your misguided wizard, embody both of these perfectly."

Artie leaned closer to the screen. At that moment he knew what he would choose, and he understood that the decision to save Qwon *was* smart. It was smart *because* it was right. After that he would figure out what to do about the rest of his mission.

"Thank you, Merlin," Artie said.

"Thank you, sire, for being so patient with me," Merlin said.

Artie clapped his hands. "So now that we're agreed, and we've gotten Bors's report, what do you think is the best way to go about getting Qwon? Should we follow Bors's advice and wait till tomorrow or use the map he provided, sneak into Castel Deorc Wæters, and attempt to whisk her away now?"

"I still think it foolish to try a special-ops rescue," Merlin said. "But I do think we can support his escape plan by distracting the witch. And the best way to do that, I believe, is by going for Kusanagi now."

Kay huffed, "So, what? Nothing's changed then?"

Merlin shook his head. "No, Kay, everything's changed.

From here forward, saving Qwon will be our primary purpose."

Artie nodded slowly. "Okay, but if Qwon is priority number one, why bother with Kusanagi?"

"Because it will vex the witch. Morgaine will sense that we are pushing forward for another of the Seven. This will preoccupy her and should help our friends."

"So off to Japan, then, eh?" came a voice directly behind Artie and Kay.

"Tom!" Kay said, jumping from her chair. "You scared me!"

"Hello, Mr. Thumb," Merlin said. "Lovely to see you. We were just discussing Qwon's blade."

"I heard," Thumb replied. "Looking forward to going to Japan. I've read a lot about it."

"It should be quite an adventure," Merlin said with a wink.

Kay pointed at the iPad. "Hey, none of that winking stuff between you two."

Merlin chuckled. "Mr. Thumb will go over everything else. The blackout Bors desires for his escape tomorrow requires my attention. Things are happening quickly now, sire. We mustn't tarry."

"Roger that, Merlin," Artie said.

Merlin hesitated. "Before I sign off, do you mind if I ask what you were discussing with Kynder?"

"He said he thinks Mordred isn't our enemy but our friend!" Kay blurted, unable to contain herself.

Thumb made a choking sound. "Amazing!" Merlin said. He stroked his long sideburns for a moment, considering this news. "Did he say *why* he thinks this?"

This was an essential question for the wizard. Merlin knew that only a short while ago Kynder had abandoned his keeper stone. He didn't know why or how this had happened, but he was pretty miffed about it. If Kynder no longer had the stone, then he might have told Artie the secret that Merlin had made him promise not to reveal: that Morgaine was the one who'd made him. If Artie knew that, Merlin was afraid that Artie would begin to question his allegiance to Merlin, especially since Artie was on record as feeling manipulated by the wizard.

That wouldn't do. If it happened, Merlin's entire plan would be compromised.

Artie shrugged. "Naw, he wouldn't say. Just called it a gut feeling."

Merlin fought an urge to breathe a sigh of relief and said, "Interesting. I don't know if Kynder is right, but since we now know Mordred holds the Peace Sword, it may not hurt to exercise some restraint next time you see him."

"I'll try to keep that in mind," Artie said.

"All right. Off to Japan, then!" Merlin said. "Once you're back, we'll decide on our next move."

"All right, Merlin. Good luck with the blackout," Artie said. "Over and out!"

The wizard swiped his finger across the screen and disappeared.

Artie looked at Kay and said, "I guess we should see what this thing has to say about Kusanagi, huh?"

"Yep. I'll do it," Kay replied, opening the sword app. "Let's see. Kusanagi. Really old, originally found in the body of an eight-headed serpent. Went missing for a long time. Some believe it's in a place called Atsuta Jingu, others think it was lost at sea. Says here it's actually in a mysterious Otherworld shrine that can only be accessed from a remote Japanese national park called Shiretoko."

"The Shrine of Horrors," Thumb interjected matter-of-factly.

"Oh, wonderful," Kay said. "Is it guarded by some psycho giant too?"

Thumb shrugged. "Unknown, lass. The Shrine of Horrors is a shadowy place. The monocle from Qwon's house is supposed to help us find the crossover that leads to it."

Artie nodded and said, "Get some rest, both of you. I'll tell the others about the plan and we can meet here at three a.m. Be ready."

𝕿𝖍𝖊 𝖒𝖔𝖔𝖓𝖌𝖆𝖙𝖊 𝖙𝖜𝖎𝖗𝖑𝖊𝖉 𝖔𝖕𝖊𝖓 𝖎𝖓 a clearing on a steep mountainside.

The party fanned out. To the east was a sheer thousand-foot drop that ended in the sea. To the west and north were dense woods. Beyond the woods they could make out a few snow-tipped mountains. To the south was a slice of forest far below, dotted with small, tear-shaped lakes. The deciduous trees were just beginning to turn and the air was crisp and clean.

Artie put Thumb, who'd reverted to his small version, on his shoulder. "Let's go that way, lad," Thumb said, pointing north to a low break in the trees. When they got there they peeked into the woods, finding a narrow path. At their feet was a rock the size of a basketball, and etched into this rock were some very old-looking Japanese characters. At the base of the rock was a tuft of long black hair.

Artie asked, "Anyone read Japanese?"

"A little," Thumb said. "That is the character for 'spirit,'" he continued, pointing with his red cane. "I believe the others say something like 'turn away,' or maybe 'behind you.'"

"Weird," Kay said.

"Hey, Art, why don't you use that eyepiece thing?" Erik suggested.

"Duh." Artie fished in a pocket. He pulled out the monocle and held it to his eye.

The world looked the same. Artie spun in a few circles, squinting through the crystal, waiting for something to happen.

"Everything's the same."

"Try tilting it, lad," Thumb suggested.

Very slowly Artie angled the lens back over his eye. When he got it just right, he stopped and exclaimed, "Oh!"

"What do you see?" Erik asked.

"It's hard to say. Tom, what is this thing?"

"It doesn't have a proper name, but its glass allows you to see through to the other side. Tilted just so, you're looking into the Otherworld. In essence, you can see the spirit world of Japan with that little thing. It has been in the Onakea family for a long, long, long time."

"Cool," Artie said. "But we're still in this world, right?"

"Correct, lad."

"Wait!" yelled Artie. "I saw something move!"

"What?" Kay asked as Lance nocked an arrow.

"Don't worry. It was small. Come on, guys. Follow me."

Artie lowered his spear and ducked into the woods. The rest of the knights followed, with Lance bringing up the rear.

Artie and his crew hunched over as they walked through a tunnel of tightly packed trees and saplings. The path led up, and after a hundred feet, the ground became very steep and choked with roots.

The path twisted and turned as they ascended. Artie recognized the trees as they changed from mountain ash to Asian spruce. The group passed an especially old and regal-looking pine tree, its gnarled bark carpeted with lichens, which seemed to mark some kind of boundary.

"Did it just get, like, way colder?" Kay asked, as they came to a stop just past the pine.

"Yeah, it did," Erik said.

Artie raised and lowered the monocle a few times. "Weird."

"What is it?" Thumb asked.

"The worlds look . . . *exactly* the same," Artie said.

"Hmm," Thumb murmured. "This world and the Otherworld must be identical in this place. Can you still see whatever it was we were following?"

Artie put the glass to his eye again. "Yeah, it's right up there." He pointed at a child-sized rock about twenty feet away.

"It'd be nice if you told us what it is, dude," Lance said.

"It looks like a fox. And you know what? I think it's waiting for us."

"A fox, you say? Do you mind if I have a look, lad?" Thumb asked.

"Not at all, Tommy." Artie held the monocle in front of Thumb's face. "You see it?"

"I most certainly do!" Thumb exclaimed. "That's a *kitsune*!"

"A what?" asked Erik.

"A spirit. In Japan almost everything—from monsters to chopsticks to toilet stalls—has a spirit associated with it."

"Is a *kitsune* a good spirit, Tommy?" Kay asked.

"Yes," Thumb said simply. "Try calling it to you, lad."

Artie brought the monocle back to his eye and made a series of clicking noises. The fox's ears turned toward the noise, then it stood and trotted down the path. To the others it was invisible, but as it got closer Artie saw that it had red eyes and golden hair. It also had several tails.

"Tom, check this out." Artie shifted the monocle back to Thumb.

The little man looked through the lens and said, "My,

this is an old *kitsune*. The more tails they have, the older they are."

"Let me see!" Kay said impatiently. Artie passed her the eyepiece, and all the knights took turns observing the curious spirit.

Erik went last. He passed the lens back to Artie, who stared through it again and, acting on a hunch, said, "Hey, *kitsune*! Kusanagi!"

The fox whined and nodded its head. Then it turned and ran down the path.

"Whoa, little dude's fast!" Artie said.

"Follow it!" Thumb said.

They took off, Artie directing them which way to go as he tracked the strange animal. It kept its distance and often disappeared, but never for long. After a while it led them off the path on an easy bushwhack that lasted about ten minutes.

Finally they reached flat ground and a little clearing. On the far side a wall of pine trees stood like sentinels.

Artie peered through the lens but couldn't find the fox. "It's gone," he said a little wistfully.

"That may be," Thumb said, "but it led us where we need to be. Look there!" Thumb pointed at two perfectly round black stones set in the earth right at the base of the wall of pines.

"The crossover!" Kay said.

"Indeed, lass," Thumb replied.

Artie took Thumb from his shoulder and placed him on the ground. Then he and Kay went about opening the crossover with the pommel. The crossover formed just like all the others, only this time the space beyond the portal was pitch-black.

Artie leaned in. He saw a clearing dotted with little paper lanterns. Hanging from the trees here and there were multicolored cloth banners covered with Japanese characters. And at the end of the clearing, also hanging from a tree, was the glinting steel of a Japanese katana.

"That's it," Artie said, but when he spoke he could hardly hear his own voice.

Weird.

He pulled back from the archway and turned to his knights, who were all yelling at him.

"What the heck, Art?" Kay said. "It was like you leaned into a pool of black ink."

"Yeah, we couldn't see you at all!" Erik said.

"Chill, guys, it's fine in there. I can see the sword—and the shrine doesn't look horror-filled at all," Artie said. "The sound's a little strange, though."

"Anything else in there?" Thumb asked.

"Not that I could see," Artie said. "Just a bunch of lanterns and a few banners."

"Nice," Erik said with relief.

"Respect, fox!" Kay said into the woods. "Thanks, wherever you are."

"All right, then," Artie said, readying his spear just in case. "Let's go and get Kusanagi." Then he turned and disappeared into the blackness, and his knights bravely followed.

Just as Artie stepped into the Shrine of Horrors, Qwon turned onto her side. She'd been tossing and turning all night, trying to shake the nerves that wouldn't let her rest.

The escape was about to commence.

The plan was straightforward: As soon as the blackout went into effect, Bors would subdue Dred and open his door. Bors would create one of his special odorless scent-locks, and under the cover of darkness Qwon and Shallot would follow him to a secret passage. They would take this and emerge on the hillside well beyond the Castel's walls. From there, they would haul butt to the rendezvous point.

Bors assured them that the Castel and the immediate area were practically abandoned, and that they wouldn't encounter much resistance during the actual escape. The real danger, he said, lay outside the Castel. Since Morgaine had dispatched most of her army to the countryside to try to find out how Merlin was stealing her power, they could run into Fenlandian forces at any time.

Qwon was pretty freaked out by all this.

She was also stressing about Dred and Excalibur. Qwon worried that she wouldn't be able to stop Shallot from hurting Dred even *after* Bors had subdued him. And as for Artie's sword, according to Bors it was just too closely guarded. They would have to come back for it, and The Anguish, through some kind of magic portal after they hooked up with Artie.

Qwon thought of all these things as she lay in front of the birdbath, her blankets pulled to her chin. Her nose was sealed with scraps of cloth against the impending fairy scentlock, and her staff was tucked under her side.

But then Dred's door unlatched. That wasn't supposed to happen yet! It opened slightly and Dred urged, "Qwon, come here!"

Qwon leaped to her feet and walked quickly to the door. Dred was framed by the light of his room and he held out his hand. His face was in shadow. "I'm taking you away."

"What?" Qwon said, her heart racing.

"She wants to execute you. She wants *me* to execute

you," Dred explained regretfully.

He retreated into his room. "Come in."

But Qwon didn't understand. She didn't understand because for the first time she could see Dred's face.

And it belonged to Artie Kingfisher.

"I don't—you look—*who are you?*" she pleaded.

The lights blinked and went out just as Dred explained quietly, "I'm his brother."

Shallot sprang into action, pushing between Qwon and Dred, her scent going crazy. Qwon yelled, "No!" but the fairy was too fast.

Dred was totally taken by surprise and immediately dazed by her scentlock. Bors, who'd been hiding in Dred's room, gave up his invisibility and helped Shallot by delivering a blow to the back of Dred's neck, knocking him out. As Dred collapsed to the floor, Bors shook one of his hands and a faint light ignited in his palm. Bors worked quickly, and before Qwon could count to five, Dred was bound to the posts of his bed with plastic zip ties and gagged with a sock.

"There," Shallot said, breathing hard.

Qwon couldn't believe it. "Why did you do that?"

"What do you mean? The plan was to subdue him. It didn't go exactly as we expected, but there he is, subdued," Shallot huffed.

"But he looks . . . he looks just like Artie."

Bors stepped to Shallot and made a series of urgent hand signals.

Qwon got her first good look at their rescuer, who apparently was a mute. He was a little shorter than Shallot but just as long-limbed. He was skinny but looked very strong. His hair was also pink and black. His skin was much darker and had a red tinge, like the color of fall leaves. His eyes were the bluest she'd ever seen.

"He says that Dred is Artie's twin," Shallot said matter-of-factly. "He says Dred just found out. His mother had been keeping it secret from him. He says we need to go, now."

Qwon knew that this last part was true and forced herself not to think about the fact that Dred was Artie's brother. She said, "Cut one of his hands free."

"What?" Shallot exclaimed.

"Cut one of his hands free, or I'm not leaving."

"No!" Shallot cried. "He's lucky I don't slit his throat for what he did to us!" Her scent was so strong Qwon could taste it.

But Bors wasn't upset. He moved to Dred's side and pressed a knife with a wavy blade into the tie around Dred's left hand. It snapped and his arm fell limply to the bed. Bors nodded to Qwon and went over to the exit. He beckoned to them and closed his hand around the light, throwing the room into utter darkness.

Shallot huffed, took Qwon roughly by the arm, and walked her to Bors. Shallot guided Qwon's hand onto Bors's sinewy shoulder and said, "Don't let go." She then stepped behind Qwon and said, "Ready."

The door opened, and as it did Qwon became aware of a very odd absence of smell through her mouth. This must have been Bors's scentlock. It smelled like nothing. It smelled like oblivion.

Bors stepped into the hall, and Qwon forced her feet to move. They went up and down stairs and seemingly around in circles. Qwon recalled the roundabout route Dred had taken when he first carried her to the courtyard. It was as if there was no end to this castle's weirdness. Qwon bumped into walls and fell down three times. All along, Bors moved with a purpose.

For several minutes they passed through Castel Deorc Wæters without hearing or seeing any sign of another person. But then they heard someone say, "Hey, who goes—unh."

It was like he'd been struck dumb. The scentlock. For good measure, Qwon stuffed the cloth into her nose a little more with her free hand.

They descended a final staircase and walked through a stone hallway. Finally Bors stopped. He turned to Qwon, and her hand fell from his shoulder. He patted her twice on the forearm, and even though she couldn't see the fairy, she understood. He was saying, "Well done."

"Thanks," Qwon whispered.

"Can we risk some light?" Shallot asked.

The answer came as Bors turned on the light in his hand.

They were at the end of a subterranean hall. Bors pointed at the wall next to him as if to say, "Here it is."

It was a small opening, low and rough. They were going to have to crawl.

"I don't know," Qwon said, taking a couple steps back.

"What do you mean?" Shallot demanded.

"That looks pretty tight," Qwon said.

"It looks fine to me," Shallot replied. "Besides, you got a better idea?"

Qwon slumped. "No."

Bors put a gentle hand on Qwon's shoulder and looked her in the eye.

"See, he says it's okay. Let's go," Shallot said brusquely.

Qwon turned to Bors. His gaze was very comforting. "All right," Qwon said. "Lead the way, Bors."

He grinned, dropped to his knees, and disappeared into the passage.

Qwon got down and peered in. The air was damp and the rustlings of a scurrying Bors could be heard from inside. It sounded like he'd already gone a fair distance. She crawled in cautiously, her eyes closed with fear. She hated small places, and her knees already hurt. As she made her way down the passage, she realized she'd never missed her old, normal life so dearly.

Dred came to just as the escapees entered the tunnel.

He was greeted with a throbbing head and his mother's nauseating voice as it beckoned him over the walkie-talkie.

"Mordred, where *are* you?"

Dred strained against his ties. Luckily, his captors had left one hand free. He pulled the sock from his mouth. It took him several minutes to get his other hand undone, and another minute to unbind his feet. When he was free, he sat and rubbed his head.

He smiled.

Qwon had escaped, and he didn't care if the fairy had too.

Dred stumbled to his desk. He grabbed a flashlight, turned it on, strapped on the Peace Sword, and picked up the walkie-talkie. "Coming, Mum," he said, and then, because he didn't want to hear Morgaine yet, he switched it off.

When he reached Morgaine's room, her doors were open, and a cool, undulating light spilled out. Dred recognized it as magic light, not electric light. She'd found some reserve of power, and Dred knew that she'd be back to her younger self, brimming with confidence.

He took a deep breath and entered.

Sure enough, Morgaine was in battle-witch mode. She floated in the air, working her hands around a gray and misty ball that flashed from within like a small thunderstorm. Eekan, the jaybird from the failed raid in Surmik, turned tight circles in the air around her head.

The witch wore a buxom purple breastplate adorned with silvery-white etchings of flowers and ribbons and lace. Her long hair was pulled into a tight bun on top of her head, and jutting from this in every direction were dozens of crisscrossing, thorny twigs. Wrapped around her head was a formfitting silver band that descended in a point over her nose and made her look like a bird. The tacky bangles she usually wore were gone, replaced with heavy brass bracelets that covered her arms from wrist to elbow. She wore poofy pink pants and had on knee-high black riding boots with pointed silver toes. Her sangrealitic dagger was strapped to her side, and she wore a pink hooded cape that just covered her bottom.

Dred had never seen her so done up.

Two other things stood out.

One was that Excalibur and The Anguish were hooked up to a generator-like thing, which hummed quietly. Morgaine must have been using the swords to help her gather strength.

The other was that the sangrealitic picture machine was sitting on a chest-high pedestal in the middle of the room.

It held two images on a split screen. One was of the empty portico where Qwon and Shallot had been kept. The other was of a scrabble of rock on some hillside. Just above the rock was a small, rough opening.

His heart quickened and his palms went cold.

"Ah, you're here," Morgaine said. She continued to work the storm in her hands as it lit up from inside in yellows and greens.

"I am," Dred said, his voice shamefully cracking.

"Give me your sword."

"Why—" But he was cut short by the grating sound of his blade flying from its scabbard and joining Excalibur and the fairy weapon at the generator. Morgaine waved her hand at Mordred's weapon, and it was quickly wrapped in wires and hooked into the array.

"I need it more than you," she explained. The little storm made a loud howl as Eekan *ca-caw*ed feverishly.

"I'll need it too," Dred said, with an amount of anger that surprised even him.

"Is that so, pet? And who would you use it against?"

Dred scowled. "I can think of someone."

Morgaine hissed as her bird dived for his head. Without landing, it pecked at his hair and beat his face with its wings. It didn't hurt him so much as piss him off even more.

Dred batted the bird away and tried to look defiant. Did she know that he'd discovered her old lab? That—and

Qwon's safety—was all that concerned him.

"Is there anything you'd like to tell me, Mordred?" she asked.

"The prisoners escaped," he said flatly.

"Yes. And you wouldn't have had anything to do with that, now, would you?"

"No." Dred figured this was sort of true, since he'd only meant to help Qwon and not Shallot. And besides, it didn't go as he'd planned. "I have a bump on my head to prove it if you don't believe me."

"Liar!" Morgaine snarled, descending to the floor. A bolt of orange lightning jumped from the storm ball and struck at Dred's feet, and he jumped back.

"I'm not lying, Mum! There was another fairy!"

"Yes, yes," Morgaine said dismissively. "Bors le Fey. I know about him. Good at sneaking, but otherwise a rank amateur. I've intercepted all of his communiqués." As she said this, she nodded her chin at a contraption that looked like a typewriter attached to an electronic gadget with an antenna. "Regardless, you're still lying. You were helping that girl. That *condemned* girl. What kind of fool do you take me for, Mordred? I know you talked to her. I know you think that you're her *friend*."

"I'm her kidnapper, nothing more."

"You are her accomplice *and* a liar!" Morgaine accused. "I know you killed my Smash! My innocent little Smash!"

The jaybird squealed as if it had lost its best friend. But Dred was happy to hear Morgaine say this. If she thought Dred, not the fairy, had killed the little spy, then that meant she didn't know about Dred's visit to the lab.

If he ever met this Bors le Fey, Dred would thank him dearly, fairy or not.

"He died quickly, Mum. And just so you know, I loved Smash. But better he die than you be able to spy on me, *your own son*! Talk about liars!"

"Pshaw!" Morgaine exclaimed as she started to spin like a top. "I am Morgaine, Lordess of Fenland, *and I have no son!*"

Silver strands shot from holes in the floor and wrapped around Dred. They were tight and as they pressed his legs together, he lost his balance. He hit the floor hard and stifled a cry. He wouldn't give her the satisfaction.

"Now that you're comfortable," Morgaine said sweetly, "you can watch the show with me. Let's see how quickly they can run."

"Aren't you going to be ready for them when they come out of that hole?"

"Yes and no, love."

Dred frowned. After a moment he said, "You're going to let them escape, aren't you?"

Morgaine rose into the air again, her voice echoing in its corners: "Of course I'm going to let them escape, you dim-witted dolt. Artie has opened another crossover—the one that will lead him to Qwon's sword—and when he returns with it, he is supposed to rendezvous with Qwon and the fairies. He believes that he can rescue her, then come back here to snatch the remaining swords and gate to Avalon. Ha! Fool. I will follow the prisoners, kill his knights, take the other swords for myself, and bring this so-called king back here as my most esteemed prisoner. Then I will take the pommel and mend Excalibur! After that, no one will be able to stop me!"

The machine that Artie's sword was hooked up to chortled and kicked, and a dark thread began to rise from Excalibur. It reminded Dred of the first time he'd seen the weapon, when it had blacked out Qwon's bedroom.

The thread reluctantly unraveled in Morgaine's direction as Excalibur shook and strained to get out of its bonds. It was plain that it did not want to lend her its power, but without the pommel it couldn't resist.

The sword's black strand struck Morgaine's hands and she cried out as the magic flooded over her.

Dred gazed at the magical blade that belonged to his brother, and for a brief moment he could see Artie there, reflected in the steel. They were perfectly identical. The same. And that was when Dred understood Morgaine's scheme. Dred had been a backup plan. If Artie couldn't retrieve Excalibur from the Lake, then Morgaine had hoped that Mordred could. But his brother was the only one who could claim the sword. Somehow Merlin had known this and succeeded in stealing Artie before Morgaine had a chance to raise him herself. That was why she was so hard on Dred. Morgaine had been stuck with him, and he served as a cruel and constant reminder of both her success and her failure.

That's why she hated him.

Dred felt sick. A clap of thunder rattled the windows, and Morgaine cackled, just like a real witch should.

Dred clenched his jaw.

"Guards!" Morgaine howled. Two elderly, remnant soldiers appeared from the shadows and hoisted Dred up. "Put him in the Vermin's Ward," she ordered. "Only one cup of water a day. No food," she said.

Dred spit on the floor as he was carried out. He said, "When you see him, I hope he kills you!"

"Now, snookums," Morgaine cooed, "I know you don't mean that."

𝔒𝔫𝔢 𝔟𝔶 𝔬𝔫𝔢, 𝔄𝔯𝔱𝔦𝔢 𝔞𝔫𝔡 his knights stepped through the mysterious, inky darkness of the crossover that led to the Shrine of Horrors, where Thumb grew back to his Otherworld size. The lack of sound inside the Shrine was a lot like being underwater. They had to shout at the top of their lungs to hear each other, and as they made their way toward the sword, Artie yelled, "Everyone okay?"

They were. So far, so good.

As Artie, Kay, and Thumb approached the first paper lanterns, a single bell dinged in the distance.

And two of the lanterns stood up on little red legs!

The knights stopped. The lanterns, which were illuminated by pleasant flickering flames, were about the size of footballs. They turned toward the group. Not only did the strange creatures have legs, but faces too. Big-eyed, child-like faces with broad, toothy grins.

They looked about as frightening as, well, living paper lanterns.

The pair wobbled toward Artie, Kay, and Thumb, and Kay exclaimed, "Aw, they're cute!"

"These are spirits too," Thumb yelled, holding the Welsh *wakizashi* in front of him.

The lanterns reached Artie's feet and pushed around his ankles like hungry house cats. "Friendly too," Artie shouted.

Kay knelt to pet one, but as she stuck out her hand, the creature opened its mouth and snapped at her fingers.

"Hey!" Kay cried, standing up. "Bad lantern!"

And then the one around Artie's feet opened wide and snapped at Artie's ankle. "Watch it!" he said.

"Ignore them, lads. Let's get the sword!" Thumb yelled.

Artie and Kay nudged the spirits aside and continued toward the hanging sword. As Erik passed a lantern, it took a crack at his ankles, and he swiftly swiped at it with Gram.

The lantern wailed like an injured animal, and to their astonishment, where there had been one lantern, there were now two.

It had multiplied.

These ran at Erik, and he instinctively swiped at them again.

He hit both, and they cried out before multiplying again. But this time, each produced two. What had begun as one lantern was now six.

"Don't hit them!" Artie and Kay yelled together, but Erik's mind was so clouded by the magical effects of the Shrine that he didn't hear them and found it impossible to stop whacking lanterns.

In all the confusion, Lance shot three of Erik's lanterns, and each of these produced four, which made eighteen!

"Stop!" Artie and Kay yelled, realizing what was happening even while the other knights seemed blind to the problem they were creating. Kay thought that maybe the Shrine of Horrors should have been renamed the Shrine of Turning Otherwise Smart Folks into Idiots. Then the bell rang three times.

Artie, Kay, and Thumb turned away from the chaos of Erik and Lance only to find *all* of the lanterns walking toward them!

"Forget them! Get Kusanagi!" Thumb reiterated at the top of his lungs, though it sounded like he was a mile away.

Artie and Kay followed Thumb toward the sword. Artie glanced over his shoulder and saw his friends fighting at least a hundred lanterns now. They were piling up and surrounding the knights' legs, almost reaching their waists. The knights didn't look to be in danger—the lanterns were nuisances, not menaces—but they definitely had their hands full. "Stop!" Artie shouted again. But it was no use.

Kay tugged on Artie's arm. He couldn't hear her at all now, but it looked like she was saying, "We're not getting closer!"

She was right. They'd gone at least fifty feet since walking into this strange corner of the Otherworld, but they hadn't gained on the sword at all.

They started to sprint. They ran twenty, fifty, a hundred feet, but still the sword stayed the same distance away.

Kay tugged Artie's arm again and mouthed, "This! Sucks!"

As Artie agreed with a nod, they each heard a whisper in their ears. The sound effortlessly cut through the muffled silence, which was really creepy.

Making it even creepier was that it was a young girl's voice speaking Japanese.

Artie, Kay, and Thumb spun in circles, but nothing was there—just the trees, the sword in the distance, and the other knights dealing with the lanterns.

Then the girl's voice came again, and this time they

each felt her breath drift across their ears!

When the three of them turned back to the sword, they were greeted by something they weren't prepared for at all.

It was about six feet tall and a foot around and it was covered, from top to bottom, in long, black, silky hair. It didn't appear to have arms or legs. In the center of its body, where a belly button might have been, was a single eye the size of a saucer, which was closed.

Artie took a step forward, and the hair thing opened its eye.

A shrill wail pierced the air, as if the eye, which was completely green, was screaming. Without dropping their weapons, Artie, Kay, and Thumb covered their ears and writhed in agony. Artie could barely think over the noise, but he had to do something. So he jabbed at the thing's screaming eye with the end of his spear.

The noise stopped and the thing fell to the ground in a heap of black hair, as if the body underneath had disappeared.

Artie and Kay looked at each other in confusion. Thumb was saying something, but it was like his voice had been stolen.

Then their hearts sank as the hair creature rose back up—and this time, like the lanterns, there were two of them.

Thankfully they weren't screaming. Not yet, anyway. The sword was right there, such a short distance away! But these hair monsters were proving to be pretty good guards. Thumb tapped Artie's foot and made motions like Artie should make a run for Kusanagi even if the things screamed, just so they could get out of there.

Artie gave him a curt nod and stepped forward.

The things opened their eyes, and this time it was much, much worse. Worse than the Mont-Saint-Michel giant, Morgaine's tornadoes, the evil boar, Lavery's saber-toothed tigers, Mordred, the old bully Frankie Finkelstein, and an angry dragon put together. It made Kay want to run home and drown herself in Mountain Dew. It made Thumb want to stop helping everyone and live out the rest of his days alone in a woodland hut. It made Artie think that being noble was stupid and that it didn't matter if Qwon didn't make it.

Seconds passed as they struggled with this excruciating spell. Artie glanced at Thumb. And the strange thing was, Thumb didn't seem to be affected anymore.

Thumb was spinning his finger through the air and mouthing some words, but Artie couldn't understand.

He might have stood there forever holding his ears against the awful wail had the child's voice not cut through the cacophony, this time speaking English with a thick accent. What it said was, "Turn away."

It took a lot of effort, but Artie forced his feet to move. Slowly, he managed to get the screaming Japanese hair monsters at his back, and as soon as his body was squarely turned to them, the wailing stopped.

Not only that, but he could hear too, and Thumb was yelling, "Turn away, turn away!"

A surge of relief washed over Artie. Without moving his head he said, "I hear you, Tom. I'm all right. Let's help Kay."

Artie sidled to his sister, who was still frozen in agony. He took Kay by the shoulders and pushed hard, forcing her around.

Artie said, "You okay?"

"Wow. Yeah. You?" Kay said.

"Yep."

"Man, I never thought monsters could be so *weird*," Kay commented.

"Looks like the others have figured out how to deal with their adversaries too," Tom added.

Instead of fighting the lanterns, Lance and Erik were slowly moving away from them. There were several hundred of the things by now, but without anyone attacking, they were losing interest.

Fortunately Lance and Erik didn't seem to have suffered

the effects of the fear scream at all.

"Now that we know the trick, I guess we can get Kusanagi," Artie said.

"Aye, lad," Thumb said.

Very slowly they backed around the hair monsters, which didn't move or spin to face the knights, even after they were past them. The screams didn't return, and Artie figured that it was the eye that they'd had to turn away from rather than the monster itself.

After a few more steps, the tip of Artie's spear knocked against Kusanagi. The impact made the same bell-ringing sound they'd heard when the lanterns woke up.

"All right, lass, cut it down," Thumb said.

Kay swiped Cleomede through the air. The rope cut, the sword fell, and Artie deftly caught it by the handle with his right hand.

They had it!

But then one of Lance's arrows split the air with a hiss and hit something behind them. Lance and Erik took off in their direction with wild expressions as Lance nocked a handful of arrows.

The hair monsters spun in place, their eyes thankfully closed, and executed deep and respectful bows. Then they collapsed.

A guttural rumble shook the air behind Artie and Kay.

Something was there. Something new.

Thumb yelled, "Run!"

Three more arrows flew through the air as Artie, Kay, and Thumb took off. As they ran, Artie looked over his shoulder and caught sight of what had materialized behind them.

It looked like a cross between an ogre and a samurai warrior. It had fire-engine-red skin, large yellow eyes, and two long white teeth like a walrus's. A ponytail of thick black hair was pulled tight on the top of its head. It was hunkered down and covered in panels of bamboo armor. Its fingernails were filthy. Each foot had a single toe with a very long claw.

Resting across its thighs was a long pole with a nasty-looking sword-length blade at one end. As it sneered at Artie the creature hoisted its weapon and brought the blunt end hard into the ground. The earth shook as the creature yelled, "Kusanagi!"

Three more of Lance's arrows flew over the Kingfishers' heads, but the guardian moved with lightning quickness—and caught the arrows. It crushed them and threw their remnants at its feet. Then it took a step, and the ground quaked again as if the power of the mountains coursed through its body.

"Oh, sugar," Kay said.

Artie stopped, spun, and let Rhongomyniad fly. The spear was fast and true, but its target was faster. The warrior sidestepped and lowered its shoulder while thrusting its hand into the air, catching the spear just like it had the arrows.

Then it grunted with satisfaction and smiled at Artie.

Artie smiled back as he commanded, "Rhongomyniad!"

The spear's shaft quickly withdrew from the warrior's grip and gave it a handful of splinters. Artie caught his weapon as the earth started to shake again.

"Let's *go*, Artie!" Kay pleaded.

Artie spun toward Lance and Erik, who were readying themselves for anything. Thankfully, this time Artie, Kay, and Thumb were able to cover ground quickly and weren't stuck on some horror-movie treadmill.

After several paces Artie glanced over his shoulder just in time to see the blade of the warrior's weapon coming down right for him! Artie leaped sideways and the blade missed, slicing across the ground with a silvery hiss. The warrior tried to grab Kusanagi, but Artie flicked it with his wrist—it was a remarkably light and well-balanced sword—and effortlessly took off one of the creature's fingers.

They had to get out of there. Artie slipped Kusanagi under his belt, pulled the pommel stone from his pocket, and said, *"Lunae lumen,"* intending to swallow his knights in a moongate, transporting them safely back to the court-in-exile.

But nothing happened.

"It won't work inside the Shrine of Horrors!" Thumb exclaimed as the trio came to a halt next to Lance and Erik. The archer let another arrow fly, but the warrior waved its pole arm defensively and knocked the arrow down.

"Through the crossover, then!" Artie ordered.

But the way was blocked by a wall of cute but annoying living lanterns.

As they paused, the warrior bounded forward and grabbed Kay by her ponytail, snatching her into the air.

"Lance, help Erik clear that exit!" Artie ordered.

"But Kay—"

"Do it!" Artie barked. Lance reluctantly turned and headed into the lanterns. Artie glowered at the frightening warrior, Thumb at his side, and commanded, "Let go of my sister!"

Artie planted a foot and threw Rhongomyniad as hard as he could, aiming well wide of his target. The spear disappeared into the surrounding trees, and the warrior gave Artie a look that said, "That's the best you've got?"

Artie called, "Rhongomyniad!" and the spear immediately boomeranged back, striking the warrior hard in the shoulder blade. With a look of shock and disgust, it reached over its body to pull the spear out, but Artie steeled himself and said fiercely, "Rhongomyniad! Come!"

The magical spear jerked forward, and the warrior made a loud, incredulous snort as the spear passed through its chest. Once free, Rhongomyniad flew to Artie and landed bloodily in his hand.

Kay had had enough. Just as the warrior brandished its pole arm to cut Kay in two, she swung Cleomede and sliced at her ponytail—which hadn't been cut since she was seven—and the warrior's blade whisked past the crown of her head as she dropped to the ground.

Artie couldn't believe it. Kay had cut her hair!

"Let's *go!*" she repeated as she passed Artie and Thumb and headed toward the mess of lanterns covering the exit.

When they reached the edge of the pile of lights, Lance emerged and said, "We can't find the crossover!"

"What should we do, Tom?" Artie asked as he looked back at the guardian of Kusanagi. It hadn't moved, but its hands were palm down and it was growling some words in Japanese.

"Oh no," said Thumb.

Rising from the ground around the warrior's feet were at least a dozen hair monsters. They didn't waste any time. The first screamer opened its green eye, and the noise came loud and furious. The knights covered their ears. Artie turned his back to the monsters, thinking it would bring him silence again, but it didn't. If anything, it made the noise worse.

But just as they felt ready to surrender, something shot out of the lanterns and flew through the air.

The *kitsune*!

The golden fox landed on top of a screamer, and the thing collapsed. It landed on another and another and another. The knights watched, still covering their ears in agony, as the cat-sized fox fearlessly took out every hair monster. The warrior tried to catch it but couldn't. The fox was graceful and blindingly fast.

"Over here!" Erik exclaimed. "The crossover!"

Reluctantly turning their backs on their diminutive hero, the knights waded through the lanterns and went through the portal, leaving the Shrine of Horrors and its horrible cacophony once and for all.

The quiet sounds of the woods were like a revelation.

Artie held the monocle to his eye, hoping the *kitsune* would jump out behind them, give them a wink, and trot off into the woods. But it never did.

"I guess we're not going to be able to save the little guy, huh?" Artie said, lowering the lens.

"They are all spirits of the Shrine," comforted Thumb,

who had returned to his miniature size. "I'm sure the *kitsune* will be fine. Probably not the first time it's had to tangle with those foul creatures."

"Fair enough," Artie said as he held up Kusanagi. "We got what we came for and I don't want to spend another second here. Let's get back to the court." Artie slipped Kusanagi under his belt and pulled the pommel from his pocket. He took a deep breath and said, "*Lunae lumen.*"

The pommel breathed to life, a moongate opened, and the knights stepped into the court-in-exile.

Immediately Bercilak came clanking in their direction waving the iPad. "Sire, sire! I believe you have a message!" he said a little breathlessly.

"What is it, Bercy?" Artie asked.

Bercilak clomped to a stop and handed Artie the tablet. "I've no idea, sire. I can't operate it. I tried doing that swipe trick you do to turn it on, but I don't think it likes my gloves."

Artie passed his spear to Kay and turned on the iPad.

Two alerts popped up. While they were off getting Kusanagi, Bors and then Merlin had sent them messages. Artie read them aloud. Bors's was first:

URGENT: Escaped from Castel, currently crossing swamp to rendezvous. Terrain is more challenging than expected. Morgaine giving chase as presumed. Have spotted two scouts, scentlocked both. Recommend meeting at rendezvous tomorrow at dawn. It is a long crescent-shaped beach and can't be missed. See you in the morning.

TTYS,
B. le F.

PS: Q excited to see friends.
PPS: Have interesting news re Mordred.

The follow-up message was from Merlin:

Sire, received Bors's message. I trust that mission for Kusanagi was successful. I have tried to reach Kynder to tell him of change in plan, but the network at the Library is still down. Recommend that you send for him only after you've reached Avalon. I will see you at the beach.

M.

Artie clicked off the iPad. "Okay. I guess we have a little time to rest."

"And try to get in touch with Kynder," Kay added.

"That too," Artie agreed.

"How's Bedevere holding up, Bercy?" Lance asked.

"The Black Knight is fine and happy to be resting in his old bed," Bercilak said. "His kitty is keeping him company. I think if you let him, he would come with you tomorrow, but I advise against it. His wound is still tender."

Artie nodded. Then he clapped his hands and said, "Naps for everybody. That's an order. Tomorrow, before dawn, we make tracks for Fenland."

𝕯red had spent the better part of the day beating on the wooden door of his dark cell, cursing the hoary guards who'd dragged him there and the witch-mother who'd cast him away. For hours, the jailers got a kick out of taunting him and calling him names. It was amazing how fast they'd turned on him. The day before he was the prince of the realm, but today he was little more than a bug.

Eventually they left, offering nothing to eat and only a wooden cup half full of rank-smelling sewer water.

What goes around comes around, Dred thought, remembering how Qwon had been served the same swill at the beginning of her captivity.

He paced. He wanted to get out and help Qwon. He wanted to stop his mother. He even wanted to help the fairy

Shallot, and he definitely wanted to thank the other one, Bors.

But more than anything, he wanted to meet his brother.

Dred kicked the cup in frustration and barked, "Where are you, Artie Kingfisher?"

"Did you say 'Artie Kingfisher'?"

Dred jumped. The unexpected voice had come from down the hall, and it had a strange accent.

One he recognized.

Dred went to the small, barred opening in his door and asked, "You're the one from—what's it called—Sweden?"

"Yes."

"But aren't you in a dragon's bubble?" Nothing, including sound, got in or out of a dragon's bubble.

"I was. But as soon as these blackouts started, it weakened and eventually it went away. Now I'm hog-tied with some pretty tough chains, and I can't move because there's one spike on my throat, one on the back of my neck, and another in between my legs."

"Oh," Dred said dejectedly.

"But what did you say about Artie Kingfisher?"

Dred paused. Should he tell this wild man from the other side?

Sure. Why not.

"He's my brother."

Dred was about to explain everything, but before he

could, a loud *clang* shook the cellblock, accompanied by a string of Swedish curse words. Then came the sound of a door being ripped off its hinges. Before he knew it, the man was standing outside Dred's cell, shining a flashlight through the small square of iron bars. Dred stepped into the light and was momentarily blinded. "Yep, you're Artie Kingfisher's brother," the man said. The light went out. "I suggest you stand away from the door."

Dred scrambled to the side. Just as he got himself in place, the door flew into the tiny room, the man entering behind it.

He shone the light at Dred's face again and said, "My name's Sami, and I've come to rescue you."

"I'll say. What happened to those spikes you just told me about?"

"Lied. Sorry."

"Why are you breaking me out?"

"An invisible guy named Bors came through here last night and told me to wait for Artie's brother," the man said. "One way or another he said you'd end up down here, and that you'd look just like Artie. He was right on both counts."

"So you've met my brother?"

"I have."

"What's he like?"

"Smart. Tricky. Although I sort of wish I hadn't met him. Then I'd be back home, feasting on roast venison, instead of standing here, wherever this is."

"But if you hadn't followed him, I would have captured him. *She* would have captured him. So you saved him."

"And now I've saved you. And you're going to return the favor. Both of you."

"How?"

"This Bors fellow said you'd be able to take me to Artie, and that Artie could get me back home. He said Artie is very powerful. He said Artie is a king."

Dred stepped forward. "He's not a king yet, but we can help him become one."

Sami held out his arm. "Lead the way, uh . . ."

"Dred."

"Pleasure to meet you, Dred. Sorry if I busted you up the other day."

Dred smiled. "Don't worry. Come on."

Dred took the flashlight and trotted out of the cell. As they wound their way up a flight of narrow, curving stairs, they heard the sound of returning guards. Sami put a hand on Dred's shoulder and squeezed past him.

Three guards appeared in single file. The two in the front had maces, and the one in the back carried a small pistol, which was a weapon not usually used in Castel Deorc Wæters.

Sami wasted no time dispatching these men. He broke the maces and ignored the gunman, who was in no position

to shoot anyway since he was in the back. In a matter of seconds the soldiers were lying in a dilapidated, moaning heap.

Sami was no joke and also a little scary.

"Nice work," Dred said, impressed.

"Thanks. Where to now?"

Dred paused. "We need to get the swords before we go
to Artie. They were in my mother's room, but I don't think
she'd risk leaving them out in the open."

"So she hid them," Sami suggested.

"Yes." Dred thought for a few moments, then snapped
his fingers. "If she wants to hide them from me too, then I
think I know where she put them." He raced off, and they
threaded their way through the Castel, heading toward the
passageway that led to Morgaine's lab.

As they arrived at the secret door, it dawned on Dred
that, very soon, he'd be leaving Castel Deorc Wæters—the
place in which he'd spent his whole life—for good. Softly
he said, "Well, this is it." Dred moved the stone in the wall,
and the hidden door grated open. "Come on."

As Dred led them through the earthen tunnel, Sami
inspected the ground. "Someone was just in here—look."
He paused and pointed at the ground.

"I don't see anything," Dred said, looking at where Sami
indicated.

"There. See that indentation in the dirt? It's very faint."

"Oh, yeah," Dred lied, still unable to make it out. He

continued down the hall, and when they reached the door to the lab he saw that it had been left ajar. He remembered how careful he'd been to close it, so he knew that Sami was right. Morgaine had been there not long before.

"This way," Dred said, pushing the door open and stepping into the lab.

They walked in silence past all the big glass tubes containing the failed attempts at re-creating King Arthur. Dred tried to ignore these biological abominations as he made his way to the back.

"What is this place?" Sami asked in a stupefied tone.

"This is where I was born," Dred said with a mouthful of venom. "It's where Artie was born too."

"I don't understand."

"Morgaine made us. She made us so Artie could retrieve Excalibur. She thought that with the sword she could finally kill Merlin. If the wizard dies, then there is no one alive in the Otherworld—or in your world—who could challenge her."

"Merlin?" Sami breathed. "Really?"

"Really." Dred stared into Artie's crib. There was a canvas bundle lying diagonally across the mattress. "Here they are."

Dred yanked the fabric, and out tumbled three weapons: Excalibur, The Anguish, and the Peace Sword.

He stuck Excalibur through his belt, sheathed the Peace

Sword, and handed The Anguish to Sami. "Think you can handle that?"

Sami turned the strange weapon in his hand, looking at it reverently. "Definitely," he said.

"Good. Now we need your tracking skills to follow Morgaine and her army. You have any problem riding a bear?"

Sami winked. "Not at all."

ON THE ORIGINS OF A CERTAIN WIZARD

𝕶𝖞𝖓𝖉𝖊𝖗 𝖘𝖙𝖆𝖗𝖊𝖉 𝖎𝖓𝖙𝖔 𝖘𝖕𝖆𝖈𝖊 𝖎𝖓 utter disbelief.

A dusty, insignificant-looking book with tiny print was laid open before him. Next to this was a giant tome full of yellowing handwritten sheets. Both contained Otherworld genealogical information, and both were open to pages that concerned one Myrddin Emrys, aka Merlinus Ambrosious, aka Merlin.

He was born in Wales, in the town of Carmarthen, in an uncertain year in the fifth century CE.

His mother was named Adhan.

His father didn't have a name.

That was because Merlin's daddy was an incubus. A demon.

Numinae sat across from Kynder. Over the past day he had regained some of his true form. He was much, much taller, even taller than Kynder now. His skin was completely green, and had patches of moss growing on it here and there. When closed, his mouth had a tendency to disappear, which freaked Kynder out a little. But this was nothing next to his eyes, which had reverted to the way they were when Artie first saw the lord of Sylvan: black where the whites should have been, with shocking green irises and snow-white pupils.

"What does this mean? That Merlin . . . *is a bad guy*?"

"Unknown, but he has been mad—crazy—in the past, and he could be again."

"A crazy guy with a ton of magical power. Great," Kynder said, sounding a lot like Kay.

"My guess is that, at minimum, he has not been honest about his motivations for everything that he has asked of you and your children."

"So the worlds don't need to be rejoined?"

"No, they do," Numinae said authoritatively, which gave Kynder a little comfort. "I just think that's not Merlin's ultimate goal. Rejoining the worlds—perhaps even pursuing the Seven Swords—for him these are things that serve a different purpose."

Kynder leaned back in his chair. Its creaks echoed

throughout the reading room. Then it hit him. "This is about Morgaine, isn't it?"

Numinae made a low humming sound. "Yes. She wants the worlds to stay separated. Much of her power would fritter away if they were rejoined."

Kynder shook his head. "No, what I mean is that for Merlin this is *only* about Morgaine."

Numinae cracked his neck, which sounded like a giant branch snapping in two. "Believe me, Kynder, I just don't know."

Kynder stood. "But you knew about this incubus thing, Numinae! Why didn't you just tell me?"

Numinae calmly said, "You wouldn't have believed me and I wasn't able to manipulate you like Merlin did. Nor would I have wanted to. I am here to help you and your children, not to tell you what to do."

Kynder put his hands on the table and leaned forward. "Will sangrealite provide my world with clean energy? Was that part true?" he asked, driving directly to the point that had pushed him willingly into Merlin's arms to begin with.

Numinae nodded. "It will."

Kynder let out a sigh of relief. "At least he didn't lie about that."

"He is not all bad, Kynder. He has helped you and the children. He saved Kay and Artie, as you told me, and he trusted you to raise the new Arthur Pendragon." Numinae paused before adding, "Even the devil was a servant of God."

"Ha! So the story goes. But Merlin is no angel, fallen or otherwise."

"None of us are."

Kynder fell back into his chair. "I have to talk to Arthur and warn him and Kay about what Merlin is, and what we think his motivations are. At this point they must be on their way to the rendezvous in Fenland. Can you get me there?"

"Of course. I can summon Tiberius and you can travel very quickly. But it strikes me as risky. Morgaine could be waiting." He paused before adding, "Merlin could be there too."

"I don't care," Kynder said, frowning. "Arthur and Kay have been risking their necks for more than a month. Besides, if Merlin *is* there and no one else has shown up yet, I think I'd like to have a few words with him."

"I should think you might. But don't be too hasty. Wizards need to be handled carefully. They can be quite . . . rash."

"Point taken. Now I have to get to Fenland."

"No, my friend. *We* have to get to Fenland."

"Great," Kynder said emphatically.

"Go and get ready," Numinae rumbled. He stood and seemed to grow a foot or more right in front of Kynder's eyes. Then Numinae shook his arm, and it turned into a giant wooden maul. "Tiberius has been summoned. We'll leave as soon as he arrives."

𝕶𝔶𝔫𝔡𝔢𝔯'𝔰 𝔣𝔦𝔯𝔰𝔱 𝔡𝔯𝔞𝔤𝔬𝔫 𝔯𝔦𝔡𝔢 𝔴𝔞𝔰 a doozy. Tiberius, whose neck had been outfitted with a double-seated leather saddle, had pulled out all the stops. He whisked them over Sylvan and across the Otherworld Sea, with clouds, sky, and stars streaking by at the speed of sound.

They arrived at a point high over Fenland several hours before dawn, four days before the new moon. Above them was the black firmament, a cosmic sieve perforated with a million points of light; below was a soft carpet of gray clouds. In the east a large storm pulsated with rainbows of lightning.

The dragon, which had not yet spoken during their trip, said calmly, "Hmmph. That tempest moves fast thisaway, and a fog rides swiftly from the other direction on a westerly front. They'll be meet'n at the rendezvous by sunup."

"Can your sight penetrate the clouds, my friend?" Numinae asked.

"Yeah, can you see Arthur?" Kynder wondered.

Tiberius leaned forward and strained his eyes on the shrouded land below. "Hmmph. They are not here. None are. All is cold and damp."

"Well, I'm glad we beat them," Kynder said.

"When do you think Fallown will arrive?" Numinae asked Tiberius. The Leagonese dragon had also been summoned to the rendezvous, just in case they needed help.

"In the last dark before the dawn," Tiberius said.

"Good," Numinae said, and patted his dragon's neck. "There's a rock in the sea a mile from the shore. You can land there. When someone shows up, we'll head in."

"Hmmph," Tiberius grumbled. "Hold'n tight."

With no other warning, he folded his wings and dropped headfirst to the earth, piercing the thick blanket of clouds. They emerged more than a minute later only a few hundred feet above the sea. Tiberius opened his wings and gently glided to a stop over a black rock.

Fenland was in the distance, a dark line rising from the water.

They waited in silence. Water lapped pleasantly at their rocky perch. Kynder closed his eyes, and Numinae and

Tiberius only spoke sparingly. After a few hours a great bank of fog overtook them. Fenland disappeared as visibility dropped to only a few dozen feet. Numinae pulled a lamp from a saddlebag and turned it on. Its green light gave the fog a sickly hue.

The sea became completely calm. Sounds vanished.

"This sure is a weird fog," Kynder observed.

Tiberius shifted his weight from one leg to the other and let out a long "Hmmmmph."

"It is," Numinae said, hastily extinguishing the lamp. "We're not alone."

A chill ran down Kynder's back as it hit him: "Merlin's here."

"Yes," Numinae said in a fierce whisper. "He mustn't see me yet. I'm sorry, my friend."

And then Numinae moved out of the saddle and appeared to become one with Tiberius, melding into the green dragon's iridescent skin right before Kynder's eyes.

Before Kynder could say anything, an unseen hand grabbed him by the neck, yanking him from the saddle. Within seconds Kynder was being pulled through the air, his feet dragging along the water's surface. Tiberius vanished in the fog behind him as Kynder heard the dragon snap his wings and surge into the air.

Kynder was being hauled through the mist as if through

a maze. The wizard was trying to confuse the dragon, and it apparently worked, because before long Kynder neither heard nor saw any sign of Tiberius.

Which was unfortunate.

But what was more unfortunate was that Kynder was having a hard time breathing. The magical hand gripping him was literally choking the life from him.

Finally he came to a stop over a narrow white-sand beach. A black bluff rose sharply to his left, and to the right was a dune dotted with tall grass. Beyond this Kynder made out the tops of the trees that populated the vast swamp of Fenland.

The sea was at his back, and in front of him was Merlin, still holding Kynder by his neck with some spell.

The wizard was dressed in a black leather robe and had donned a simple linen cowl. Fog billowed from the bottom of his clothing, as if it were the source of the mist covering the sea. He pointed the owl-head of his cane directly at Kynder's chest.

He did not look happy.

"Where is the stone that I gave you?" the wizard demanded.

Kynder clutched at the wizard's invisible hand. He couldn't talk. He was getting light-headed.

"Pshaw!" the wizard spit. He brought the head of his cane down swiftly, breaking the enchantment that held

Kynder. A loud *crack* rang out over the beach as Kynder collapsed to the ground, a sickening *snap* coming from his right leg.

"My leg! You broke it!" Kynder wailed.

"Did I? So sorry," Merlin said insincerely.

"What happened to you?" Kynder asked, trying to stay still, afraid to move his leg at all.

"Nothing happened to me. This is who I am," Merlin said darkly.

"I see," Kynder said with a note of resignation. "Well, I gave the stone away."

"To whom?"

"Numinae."

Merlin made a throaty sound of disgust. "And what, pray tell, did that *thing* have to say about it?"

"He said it was a keeper stone, that it kept me from doing certain things—namely, looking into who *you* are. He said I didn't need it to be in the Otherworld, which is clearly the case. He said you were manipulating me."

"How . . . *revealing.*"

"And he said you were lying to Arthur."

The wizard blew out his cheeks. "I did nothing of the sort. I have been faithful to all of you. That's more than I can say of you, Kynder. You should have stayed at the Library. You should have kept the stone."

Kynder let out a quick breath. "So I could remain

ignorant of what really motivates you?"

Merlin waved his cane dismissively through the air. "Ignorance is safety, Kynder Kingfisher. As a father, I would expect you to know as much."

Kynder shook his head. "Man, you have a lot to learn."

"*I* have a lot to learn? From whom?"

Kynder's leg began to feel very warm. He tried to see if the bone had broken the skin, but because of the way his leg was bent under him, he couldn't tell. "Maybe from me," he said. "Maybe from Numinae. But definitely from Arthur. He's loyal. Noble. He *helped* you."

Merlin chuckled. "Ah, nobility. I was just speaking to Artie about that. It's true that Artie is noble. Nauseatingly so. Trust me, I know noble better than any living thing. Arthur the First was disgustingly noble. And don't get me started on his knights. Gawain, Perceval, Tristan—they were impossible. Please, save me the lecture."

Kynder felt like he was the one being lectured to but didn't bother to point that out. "And you told Artie you thought he was noble too? Just to manipulate him?"

"Of course. Flattery is an extremely effective motivator."

"He's a kid, Merlin."

"I don't care," Merlin barked. Kynder noticed that the overcast sky was beginning to lighten. Dawn was nearly upon them.

"Man, you're ruthless."

"Yes."

"And all you want is revenge on Morgaine, isn't that right?"

"Yes!" Merlin said. A powerful crack of thunder rolled over the hill from the direction of the swamp, and the clouds there began to let down a curtain of rain. Merlin cried, "That witch ruined my life. She *stole* it. She and her agents exiled me to the other side of the world. You try being imprisoned for a thousand years and see how you like it. She deserves nothing but death for what she did to me."

Kynder looked away. "Figures you'd be this way, since you're a . . ."

Merlin narrowed his eyes and asked, "A what? What do you think you know?"

Kynder didn't answer at first. He was preoccupied as his hand gently probed the jagged edge of a tibia jutting from his leg. Finally he said, "I know what your father was, Merlin Ambrosius."

Merlin recoiled. The fog obscuring his feet thinned, and he drifted to the ground. He leaned close to Kynder's face, eyes red with fury, tattoos writhing like snakes. He was terrifying.

"Don't speak of my father!" he boomed. And then, in a fierce whisper, "The boy cannot know."

"Of course he can't. He would never help you if he knew that you were a half demon, hell-bent on revenge over everything else."

Merlin spit an oyster of phlegm into the sand.

"But why Arthur? Why my son?"

"He is not your son! He is an experiment. And I couldn't escape without him."

"Oh my god," Kynder said heavily, realization dawning. "That's why she made him."

"Yes."

"Because only he could get Excalibur and free you, and she couldn't kill you *unless* you were free."

"Yes."

"And you knew this all along?"

"Of course! The witch and I are mortal enemies, but sometimes even enemies must pursue common goals so that one day they may meet."

"So all this is just to settle some stupid score?"

"Not stupid to me or her. And if it matters to you, she does want to keep the worlds separated. She doesn't care if your world destroys itself."

"But you don't either."

"No. Why would I? In truth, your world's atmosphere is already poisoned. It has passed the tipping point. It cannot be saved."

"But that's no reason not to try! And what about the Otherworld? Won't the Otherworld fall too, if our side falls first?"

"Eventually, yes."

"And you don't care about that either."

"No."

Kynder fought back a ball of acid rising from his stomach. "Why do you need Arthur now? Why can't you just kill Morgaine by yourself? A big wizard like you . . ."

Merlin gave Kynder a smart-aleck smile and said, "Because in spite of my feelings about him, Artie is powerful, so why *not* use him if it increases my chances of killing Morgaine? Why not stand against her with the one who wields Excalibur at my side?"

At the mention of Excalibur, Kynder was struck with a revelation. Now he understood why Excalibur wanted Merlin dead!

He also understood that Merlin could not know what he'd just gleaned. The secret was for Artie, and Artie alone.

Kynder forced this revelation from his mind, and tried to distract Merlin by asking, "Taking control of the Seven Swords is as important to you as gathering Artie and his knights. Isn't it?"

"More," Merlin said, sounding surprisingly honest. "Steel is stronger than flesh."

"What are you going to tell Arthur when he gets here?" Kynder asked.

Merlin smiled. "What are *you* going to tell him, Kynder?"

"The truth. That he's being used. That you're disingenuous at best."

Merlin made a *tut-tut* sound and shook his head disapprovingly. "Arthur—yours and the one that came before—is nothing but a vessel. Both were created to be used. Both only exist for purposes at hand. You won't tell him anything. Least of all the truth."

"The heck I won't," Kynder said.

Merlin stroked his chin and said with a heavy air of conceit, "Let's see. Shall it be death or amnesia for you, dear Kynder?"

Kynder didn't give him the pleasure of a response.

"I certainly don't need you anymore," Merlin continued. "You were here to raise Artie Kingfisher, and you did."

Merlin rose into the air and held his cane in both hands across his body. White wings of fog unfolded from behind him as his power grew, his staff beginning to glow brightly.

Kynder had failed his children, and he felt like a total idiot for it.

"I like you, Kynder, in spite of your defiance," Merlin continued. He nodded, as if to himself. "Yes. I think it shall be amnesia, perhaps preceded by a rather long coma. To keep you from meddling."

Kynder couldn't move. His leg was hot now. This was it. Noiselessly, the light from Merlin's cane shot at Kynder's head.

But then, as if from nowhere, Tiberius darted between them. The wizard howled, and for Kynder, everything went black.

IN WHICH THE RENDEZVOUS COMMENCES

𝕬𝖗𝖙𝖎𝖊 𝖆𝖓𝖉 𝖍𝖎𝖘 𝖐𝖓𝖎𝖌𝖍𝖙𝖘 𝖌𝖆𝖙𝖊𝖉 to Fenland just as Merlin grabbed Kynder off Tiberius's neck. None of them knew that Kynder was even there, or that Merlin had snatched him, or that Kynder was in deep doo-doo.

"Man, why can't these *lunae lumen*s ever put us exactly where we want to go?" Erik complained as he stared at his feet.

They were ankle deep in black muck that made crude sucking sounds as they struggled to get onto firmer ground. The sky was just beginning to brighten, though it wasn't going to brighten much because it was pretty obvious that a storm was coming.

Which made Artie's and Kay's hearts sink a little, since storms usually meant Morgaine.

"Aw, this is nothing, dudes," Lance said. "You should see Iraq in August. At least it's not a hundred and twenty degrees in the shade!"

Artie stepped onto a pile of rocks, Kay and Thumb joining him, while the other knights gathered at the opposite side of the mud pit.

"Any idea where we are, Tom?" Artie asked.

"Well, definitely Fenland. And we're near the sea. I can sm—"

Lance held up his fist and cocked his ear to the swamp.

"What is it, lad?" Thumb whispered.

Instead of speaking, Lance twirled a finger through the air and pointed at the thick tangle of bushes behind them. Then he quietly nocked an arrow as Erik drew next to him. Artie and Kay stood shoulder to shoulder, and Thumb knelt, the Welsh *wakizashi* fast across his body.

They waited. Artie didn't say anything, but he had an overwhelming feeling that Excalibur was nearby. Could Bors have managed to retrieve his sword?

Finally they heard footsteps. Breathing. The muffled sound of a girl clearing her throat.

Then the smell of the sea left Artie's nostrils. No, not just the sea—*all* smells had been sucked into a void. It was a little disorienting but it didn't really affect Artie so much. Unbeknownst to him, Excalibur's scabbard protected him from the fairy scentlock.

But not the other knights. Their faces went blank and they dropped their weapons to their sides.

Several tense moments passed before the grass parted, revealing two of the strangest-looking people Artie had ever seen. Both were incredibly thin, and the proportions of their long-limbed bodies were practically alien. Their pulled-back hair was pink with black streaks. Both had bright blue eyes, but the boy's were ridiculously blue. The girl was so beautiful Artie had a hard time raising his spear to her.

But he didn't have to because they didn't attack.

They were the fairies, Shallot and Bors le Fey.

Artie peered past them. Standing in the grass was Qwon Onakea, who had a couple of giant wads of cotton stuck in her nostrils.

"Qwon!" Artie yelled.

"Artie!"

Artie dropped his spear and Qwon dropped some kind of mace, and before either of them knew it, they were locked in a really big hug.

Artie had never felt so good.

And neither had Qwon.

"I'm sorry I couldn't save you," Artie whispered directly in Qwon's ear.

"Aw, don't sweat it. I wouldn't have believed any of this stuff if you had." Then she grabbed Artie by the shoulders and pushed him away and asked, "Are you okay?"

The fairies stepped forward, their faces twisted by curiosity. "You *do* look just like the Fenlandian," Shallot marveled quietly. Bors reached out and touched her arm as if to say she shouldn't bring it up.

"Huh?" Artie asked. Shallot *was* beautiful, but her teeth, which were jagged and pointy, were just nasty.

"I told you," Qwon said.

"What's she talking about?" Artie asked.

"It's a long story, Artie," Qwon said.

The girl fairy pointed one of her weapons at his chest and said, "So you're the king?"

Artie smiled and said, "Yep. And you must be Shallot le Fey."

"I am. But I'm a bred warrior. You look like a . . . a . . ."

Qwon smiled proudly at Artie and said, "Yeah, he's a nerd all right. Or was, anyway, until he beat up Frankie Finkelstein on the first day of school."

Shallot rolled her eyes. Artie bumped Qwon's shoulder and said, "Thanks, Q. Shallot, are you guys freezing my knights?"

Bors stepped forward with an apologetic look. As if on cue, the others started to come back around.

Qwon pulled the cotton from her nose and said, "They call it a scentlock. His is odorless, and Shallot's smells like the awesomest bouquet of flowers ever."

Artie raised his eyebrows. "Cool. You must be Bors,

then." The fairy nodded, and then suddenly knelt before him.

Shallot looked away slightly and said, "He's nicer than me."

"Bors is a mute," Qwon said. "And we wouldn't be here without him."

Artie bowed to Bors. "Stand up, dude. I may be king of the Otherworld, but I can't thank you enough for bringing my friend back."

Bors stood and nodded deeply to Artie. Artie nodded back. He already liked Bors.

Kay, free from the scentlock, ignored the fairies and ran to Qwon, yelling, "Q!" The girls gave each other a big hug.

"What happened to your hair, Kay?" Qwon gasped.

"Oh, I cut it off," Kay said flippantly. "This Japanese guy made me do it."

"Hey, Qwon," said Erik from across the mud pit.

"Wait, *Erik*?" Qwon squeaked.

"Yeah," he said proudly, standing up extra straight and showing off Gram a little.

A million questions ran through Qwon's mind.

Thumb pulled up next to Artie and nodded at the fairies. "Qwon, this is Tom Thumb," Artie said.

"*Tom Thumb?*" Qwon asked dubiously.

"That's right, lass," Thumb said.

"Okay, if you say so," Qwon said slowly.

"I almost forgot—I have something for you, Qwon!" Artie reached into his belt and pulled out the ancient Japanese katana.

At first Qwon didn't understand what she was looking at. But then everything her grandfather Tetsuo had taught her about swords and her heritage and Japanese folklore washed over her. She glanced back and forth between Artie and the weapon and finally asked, "Artie, is that . . . *Kusanagi?*"

Artie nodded and Kay said, "Sure is, Q."

She reached for it and began to ask, "But how did you . . . ?"

Artie said, "That's a long story too. I'll tell it to you after you tell me yours." He flipped the sword around and presented it hilt first to its rightful owner, Qwon Onakea.

She held her hand around the hilt before gripping it. The sliver of air between hand and sword tingled with electricity.

Then she grabbed it.

Qwon's eyes widened and her mouth broke into a large smile. Her free hand automatically joined the one holding the sword. Kusanagi was doing its thing, just like Excalibur had for Artie and Gram had for Erik. Whole histories coursed through Qwon's mind, and her bones and muscles twitched with the sudden knowledge of sword mastery.

She was officially a kick-butt swordswoman.

"You guys all right?" Lance called from the other side of the mud pit, breaking everyone's reverie a little.

"Yep, we're fine," Kay said. "Qwon and Kusanagi just met, so they're having a moment."

"Cool," Lance said.

Artie said, "Lance, this is Qwon, Shallot, and Bors." They exchanged greetings and then Artie said, "So now that we're all here, do you think it's safe to go to Castel Deorc Wæters and grab the remaining Seven Swords?"

Bors nodded.

"Wonderful. Ready, guys?" Artie asked. Now that he'd found Qwon, he was looking forward to getting out of there. Being on Fenland gave him the willies.

But before anyone could answer, a loud noise echoed through the swamp.

"What was that?" Kay asked.

"It came from over there," Lance said, pointing toward the sea.

The party mucked through the swamp and started downhill. The ground became sandy, and eventually they reached a tall grass-covered dune. Lance led the way as they charged up it. Right before reaching its top, he dropped to his stomach and crawled to the edge. The other knights did the same. Lance grabbed his bow and got an arrow ready. In the day they had to regroup, Lance had trained with Orgulus—it was a pretty sweet sword—but his instincts still led him to his bow and arrows.

A few hundred feet away, in the middle of a crescent-shaped beach, were two people, one on the ground and another standing on what looked like a column of mist. The figure on the mist had its back to Artie and his friends.

"Artie, is that . . . your dad?" Erik asked.

"I think it is!" Artie said breathlessly. Kynder was sprawled on the ground and did not look good. "What's he doing here?"

"Who's that other guy?" Kay demanded.

"Oh, no," Thumb said. "That's Merlin," he said ashamedly.

"*What?*" Artie said, shocked.

"I recognize his cloak. He used to wear it a lot back when he was more . . . disturbed."

"What do you mean, 'disturbed'?" Artie asked. Kynder and Merlin were definitely arguing about something.

"Merlin is old, and has not always been well," Thumb tried to explain.

Kay couldn't believe it. "Isn't that, like, important info, Tommy?"

"I thought he was better. I swear it. These past few hundred years, he's been a different man."

Another crack of thunder rolled through the sky.

They watched in horror as Merlin leaned close to Kynder.

"Did that jerk just *spit* at Dad?" Kay said, starting to get up. Thumb grabbed her by the hand and pulled her hard back into the sand.

"Should I—should I shoot him, Art?" Lance asked as if he couldn't believe his own words.

"I—I don't know. Tom?"

"I don't know either, lad," Thumb said. "I can't believe this. . . ."

They watched as Merlin rose into the air and held his cane across his body. The mist gathered behind him in the shape of two great wings.

"Lance, I think you *should* shoot Merlin," Kay said hollowly.

"Yes," said Artie. "Shoot him, Lance."

"But that's Merlin! Our Merlin!" Lance exclaimed.

"Shoot him!" Artie ordered.

A bright light gathered in front of Merlin. Kynder glared up at the wizard in defiance.

Thumb steeled himself and said, "Do it now, archer! Don't miss!"

Lance stood. He emptied his head and then imagined the spine, the lungs, the heart of the wizard Merlin.

His fingers slipped from the arrow's fletching, and the bowstring jumped. Just as the arrow took off, Shallot pointed into the fog over the water and yelled, "Look!"

Darting out of the mist was their friend Tiberius, and

right behind him was the golden dragon, Fallown.

Tiberius snaked between the wizard and Kynder, and the bolt of energy shooting from the wizard's staff split and hit them both. Kynder flew back several feet and landed in a shower of sand. Tiberius crashed hard into the ground headfirst, while Fallown overshot the attack and rose back into the mist.

In the same instant, Lance's arrow hit Merlin squarely in the back. The wizard howled in pain and spun around. He scanned the dunes, searching—and quickly spotted those who had attacked him.

He did not look pleased.

𝕬𝖗𝖙𝖎𝖊 𝖆𝖓𝖉 𝕶𝖆𝖞 𝖘𝖎𝖒𝖚𝖑𝖙𝖆𝖓𝖊𝖔𝖚𝖘𝖑𝖞 𝖛𝖆𝖚𝖑𝖙𝖊𝖉 over the edge of the dune and ran toward Kynder, the rest of the knights on their heels. The siblings should have been thinking of Merlin and that awful look he gave them, but all they wanted was to know if their father was okay.

As they made their way across the beach, Merlin looked at the arrowhead that had entered through his back and was now sticking out of his chest. He put a hand around the shaft and pulled it out. A dark jet of blood shot from his chest before he healed himself.

Artie and Kay ignored this, passing Merlin and continuing headlong for Kynder. But Thumb found it impossible to ignore his old friend Merlin. When he reached the bloodied wizard, he skidded to a halt and yelled, "Why?"

Merlin sounded pretty unconvincing when he pleaded, "It's not how it looks! Let me explain!"

But there wouldn't be any time for that. The rain finally began to fall in heavy, drenching drops. The wind gusted. A web of lightning shattered the clouds.

Morgaine had arrived.

Merlin said nothing more and flew away from the knights toward the source of the storm, toward Lordess Morgaine. The knights and fairies, unsure what to do, waited in the middle of the beach as Artie and Kay sprinted past Tiberius, who was badly dazed and possibly wounded, and threw themselves into the sand next to Kynder. Dropping Cleomede, Kay vigorously shook Kynder's arm while Artie took his face in both hands. Kynder's huge, square eyeglasses from 1985 lay across his face at an angle.

"Artie, look!" Kay exclaimed. She stared at Kynder's leg, which was bent completely backward. Bones on both sides of the break stuck out. His shoe and sock had somehow come off, and his foot was the color of the gray sky overhead.

Artie screamed, "Dad! Can you hear me?"

Kynder's eyes fluttered and his lips moved, but there was no voice. Kay let go of his arm as Artie tried to wipe the rain from Kynder's glasses and put them back in place. He ripped off the scabbard and laid it across his dad's chest, but it didn't seem to have any effect.

"Is it working, Artie?" Kay asked desperately.

"I-I don't think so," Artie answered weakly.

"Why not?" Kay shouted.

"I don't know." Artie gazed up at his sister. "I don't know what to do, Kay!"

Kynder tried to speak again.

"What's that, Dad?" Artie asked, leaning close to his father's mouth. It was difficult to hear over the rain as it began to hiss across the beach.

A bare whisper passed Kynder's lips: "Ex . . . Ex . . ."

"Excalibur?" Artie asked. As he named his sword, he felt again that it was close, and that it wanted to be reunited with him as soon as possible. Kynder nodded ever so slightly. "What about it?" Artie asked.

"It . . . You . . . Mer . . ."

But it was too much; his injuries were too great. It wasn't just his leg. Getting zapped by Merlin was obviously no fun. Merlin's magic must have been why the scabbard wasn't working.

"I'm going to kill that wizard," Kay said seriously.

"All right, Dad, hang in there," Artie urged, ignoring Kay. "Let me get everyone and we'll *lunae lumen* back to Shadyside. We'll get you to a hospital, okay?"

Kynder smiled weakly. Thunder rumbled behind them. Kay looked back in the direction they'd come from and said, "Oh, this is just wonderful."

Artie looked too. The dune they had just been on was now dotted with a dozen soldiers like the ones they'd fought in Surmik. More were coming too. They were getting ready.

Only this time, they weren't just foot soldiers.

They were bear soldiers.

Kay looked at her brother. Her mismatched eyes were lit with purpose. "Art, take Dad and get out of here."

"No way! I would never leave you here!"

"Do it!"

"No!"

"Ugh!" Kay cried in frustration. She grabbed Cleomede and stood.

And just then Kynder's body began to shake. "Wait— what's happening?" Artie squealed.

They watched as Kynder's eyes closed and his body went limp. Artie shook Kynder's rain-spattered face. He pounded his chest. He pushed the healing scabbard hard into his father and yelled his name. Kay screamed his name too. But there was nothing. No breath. No life. Rain lashed their bodies and made their hands go cold.

"No! Dad! No!" Artie yelled desperately. He just wanted all this to end. He wanted to be home, to be safe, to never have heard of the Otherworld or been burdened with its problems. He wanted to be playing video games, and sneaking cans of Mountain Dew into the house, and even going to school. He didn't want to have to fight a witch or bear soldiers, or find his long-lost magical sword. He didn't want to be king of anything, least of all some whacked-out fairy world where anything could happen.

Where fathers could die.

Artie lifted his head, squinting his eyes against the rain and tears, when Kynder's body shuddered again and his breathing resumed. Artie was shocked, ecstatic, whooping with joy as Kynder looked Artie square in the eye and hissed, "Get to Avalon!" But then he lost consciousness again, his breath short and labored—but at least present.

Artie had a hard time dealing with the adrenaline shooting through his every fiber. This was all his fault. This was all his fault. Artie Kingfisher had almost killed the person he loved more than anyone in the world.

This was all his fault.

"Artie, what do we do?" Kay asked helplessly.

"Hmmmph," Tiberius said before Artie had a chance to answer. "Hmmmmmmmph!" the dragon said again more forcefully.

Tiberius didn't look so hot, either. When he'd careened into the ground, he'd been dragged across a sharp spur of rock jutting from the sand, and now golden blood flowed freely from a two-foot gash on his neck. "His life force fades," Tiberius murmured.

"Do something, Tiberius! Please!" Kay pleaded.

"Move, Kingfishers," the dragon crooned as he trained his rainbow eyes on Kynder. Black, crinkly smoke began to rise from Tiberius's nostrils. "Move!" he repeated.

And then someone they didn't expect appeared to step right out of the dragon's body. "Numinae?" Kay asked, her head spinning with confusion.

The forest lord stood at full height and said, "Arthur Pendragon, Tiberius can keep your father from dying, and preserve his mind before the wizard's amnesia spell can take root. Please move."

Artie wiped his arm across his eyes and pulled Kay toward Numinae. Tiberius struggled to lift his head and then breathed a jet of black smoke on Kynder's broken body. Quickly, the black stone unfolded around their dad in the shape of an elongated egg, encasing him like Han Solo in carbonite.

Tiberius let out a long and exhausted, "Hmmmmph," and then closed his eyes.

Numinae put a hand on his dragon's neck and whispered something in his ear. Then Tiberius shook as muffled snapping noises came from inside his body, and spots all over his brilliant green skin began to turn black. The spots grew and hardened, and in a matter of seconds Tiberius became like the black stone that he'd just breathed on Kynder, although not in the shape of an egg. Instead he'd been transformed into a statue.

"Is he preserved, too?" Kay asked.

"No," Numinae said. "Tiberius used his last bit of energy to save your father."

"You mean Tiberius is dead?" Kay asked in a wavering voice, tears streaming down her cheeks. Her stomach was a twitchy mess and she felt like she was going to vomit.

"Yes. But if you can get to Avalon," Numinae said sternly, "you may be able to revive Tiberius. You'll know better than me once you arrive at your castle."

"And Kynder?" Artie asked.

"Nothing can hurt him now. He is alive in there, but barely. Since we can no longer rely on the wizard, we will have to find the Grail to ensure that he will be fully revived," he said.

"The Grail? You mean the *Holy Grail*?" Artie asked.

Numinae nodded.

Kay wiped tears from her eyes and asked, "You sure we can get our dad back?"

"I swear it to you," Numinae said. "He is my friend. I will not rest until he is back in your arms, alive and well."

Artie rubbed his tear-filled eyes. Numinae placed a gnarled hand on his shoulder. "You have to be strong now, Arthur. You too, Kay."

"I know," Artie responded weakly. Kay said nothing.

They stood in silence for a few moments, and then they heard Thumb and Lance cry, "Take cover!" The knights were scrambling for a place to hide, but since they were on a beach, there wasn't one.

Which sucked.

Because the air was not just full of rain, but also a ton of arrows.

The projectiles arced up against the deluge and were about to make the turn back to earth, where they would kill or maim as many of Artie's knights as possible. The knights stood together and waved their weapons over their heads, hoping to deflect whatever arrows might fall down on them.

But then Merlin, who was closer to Morgaine's army amassing on the crest of the dune, raised the owl-headed cane and all the arrows quickly changed course, like a school of fish dodging a predator. He waved the cane again, and the shafts scattered in all directions, a few even turning back on the Fenlandian soldiers and striking them down.

"What is going *on*?" Kay exclaimed. "Is he on our side or not?"

"He's on *his* side," said Numinae as a bolt of lightning arced from the swamp into the sky, accompanied by a long, gut-wrenching wail.

"Was that . . . ?" Artie trailed off.

Numinae nodded. "Morgaine. She is here." Then he held up his maul-arm and said, "Arthur Pendragon, we must fight!"

"What? No! Let's just gate out of here!" Kay said, her eyes bloodshot and glassy. It was maybe the first time in her life she'd ever wanted to run from a fight.

"If you run now, it will mean leaving Kynder here," Numinae said.

Artie swallowed hard. "He's right. We couldn't carry him through the gate."

"What about that other dragon?" Kay asked. "He's strong."

"Fallown could pick him up, but a moongate is not big enough for a dragon," Numinae said. "The only way Kynder gets off this beach is if you open the gate to Avalon while you're standing around him."

"How the heck are we going to do that, Numinae? We've only got four of the swords!" Kay's voice shook with fear. "Artie—let's stick to the plan. Let's go down there and get the others, gate to the witch's castle, get the missing swords, gate back here, and then jet to Avalon with Kynder!"

"No," Artie said.

"What do you mean, 'No'?" Kay demanded, spittle flying from her lips.

"Excalibur isn't at the Castel anymore." Artie pointed

Flixith at the dune. More soldiers had lined up along it. "It's near. It's not with the witch, I can feel that much, but it is near."

Kay's shoulders slumped, while Artie's straightened. "Kay, I need you. We're going to fight for Kynder. Here. Now. We'll worry about Merlin later. We're going to fight, get my sword, and then find a way to get the other two. I need you to be strong, Kay. Be strong for Kynder, Kay Kingfisher!"

Kay ran a hand through her short hair and looked at her brother. "All right," she said. She whisked Cleomede through the air. "All right!" she repeated with conviction.

"That's my girl," Artie said.

"I will fight with you too, sire," Numinae said reverently.

"You better!" Artie said, slapping the Sylvanian lord on the back.

"As will the golden dragon," Numinae said.

At this point the other knights came running down the beach, their faces creased with confusion, fear, and excitement. As they arrived, Numinae pointed his face to the sky and made a low, lumbering sound. Fallown swooped from the clouds, picked him up, and threw him onto his back.

"That's Numinae, isn't it?" Lance asked in awe.

"Yeah," Artie said. "He's with us."

"How's Kynder?" Thumb asked, placing his hand on the oblong stone that contained Artie and Kay's father. "And Tiberius?"

But before Artie could answer, the unseen archers launched another volley. Merlin was still in place farther down the beach, and the knights watched him cast another spell. This time the arrows never slowed or changed trajectory. They just kept rising into the air and vanished in the clouds.

But not a moment later they returned, heading right back for the dune. They disappeared behind the line of bear soldiers, and Artie and Kay could hear the faint cries of dozens of men.

"I still don't understand what Merlin's doing!" Artie said. "Is he fighting for us or what?"

"I don't know," Thumb said.

"And I don't care," Kay said. "I still want to kill him."

"Artie, is your dad in that *rock*?" Qwon asked.

"Yeah. He's alive in there . . . kind of."

"So, what now, dude?" Lance asked, more concerned with the fight at hand.

"Yes, what now, lad?"

Before Artie could answer, there was a great flapping sound, followed by a high screech.

They watched as a purple-skinned dragon rose from the swamp behind the dune. Its green-feathered wings pushed hard at the air. For a moment the knights were reduced to spectators as it wailed again and then breathed a jet of black liquid at Merlin. The wizard casually held up his cane, and the dragon's breath attack formed a ball around him and fell away.

The wizard was fine, rising slowly into the air.

Lightning jumped from the back of the dragon's neck, which held a saddle and rider.

"Morgaine," Thumb said bitterly.

"On Scarm, no less," Shallot added.

Then it hit Artie. He knew exactly where Excalibur was.

"Now we fight," Artie barked, knocking Flixith against Rhongomyniad's shaft. "Now we fight for Excalibur and for Tiberius—and for Kynder!"

The other knights were silent, their muscles twitching with anticipation. Shallot hissed like a cat.

Artie swallowed hard and glanced over his shoulder. Fallown, Numinae on his back, had taken up a position behind them. A sharp green glow framed the lord of Sylvan like a corona.

"I don't think I'm ready for this," Qwon said shakily as she moved between Artie and Kay.

"Stay close. We've got your back," Kay said.

Artie took a step forward. He was like another person. It wasn't just that he was motivated by heartbreak and vengeance. He was bigger. He was nobler. He was more kingly.

The bears snorted in unison. Morgaine raised her hands. Merlin did too. The fight was about to commence.

Artie glowered and pointed his spear through the line. "Someone back there has my sword, and I intend to get it."

Morgaine spurred Scarm, and the dragon pushed toward Merlin, her scaly skin wet and glistening from the storm. The wizard spawned his giant white wings and rode them away and into the clouds. Scarm tilted her body, pumped her wings three times, and bolted up. As she vanished in the cloud it lit up with orange lightning, and thunder ricocheted around the beach, filling the knights' ears.

At the same moment, the bears charged off the dune. Artie looked at his friends intently and ordered, "Fall back and use Tiberius's body for cover. Lance, empty your quiver—show no mercy! Erik, when they get closer, go crazy, but stay with the others. Don't split up!"

Bors tapped Shallot and signed frantically. She said,

"Bors'll make a strong scentlock called a scentwall. Stuff your noses if you can."

"Good!" Artie said.

The bears were a third of the way to them.

A terrible explosion came from overhead. Merlin and Morgaine had locked horns. Most looked up. Artie didn't.

"Don't think about them!" he said. "Take cover behind Tiberius!" Lance pulled Erik and Qwon to Tiberius, while Artie stepped toward the charging soldiers. Kay did too. She was scared, but she wasn't going to leave her brother now.

Bors walked a little farther up the beach, waving his hands through the air. Kay cut some cloth from her undershirt and stuffed it in her nose. Thanks to Excalibur's scabbard, Artie was immune, so he didn't bother.

Kay swung Cleomede back and forth around her body. She looked seriously hard core.

The bears were thirty seconds away.

The air around Bors shimmered like it was giving off heat.

Lance unleashed a fireballer that passed within inches of Artie's head. It landed in the sand a hundred and fifty feet away and exploded, felling half a dozen bears and their riders.

Thumb stuffed his nose too and said, "I'm with you, lads!" He did a few tight flips, the Welsh *wakizashi* zinging through the air.

"Glad to hear it, Tommy," Kay said with a big smile.

Shallot stood fast next to Artie. "Me too. I'm sorry I underestimated you, sire."

Artie shook the rain from his head. "Don't sweat it. I'm just glad you're here."

Artie reeled back and threw Rhongomyniad. It hit a bear square in the chest, rode through its body, and knocked the rider behind off his mount. Artie called the spear's name, and it came zipping back, skewering another rider on the return.

"Nine down, a hundred to go!" Kay yelled.

The din of pounding rain and charging bears filled their ears.

And then the animals roared.

Which would have been terrifying if Fallown hadn't flown over their heads at the same moment, spraying gold and silver glitter directly at the charging line. Artie and Kay were both struck by how innocent the dragon's fairy-dust breath appeared; when a large group of riders galloped through, it collected on their bodies, and they looked kind of ridiculous.

But then the glitter started doing its thing, and the bears and riders began to disintegrate. The resulting dust was carried forward by the fizzled riders' momentum before drifting down to the sand.

Just like that, the riders' numbers were nearly halved.

"This is gonna be easy!" Kay exclaimed, as Lance's

arrows streaked the air and felled riders left and right.

"No, it won't," Shallot said. "Fallown's breath attack isn't limitless. It'll be another ten minutes until he can do it again."

"Maybe it doesn't matter," Artie said, watching Bors intently.

The mute fairy stood his ground and did a little jumping-jack as a pair of bears turned and headed directly for him. His scentwall moved away from him and missed the two charging bear riders, but it hit the larger groups on either side. Ten from each flank came to a grinding and delirious halt. The bears fell heads-and-shoulders into the ground and sent up showers of sand, a few skidding to a stop not ten feet from Artie and the knights.

They and their riders were enthralled and utterly use-less.

Artie watched the two bears that were barreling toward Bors, his heart pounding. The fairy was going to get hit. But then, just before the bears reached him, Bors spun in a tight circle and completely disappeared. One of the bears spooked and changed course, crashing sidelong into the other and throwing both of their riders a dozen feet onto the beach. The sound of shattering necks was horrendous.

Twenty riders who'd avoided the scentwall pulled up, flanking the knights. The bears snorted and growled. The riders shouted as some shouldered their crossbows and began to fire. Kay deflected a couple bolts with Cleomede; Shallot—who was insanely quick—simply dodged them. Artie blocked one with Flixith, but another hit him in the back and knocked him to his knees. The graphene shirt stopped it from penetrating his body, but it still hurt like crazy. Excalibur's empty scabbard took care of whatever bruise it left, though, and he quickly got up.

The sky boomed overhead. The purple dragon, still hidden in the clouds, screamed. A woman's voice came from above, reminding the soldiers, "Don't kill the boy!"

At which point the riders dropped their crossbows and drew swords.

The bears on the right charged. The ones on the left broke off to attack Lance, Erik, and Qwon near the petrified bodies of Kynder and Tiberius. Erik launched into berserker mode as Fallown, down the beach, broke toward them to help.

Within seconds Artie, Kay, Thumb, and Shallot were surrounded by bears. And up close they were scary big. The knights formed a circle, each taking a quadrant. A few beats passed before a paw as big as a dinner plate swiped at Kay; she flashed Cleomede and took it off cleanly. But the bear didn't care. It planted its stump in the ground and leaned forward, baring its teeth. With one swipe, Kay sliced through the bear's jaw, swept her blade up, and cut the rider's sword in two.

"Ha!" she blurted.

But she didn't see the bear's other paw coming.

It hit her across the shoulder, which lit up in pain. As with Artie, her graphene shirt prevented the bear from drawing blood, but it knocked her over big-time.

Meanwhile, Shallot put up a scentlock that quelled the bear in front of her, but because of the angle of attack, not its rider. This man was fast and tall and armed with a long halberd. He stood in his saddle and brought the point of his weapon down on Shallot, jabbing wildly as she sidestepped the attacks with her amazing speed. The soldier was about to land a good hit to her midsection when she suddenly disappeared, just like Bors. The soldier stabbed at the air and looked around confusedly before Shallot reappeared directly in front of him atop the bear, straddling his weapon. Quickly and mercilessly she brought down two of her short, wavy fairy blades and hit the soldier in the neck.

She looked to Kay, who was trying to get up after being knocked down, and jumped over to help her.

Meanwhile Thumb was going crazy, battling a bear and rider of his own. He bounced all over the place, scoring several quick, deep cuts in the bear's forelegs. He worked his way onto the animal's back, and before the rider knew it, she was defending herself against the smallest warrior she'd ever seen. The bear turned a tight circle as the rider parried Thumb's furious attacks. For a few moments the soldier held her own, but then Thumb sailed into the air. The rider twisted in her saddle, but it was too late. The Welsh *wakizashi* had already found its way into her back, and was being driven painfully into her kidney.

Another down.

Artie was dealing with two bears simultaneously. The riders on these each had one of those silver whips and they were trying to get one around Artie so they could take him prisoner. Artie quickly realized that his spear wasn't helping because it put too much distance between him and the bears—distance that the soldiers could use to wrangle him with their whips.

He was about to throw the spear at one of the riders when he saw that Kay was still on the ground. Shallot was already sailing to Kay's aid, but the rider over Kay was about bring what was left of his sword through the top of Kay's head.

Artie threw his spear at Kay's assailant, taking his sword arm clean off. The soldier cried out in pain as Shallot finished him off.

Artie turned back to his bears only to see the tasseled end of a whip flying at his face. He ducked under it and slid beneath the bear in front of him. He drew Carnwennan from his belt and drove it into the bear's musky belly. Before it could fall on him, he scampered away between its hind legs, and severed a tendon behind its knee.

The bear collapsed and wailed.

Artie stood and surveyed the field. Lightning illuminated the beach like a strobe light. The witch and the wizard—still shrouded by the clouds overhead—were really going at it. Fallown was near the other knights, dispatching bears and riders with diving attacks. Numinae was still on the golden dragon's neck, knocking heads with his giant maul arm. Lance and Erik—and Qwon too, her blade trailing blue streaks as it danced through the air—were holding their ground.

They were doing all right.

Artie tried to empty his mind and concentrate on his sword. *Where is Excalibur?*

A bear jumped in front of him, breaking his concentration. He raked Flixith across its wet nose. It roared, and then, before he knew it, a whip was around his neck.

Artie flailed at the cord as it snaked around him. He twisted to try to get a better angle to cut it, but only succeeded in wrapping himself up some more.

Then another whip caught him around a foot. This one was yanked hard, and he fell to the ground. Flixith went flying. He tried to cut his way free with Carnwennan but before he could get started, his arm was lashed to his side.

He found himself staring up at the sky, rain falling

directly into his squinting eyes. Another great boom rattled the clouds and then, to his dismay, he saw Merlin falling through the air, looking seriously unconscious or possibly dead. But before he hit the ground, he turned into a column of mist, and this quickly morphed into the shape of an owl. The diaphanous bird squawked and then flew into the fog that blanketed the sea, beating a fast retreat.

The wizard had left the fight, and despite Artie's confusion about Merlin, his heart sank.

Scarm broke hard through the clouds, water streaming from her great feathered wings. Morgaine jumped from her perch and stopped in midair, her hands held up as lightning bolted from the storm and gathered in her palms.

From the corner of his eye, Artie saw the purple dragon attack the golden one. Numinae jumped to safety as Scarm coated Fallown in scalding oil, the golden dragon wailing in agony before falling silent.

Morgaine then peppered the beach with some kind of rapid-fire magic, each strike making a noise like an electric shock. One, two, three, four, five, six, seven. Artie used all his strength to crane his neck around and saw that each of his knights, and Kynder's stone, had been caught in some kind of glass-like bubble. The rain gathered in sheets on these, coating them. An unarmed Lance and an armed and defiant Qwon were together; Kay, Thumb, and Shallot were yelling from their individual bubbles, but no sound escaped the floating prisons; Erik bounced around his like a pinball, still fully raged up.

They were *not* doing all right. The fight was over. They had lost.

Even Numinae had been captured. He was strong and determined enough to break out of his bubble, but Morgaine just kept launching new ones in his direction.

Artie had failed.

Morgaine lowered herself as Artie was dragged roughly along the sand. More archers jogged down the beach, and two more bear riders, who had not partaken in the fight, trotted easily behind them at a distance.

Artie's spirits rose slightly as he realized that it was one of these who held Excalibur. But how was he going to get it?

Scarm glided softly to the ground. She shook off the rainwater like a drenched dog before striking a proud and victorious pose. She was riveting, both terrible and awe-inspiring, just like Morgaine's tornadoes had been. The dragon cocked her head and looked at Artie as if she couldn't see why this boy was worth so much trouble.

Morgaine moved her hands through the air, and the bubbles containing his friends drifted together. It was at this moment that Artie realized that Bors hadn't been caught! There was still a sliver of hope.

Artie locked eyes with Morgaine and asked, "What are

those things around my friends?"

"Dragon's bubbles," Morgaine said with a kindly voice. "No way in or out, I'm afraid."

Artie was hoisted to his feet by an invisible hand. He was drenched and cold. He was frightened, but he composed himself and said, "You're not that scary-looking up close."

Morgaine pushed a stray lock of hair behind her ear. "What, even in my warrior dress?"

"Yeah, you kind of look like a mom."

"Oh, I'm glad you noticed, dear."

She shot another bubble at Numinae, who didn't pause in trying to escape. He was livid.

What was left of the bear soldiers had taken positions behind Scarm. The pair of officers protecting Excalibur were all the way at the back.

How *was* he going to get his sword from them?

And where was Bors? Where were Lance's bow and quiver?

"You aren't very scary-looking either, Arthur Pendragon. You look exactly like I knew you would," she said snidely.

"What are you going to do with us?" Artie asked, his voice shaking with anger.

"Unfortunately I have to keep *you*," Morgaine said with a sigh.

"And my knights?"

The witch went wide-eyed and began to giggle, which quickly turned into a full-throated belly laugh. Tears came to her eyes and she turned to Scarm, who was also chuckling. "Knights! How . . . medieval."

The dragon nodded.

Morgaine shot another bubble at Numinae.

"Your 'knights' are completely expendable, now that I have you. They won't leave this beach alive."

"Why haven't you already killed them, then?" Artie asked coolly.

The witch respected his calm. "Some of them hold things I need. Can't risk destroying them in the process."

"The Seven Swords?" Artie guessed.

"Yes, but by my count only four remain with you. I have the others."

"Yeah, I know."

She launched yet another bubble at Numinae.

Artie asked, "And what about the wizard? Why did he run?"

"We'll talk about that later, dear."

"Stop calling me dear."

"Oh, come now, *dear*!" Morgaine mocked, looking at the dragon again. Even some of the soldiers laughed, though their laughs seemed disingenuous. "You fought well today, truly, but there is no hope now. Sorry, child."

Something about the way she said "child" made Artie's skin crawl. He couldn't bear to look at her anymore and cast his gaze to the dunes in the distance. *Where is Bors?* Maybe the fairy also knew that one of those soldiers at the back had Excalibur. Maybe Bors was going to lift it from him and deliver it to Artie!

Hoping to see some sign of the missing fairy, Artie eyed the officers at the back. The smaller one wore a simple helmet that obscured his face. The bigger one reached up and pulled his own helmet from his head and looked straight at Artie.

Artie couldn't believe it. It was Sami!

Artie forced himself to remain expressionless, but his heart and mind raced as he watched the smaller officer unsheathe Excalibur. Even without any sunlight, the blade glinted at Artie like it was winking at him. They were so close to being reunited.

Carefully the smaller soldier handed Excalibur to Sami, who nodded meaningfully to Artie. Artie could tell that the superstrong Swede was only waiting for a signal and then he would hurl Excalibur to him.

Artie looked at Morgaine. "It was foolish of you to bring Excalibur with you, Lordess Morgaine."

She furrowed her brow and asked, "What? I'm not that stupid, child."

She didn't know. The door called hope was flung wide!

"You can't feel it, then?" Artie asked.

"Of course not, because it's not here," the witch foolishly insisted.

Artie smiled ever so slightly. "Interesting. I guess you're not as powerful as you think you are."

IN WHICH ARTIE AND EXCALIBUR ARE REUNITED, AND WHAT ENSUES

32

The sword sailed through the air in a tall arc, and time slowed for Artie.

A lot.

It was like when he'd gotten Excalibur from the Lake— but there was more to it. It wasn't just time that had changed, but awareness. For a few moments he knew everything that was going on in precise detail.

There were exactly seventeen archers left, and twelve riders, and fifteen bears. Morgaine had fifteen metal cuffs on each forearm. There were twenty-three gulls skirting the water's surface off the beach. The bear closest to him, which was the biggest, had one eye. Artie's knights had killed or injured seventy-eight riders, seventy-five bears, and fifty-five archers. Excalibur had flipped thirty-two times. Morgaine had cast five dragon's bubbles on Numinae.

The forest lord had just burst his current bubble and its skin was peeling back in slow motion, and Morgaine was preparing to cast another.

Sami was jumping off his bear, getting ready to take out the remaining archers, while the guy next to him had taken off his helmet.

Mordred.

Kynder had been right. Mordred was not his enemy. He was not his enemy because Artie knew with dead certainty that he was his brother.

Artie's heart swelled. The sword was right in front of him now. It had stopped spinning and was coming point down for his body. Artie breathed in, making himself as thin as possible. Excalibur couldn't cut him, he knew, but he needed to make room for his weapon between the whips and his body. Effortlessly it slid between the coiled strands, twisted, and the magical silver whips fell to pieces.

In a fluid motion, Artie sheathed the dagger Carnwennan, reached up and caught Excalibur, pulled out the pommel, and placed it on his sword's hilt. The sword glowed so bright that Artie had to shut his eyes, but even with his eyes closed, he knew exactly where everyone and everything was.

Including Bors, who was down the beach to his left and armed with Lance's bow and arrows! And including

The Anguish and the Peace Sword, which were safe with Mordred and Sami. All Seven Swords were there!

Artie held Excalibur one-handed and called Rhongomyniad. The spear jumped up and flew to his hand. Then Artie yelled, "More light!" and a blinding shock wave burst from Excalibur's blade. In its wake, time ramped back up, resuming its usual pace.

Morgaine screamed, full of wrath and terror. She, along with the bears, soldiers, archers, and Scarm, were momentarily blinded by the ancient sword's light, while Artie's friends were unaffected.

Numinae, free from his dragon's bubble, conjured millions of tiny slivers of wood and let them fly at Morgaine. Bors, visible now, let one of the limitless arrows Merlin had gifted Lance fly at the witch. Artie hurled his spear.

Each of these attacks arrived at the same time from a different angle. Morgaine managed to deflect the spear, though its shaft smacked hard into her head; the arrow drove through her back; and the Sylvan lord's magical splinters swarmed her like a hive of angered bees. Stricken, she fell to the ground, unconscious.

Morgaine's soldiers went wild in their confusion, and Numinae took advantage, bursting the dragon's bubbles of the other knights. Bors ran in their direction, firing at will at the riders. He wasn't as accurate as Lance, but he was still pretty good.

Sami was in the back, knocking the heads of the archers together like he was in a cartoon. He moved quickly, and the archers didn't have a chance.

Mordred spurred his war bear and was hurtling toward his brother. It was pretty surreal to watch. Artie thought this kid—who was slightly bigger but otherwise his *exact* double—looked a lot more heroic than he ever did, but what did he know.

Excalibur hummed, alerting Artie to an incoming crossbow volley. He whisked his blade through the air, slicing the bolt to pieces. He looked at the rider who'd shot it and shook his head.

Not smart, dude.

Artie sprang forward. Having Excalibur back felt so good.

The knights, free from the dragon's bubbles, engaged what was left of Morgaine's forces.

As Mordred's bear sailed past Shallot, Artie's twin threw a long, strange-looking weapon to the fairy. She saw it instantly, vaulted over a soldier, and caught it in midair. Then she did some things Artie had never seen before. Shallot, armed with her birthright, was a terror. She flew through the field of battle contorting her long body around The Anguish, twisting and tumbling, stretching in all directions, and meting out severe punishment. The fighting was fierce but lopsided, especially once Sami drew into their circle. When he came close, he nodded at Artie, and Artie, beaming proudly, nodded back.

Kay arrived at Artie's side as Mordred's bear skidded to a stop in front of them.

"Arthur," Mordred said.

"Mordred," Artie returned.

"Holy mirror image, Batman!" Kay squealed.

The brothers ignored Kay. They were too entranced with each other. "Nice to see you, Brother. But call me Dred."

"And call me Artie." They shared a knowing smile as the sound of clanging metal and moaning bears echoed across the beach.

"So you're the Peace Sword guy, huh?" Kay asked as Dred smiled at her.

But then the Fenlandian dragon rose behind him. How had they forgotten about Scarm?

Numinae was standing guard at Kynder's stone. Thumb, Lance, and Qwon were with him, and Erik was close by, still in full berserker mode.

The dragon sprayed her hot oil breath at this gathering of knights.

Numinae raised his hands, and the air shimmered with a green light all around. The oil hit the light and evaporated into a dense cloud of smoke. The dragon brayed and breathed again. Numinae fell to his knees as he put up another shield. They went one more round, but the third shield was clearly smaller and weaker. Oil seeped through here and there. Lance was splashed on the thigh and fell to one knee, screaming in pain.

The dragon had just started another attack aimed at Numinae and company when Sami tossed a bear right at her. "Chew on this, you dumb snake!"

"Bors!" Lance called, his teeth clenched against the scalding pain. "You've got one arrow left!"

Bors looked in the quiver. Actually, there were two, but he knew what Lance had in mind.

Artie ran toward Sami, and Dred and Kay joined him. The dragon shifted her attention to this group and prepared to shoot oil on them.

Bors let an arrow fly.

The dragon's oily breath was in midair when the arrow hit it. The oil lit up like a fuse as fire traveled up and toward the dragon's head. Bors had shot a fireballer!

The conflagration traveled into the dragon's mouth and out of her nose. For a second Scarm looked like she was choking on something—then her head blew up.

"Take that!" Kay yelled as the rest hooted and hollered.

When the excitement died down, Dred nodded in the direction of his unconscious mother and said, "Brother, we need to leave here."

"Yeah, I know," Artie said.

That was when it hit him. It was why he'd felt so weird when she called him "child." Morgaine wasn't his biological mom, but he knew that she was the one who had made him. She was the person who had brought him into the world.

"Let's go, guys," Artie yelled. Everyone gathered by Kynder's stone and shared a quick round of hugs and handshakes. Numinae was weak but on his feet. Qwon had big embraces for both Artie and Dred—maybe even a bigger hug for Dred, which kind of ticked Artie off. But he wasn't going to let that spoil their victory. It felt a little hollow anyway, what with Tiberius dead and Kynder frozen in a huge chunk of black rock.

Dred put his arm around Artie, and Kay shook her head at seeing them together. "Man. *Two* of you! This is just too darn freaky!"

"All right, here we go. New Knights of the Round Table, get out the Seven Swords," Artie ordered softly.

Then he held Excalibur straight out in front of him. It was glowing slightly.

"Shouldn't we wait for Bors?" Qwon asked as Bors ran toward them across the sand.

"He'll make it," Artie said. "We need to open the gate to Avalon."

Cleomede was next. Kay laid it across Excalibur, which got brighter. Then came The Anguish and the Peace Sword. Excalibur got a lot brighter.

Erik added Gram, and Lance pulled Orgulus from his belt. He put it in, and Excalibur hummed.

Artie looked at Qwon. "Well, what are you waiting for?"

"What—what's happening?" Qwon asked, overwhelmed by the day's—the week's—events.

"We're all about to level up, like, big-time," Kay said decisively.

Artie smiled at his sister. This *had* all started with a video game, after all.

Bors was only a hundred feet away.

Qwon shrugged and got ready to slap Kusanagi onto the array of legendary swords.

But then Bors was picked up midstride and torn in half! Shallot cried out and clutched her chest. The halves of his body turned into fairy dust as they flew through the air. Lance's bow and quiver twirled over the sand noiselessly.

But there was no time to mourn. Rising on a black column of air was Morgaine. On the other side of her, the sea grew in a wall of gray foam. The witch was swirled with wisps of smoke. Her dark, mismatched eyes burned out of their sockets, and her rust-colored hair stood on end.

Qwon brought Kusanagi down on the fan of swords. They began to vibrate violently, and the sword bearers had to hold on tight with both hands.

"Now, lad!" Thumb screamed.

"Do it!" Numinae said at the same moment.

The witch held her hands—which had become freakishly large, with fingers as long as walking canes—in front of her. Manic flames and lightning laced her digits.

The swords became blazing hot, but none of the knights could relinquish them. They were joined as one—the knights to their swords, the swords to each other. They cried out as Morgaine unleashed her spell. King Artie Kingfisher shut his eyes and forced his quaking body to say the words: "*Lunae lumen!*"

There was a blinding orange flash as Morgaine's fire and lightning exploded into the sand. As the sand and smoke and ozone cleared, the witch stared feverishly at the ground, her zealous eyes darting in their sockets.

But all that was left on the beach was a crater, and the bodies of three dead dragons, and the remains of her defeated army.

Fury consumed Morgaine's every fiber.

Because Arthur Pendragon and his noble knights were gone.

Gone to Avalon.

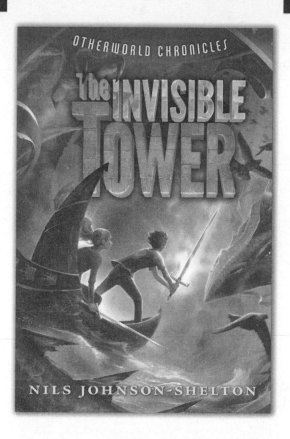